Fresh Eggs

by

Rob Levandoski

THE PERMANENT PRESS
SAG HARBOR, NY 11963

Library of Congress Cataloging-in-Publication Data

Levandoski, Rob
Fresh Eggs / Rob Levandoski
  p. cm.
ISBN 1-57962-048-5 (alk paper)
1.Human-animal relationships--Fiction. 2. Fathers and
daughters--Fiction. 3. Animals--Treatment--Fiction.
4. Eggs trade--Fiction. 5. Chickens--Fiction. I. Title

PS362.E8637 F74 2002
813'.54--dc21   2001036612
                                     CIP

Printed in the United States.

THE PERMANENT PRESS
4170 Noyac Road
Sag Harbor, NY 11963

To Jenifer and Kary, My daughters.
Thanks for growing into such wonderful women.

PART I

"Farming is not a game of chance. Nothing grows by chance. Not even the weeds. Neither does a crop grow in a day. If we want results we must wait. This is rule one of the farm."

Ohio farmer Will H. Evans, 1891

One

CALVIN CASSOWARY SITS alone at the table in the breakfast nook. His fingers are wrapped around the coffee mug First Sovereignty Savings Bank gave him when he took out that quarter-million-dollar loan. It's 5:30 a.m. Rain is streaming down the window. Out in the chicken yard Captain Bates is crowing. The big dumb rooster has been crowing for a half hour. Calvin wishes he would shut up. Jeanie is going into labor any day now—maybe any minute now—and she needs all the sleep she can get.

When Calvin lifts his elbow to take a sip, the table wobbles. The table has been wobbling under the elbows of Cassowarys since the presidency of Ulysses S. Grant. It was built by Calvin's great-great grandfather, Henry Cassowary. Henry spent a year with the Shakers when he was a young man. He left hating everything about them except their furniture. So years later when Henry got the bug to make a new kitchen table for his growing family, he built it in the no-nonsense Shaker style. Except for that one short leg, it came out pretty good, too.

Calvin finally sees what he's been waiting for, the blurry lights of Helen Abelard's Pontiac zeroing in on the plastic *Gazette* box at the end of the driveway. He struggles into his waterproof poncho and heads out for the paper. He takes his coffee with him. As Helen pulls away, her headlights wash across the FRESH EGGS sign on the front lawn. It's a wooden sign, red letters painted on white. In the rain it glows like Las Vegas neon.

Calvin isn't happy with the rain, though everybody's corn-fields sure need it. The rain means another go-slow day on the new layer house. The crew from Buckshee Construction can't help it if it rains, of course, but that first truckload of young Leghorns from Gallinipper Foods will be arriving on the seventh of July, layer house or no layer house.

Halfway to the road Calvin stops and takes a sip of coffee.

There is the smell of cow manure in the air, but there are no longer cows on the Cassowary farm. Calvin sold them off six months ago. He also had his father's six remaining hogs slaughtered and he gave the goats to Dawn Van Varken. He kept Biscuit, the Shetland sheepdog his mother rescued from the pound just a week before his dad died. He also kept the cats and the little flock of Buff Orpington hens his mother used to tend.

Calvin Cassowary has bitten off quite a mouthful for a kid of twenty-four with a B.A. in Fine Arts. While his old high school buddies are still talking about the kind of cars they'd buy if they had the money, he's risked the family farm on a quarter-million-dollar loan to go into the egg business—not the kind of egg business his grandfather started in the 1920s, but a real, full-tilt egg operation, with a layer house as long as a football field and 60,000 Leghorns, each hen pooping two Grade A eggs every three days for Gallinipper Foods.

Quite a mouthful. But what's a man to do? When your father drops dead from a heart attack at fifty-two? When your older brother opts for a career in the Navy? When your mother remarries and moves to Columbus? When the deed to the farm suddenly has your name on it? When you've got a wife carrying your first baby? You give up your dream of being a high school art teacher. You sign a contract with Gallinipper Foods. You borrow a quarter-million bucks. You do whatever it takes to keep the family farm in the family for at least one more generation.

Calvin pulls the *Gazette* from the tube and, despite the rain, reads the top story: Watergate Special Prosecutor Leon Jaworski has taken his demand for sixty-four taped presidential conversations directly to the Supreme Court. It looks like Nixon's days are numbered, which makes Calvin happy. He hates Nixon. Hates him for those bulldog jowls and all the kids he kept sending to Vietnam. "They got you this time, Dickie boy."

It's not easy for a Cassowary to hate a Republican president. The Cassowarys have been voting Republican since Abraham Lincoln took up the cause in 1860. His granddad didn't even vote for Franklin Roosevelt during World War II. But Calvin sure as hell didn't vote for Nixon in '72. He voted for George McGovern. Everybody in the art department at Kent State University voted for George McGovern.

Still, Calvin knows he owes his degree to Nixon. If Nixon hadn't kept the war going, he wouldn't have gone to college. No Cassowary had ever seen the need for an education. Calvin hadn't either. He did, however, see the need for a 2-S draft deferment. And he held onto that deferment for four years, majoring in the only thing he was even remotely good at—drawing pictures.

At first drawing pictures was just an easy way to stay off that plane to Vietnam. But as he drew, and painted, and sculpted in clay, he also began to see it as a way to escape the farm—the farm that had kept the Cassowarys pinned down for five generations, while the rest of America was living it up in the suburbs. Hard as it was to believe, the war in Vietnam outlasted Calvin's four years in college. So he took out another student loan and enrolled in the College of Education.

Once the war was over he planned to run just as fast as he could to one of those suburbs and teach other kids how to un-pin themselves from the expectations of their families and their presidents. Brown-eyed Jeanie Marabout was going to run off with him, he with his art degree and she with her degree in English. They'd get teaching jobs and buy a big old rickety Victorian and they'd fill it with his paintings and her books, and eventually some kids. Then just three weeks after graduation his dad dropped dead, and everything changed.

That FRESH EGGS sign at the end of the driveway is the same sign his grandfather, Alfred E. Cassowary, erected in 1928, two by three feet, one inch thick, cut from a piece of floor planking from the old barn.

Alfred was a prosperous farmer always looking for ways to become even more prosperous: he bought eighty acres of worthless swamp from Louie Flexner, and with the help of a couple of long ditches and a windmill, doubled his corn acreage; he bought thirty acres of jungle from Harold Van Varken, cut out everything but the maples, and in a few winters had the best sugar bush in Wyssock County; he fenced off a corner of the old potato field, added thirty-three young Rhode Island Reds to his small flock of New Hampshires, almost overnight establishing the best drive-in egg business in the township.

"What's your trick, Al?" Minnie Rogers asked every time she pulled in for a dozen or two. "Them's the fattest eggs I've ever laid eyes on."

Being a modest man, Alfred always shrugged off the question. But he knew the answer. It was the rooster riding the backs of his hens that made those eggs so big and rich, a big black-feathered mongrel cock named Buster, the fifth-generation grandson of Maximo Gomez.

Alfred's granddad on his mother's side, Chuck Cowrie, had acquired Maximo Gomez in Cuba during the Spanish-American War. Granddad Cowrie was a supply sergeant in the nine thousand-man expeditionary force led by Major General W.R. Shafter, deployed for the duration of that funny little war in the coastal town of Baiquiri. Maximo Gomez was a champion fighting cock, named in honor of the general-in-chief of the Cuban revolutionary forces. He was a nine-pound Spanish, with shiny black feathers, a bone-white face, a tall red comb, wattles the size of chili peppers. There wasn't a cock in Baiquiri that hadn't been spurred senseless by him. Nor was there a campesino within twenty miles who hadn't happily paid the cock's owner, a brothel owner named Calixto Cervera y Cisnaros, two or three centavos for the honor of letting Maximo Gomez ride the backs of their hens. Chuck Cowrie, an experienced cock fighter himself, paid Señor Cisnaros one hundred dollars American for the bird, an enormous sum in those strife-filled years in Cuba, even for the proprietor of a brothel.

Granddad Cowrie smuggled Maximo Gomez back into Florida in an ammunition crate. After a few years touring the barns and pool halls of Western Ohio and Indiana, Maximo was retired to the Cassowary farm in Wyssock County, where he immediately proved himself king of the roost and sent his hot Spanish blood coursing through the veins of the Cassowary's plump and placid New Hampshires. And that's why Alfred Cassowary did so well selling eggs in the twenties and thirties, and why even today, now and again, one of the Cassowary roosters sports black tailfeathers.

The *Gazette* thoroughly read, Calvin eats a quick bowl of shredded wheat and then goes upstairs to check on Jeanie. "Looks like it's going to rain all day," he says, kissing her big belly.

Jeanie hadn't complained one iota about their change in plans when his dad died. She packed up her books and dreams and moved with her new husband to the farm. She got a part-time job at the library in Tuttwyler and put in all the days she could as a substitute teacher, right up until a week ago. "Maybe I should call off today," Calvin says. "You look about ready to pop."

"I feel about ready to pop," Jeanie says. She's gained weight in her face since becoming pregnant and her doughy cheeks flop over the corners of her mouth when she smiles. "But you go ahead. I'll call Dawn if something happens."

Calvin knows he should drive the school bus that morning. They need the money. Still he's worried. "What if Dawn isn't home?"

Jeanie tries not to laugh, but does. Her belly swells like a wave. The baby inside her bobs like a rowboat. "Five boys? Five hundred hogs? When isn't Dawn Van Varken at home?"

Before leaving for the bus garage, Calvin goes to the chicken coop to feed Captain Bates and the sixteen remaining Buff Orpington hens. It's a small coop, just twelve by twelve feet. The outside yard is twenty feet wide and forty-four feet long. Raining as it is, Captain Bates and the hens are inside the coop today. Calvin scatters a large scoop of cracked corn. The hens go crazy.

Calvin does not like the way Captain Bates is looking at him, or, more correctly, not looking at him. The rooster's head is turned sideways, close to the floor, as if looking for something to eat. Calvin doesn't know a lot about chicken behavior, not yet, but he knows that's a fighting posture; any second that rooster's toes could be in his face.

It's hard to say just what kind of rooster Captain Bates is. Over the generations many different varieties of chickens have been introduced to the Cassowary flock, most recently the Buff Orpingtons, a hale and hardy breed renowned for their big beautiful brown eggs. So who knows what kind of rooster the captain is, except that, like all the Cassowary roosters, his blood goes back to the famous Maximo Gomez. He's a huge caramel-red cock with fiery wattles, floppy comb, and shiny black tail feathers that curl around and almost stick him in the ass.

Captain Bates does not particularly like Calvin either. He misses Betsy, the mother of this worthless man. Betsy always sang to him and his hens, a song with endless verses called "How Are My Chickie-Chickie Cluck-Clucks Today?" Besides singing, she always gave them an extra half-scoop of cracked corn. And when she reached under his hens for their eggs, she did it slowly and respectfully, with a friendly, "Thank you, ma'am." This Calvin just jams his hands under them, as if a peck on the knuckles will kill him, and jerks out their eggs with the grace of a starving opossum.

More than anything, Betsy was respectful to *him*. "You're in charge now, Capt'n Bates," she'd always say before leaving the coop. This Calvin just slams the door. Whatever happened to Betsy anyway? Did she get old? Stop laying? Did they eat her?

The old rooster has no way of knowing that six months after her husband died, Betsy went to her 30th high school reunion in Columbus and met an old boyfriend, a widowed insurance agent named Ben Betz, and, without consulting her children or her chickens, accepted his marriage proposal, transforming herself from a farm wife named Betsy Cassowary into a suburban wife named Betsy Betz, putting his fate, and the fate of his hens, in the uncertain hands of this *Calvin*.

12

Two

CALVIN CASSOWARY DRIVES his Pinto to the bus garage in Tuttwyler and starts his morning high school run. There are only ten days of school left, counting the three-day Memorial Day weekend, and the kids on the bus are loud and antsy. Before starting his junior high school run he calls Jeanie and makes her swear she's not in labor. He also calls Dawn Van Varken and makes her swear she won't drift more than twenty feet from her phone. He rushes home as soon as his elementary run is finished, driving right past the Pile Inn, where fellow school bus driver Paul Bilderback is waiting to have coffee with him.

It's raining hard when Calvin pulls into the drive. The crew from Buckshee Construction is huddled inside the tractor shed. Inside the house he finds Jeanie on the living room sofa, watching *Phil Donahue*. She's got several pillows wedged behind her and there's half a glass of orange juice balancing on her belly. "You didn't stop for coffee with Paul?" she asks.

"Paul isn't nine months pregnant."

Jeanie pounds some air into her pillows. "Paul's a lucky man."

Calvin kisses Jeanie on the forehead and goes back out on the porch. If the crew from Buckshee Construction has accomplished anything this morning, he can't see it. He checks the sky. Nothing but gray. He goes inside and opens a can of tomato soup. He makes it in the Cassowary style: half a can of water, half a can of milk; tablespoon of real butter, quick shake of pepper.

So with Jeanie on the sofa, the construction crew dragging their asses, Calvin ladles himself a bowl of soup and opens one of the Proper Poultry Management manuals given him by Norman Marek, Gallinipper's Midwest producer relations manager. This one is titled, "Feeding Standards and Rations." Every time he lifts his elbow to take a spoonful of soup or turn a page, the Shaker-style table Henry Cassowary made wobbles.

But Calvin doesn't feel the wobble, no more than his father felt it, or his grandfather, or any of the fifty or sixty Cassowarys who'd sat around that table over the generations. But he sure feels the presence of those other Cassowarys. Generation after generation, they took care of that farm, making sure the farm took care of them. And he will do the same. And he's sure that with the help of Gallinipper Foods, he'll find fulfillment and joy and financial success, even if running the family farm is the last thing in the world he wants to do.

Things are scary right now. But pretty soon the old Cassowarys will be looking down with pride, and that baby in Jeanie's belly will be looking up from its crib with pride. So what if he hadn't planned on being a farmer? Great-great grandfather Henry hadn't planned on it either.

Henry Cassowary was the son of a Cincinnati barrel maker. He grew up planning to work on his uncle's grain barge, floating up and down the Ohio and the wide Mississippi, collecting scandalous first-hand experiences like the ones his cousins bragged about. But that dream ended in 1847 when nineteen-year-old Henry met Hannah Drindlekeid.

Hannah was devoutly religious. A month after she accepted his marriage proposal, she decided that instead of a traditional marriage encumbered by carnality and children, they would live chaste, ethereal lives in the service of Jesus Christ, as members of the United Society of Believers, as Shakers.

Henry was all for carnality and children; yet, how could he resist the wishes of this wonderful woman who used words like *chaste* and *ethereal* and aspired to an elevated existence? Immediately after the wedding they boarded the stagecoach for the Shaker community in Union, carefully avoiding even one night of sexual temptation.

Just as Hannah had put her trust in God, Henry now put his trust in Hannah. He went to work in the carpentry shop, rewarding each long day of labor with an hour of shoveling manure in the cow barns. He dutifully attended all the Sabbath services and sang all the joyous songs and learned to dance and twitch. He admired his wife from afar, the roundness of her hips and fullness of her bosom, the delicate white chin protruding from her bonnet, the serene motion of her tiny hand when she scattered cracked corn to the chickens.

Summer and autumn flew by. But the winter kept its toes on the ground and no amount of carpentry or manure-shoveling made the days pass. By the time spring finally arrived, Henry was shaking all the time, not for the love of God, but for the love of his wife, and on the Friday before Easter when he was fitting the hen house with new perches, Hannah came in to gather eggs. "Sister," he said. "Brother," she said. Before he knew it he had her flat over the feed bin. The rooster started squawking and the hens clucked and flapped and Henry did to Hannah what that rooster regularly did to his hens. What Adam did to Eve at the serpent's urging.

Afterwards Henry ran as fast as a rabbit across the neat Shaker fields, and through the neat Shaker woods, jumping the neat Shaker fence rows, until he reached the road. He walked all the way to Cincinnati, filled with shame and relief. After a while he signed on with the CC&C, the Cleveland, Columbus and Cincinnati Railroad, and was sent north to Wyssock County, to help build a trestle over Three Fish Creek. It was here that he met Camellia Bloom, an earthy young widow with a farm. Henry wrote Hannah and asked for a divorce, which she granted with Shaker joy. On a rainy day just before Halloween, Henry and Camellia were married, and the Bloom farm passed into the ownership of the Cassowarys. Sometime during the presidency of Ulysses S. Grant, Henry built that wobbly table.

Shortly after one o'clock Marilyn Dickcissel pulls in for her weekly two dozen. Calvin dog-ears his manual and rushes to the refrigerator for the eggs. If Marilyn gets her foot in the door she'll spend half the afternoon yakking about her dog grooming business.

He reaches the porch just as Marilyn is navigating the stone steps. "Two dozen, right?"

Marilyn does not like being intercepted. "How's our Jeanie?" she asks.

"Sleeping."

She frowns and digs into her purse. "You're still gonna sell brown eggs after you get that big operation of yours running, ain't you?"

"Until the old hens die off."

She hands him four quarters. "White eggs ain't no good for pies."

He hands her the cartons. "An egg's an egg."

She flips her spent cigarette into the shrubs. "An egg's an egg my Ohio ass."

There's a break in the rain and the construction crew gets busy, completing an entire wall of metal sheeting by the time Calvin leaves for his afternoon bus run. When he gets home he finds a note fastened to the screen door with a safety pin. It's in Dawn Van Varken's handwriting: *Jeanie's water broke. Meet us at the hospital.*

Rhea Cassowary weighs four pounds, thirteen ounces. She's seventeen and a half inches long. She's got brown eyes. Quite a head of hair. She has all her toes and fingers and all her other little body parts appear perfect.

"Rhea? Why Rhea?" Calvin's mother, Betsy Betz, asks when he calls her from the hospital.

"You know Jeanie and her literature," he says. "Apparently Rhea was the oldest of the Greek gods. Mother of the universe."

"Don't you think that's a lot of responsibility to put on a little nubbin, Calvin? Mother of the universe? Thank your lucky stars you didn't have a boy. She might've named him Jesus the way the Mexicans do."

Calvin laughs. "You're close. She was set on Moses."

"Oh Lord," his mother moans. "I'm glad I didn't go to college and get my head filled with such foolishness."

Rhea is brought home after just three days in the hospital. When the crew from Buckshee Construction sees Calvin's Pinto pull in, they gather on the side of the drive to applaud. Calvin just wishes they'd go back to work.

Calvin's mother has driven up from Columbus and Jeanie's mother and father have driven down from Toledo. Neighbor Dawn Van Varken has walked over with enough tuna and noodle casserole to last a week. Inside, the kitchen counters are covered with casseroles from other neighbors. Jeanie's mother takes tiny Rhea while Jeanie heads for the bathroom. Calvin pours himself a cup of coffee and watches the crew as it slowly gets back to work. The cage-units are being delivered first thing Monday morning and the roof had better be on. Automatic feeders are coming Wednesday. Egg conveyors Thursday.

Calvin feels Jeanie's arms around his neck. "Let's take that beautiful daughter of yours upstairs," she says. Everyone files up the narrow stairs. Every step creaks.

They fill the first room at the top of the stairs. It's a small room, nine by nine, with one window that looks out over the creek valley to the south. The walls, like all the walls in this old house, have several wavy layers of wallpaper over them, and who knows how many coats of paint. Not long after she found out she was pregnant, Jeanie painted the walls a pale peach and pasted a paper border around the ceiling with green turtles riding tricycles and blue geese jumping rope. The crib is Calvin's old crib, freshly painted white. The mattress is new, a gift from Jeanie's mother. Calvin's mother bought the curtains, Beatrix Potter rabbits harvesting enormous carrots and cabbages. There are several boxes of disposable diapers stacked in one corner like bales of hay.

"This room is so cute," Jeanie's mother says.

"It's the old Cassowary birthing room," Calvin's mother tells her. "Calvin wasn't born here—I put my foot down about that—

but Calvin's father was born in this room and his father and all the Cassowarys going back to old Henry's seven kids."

Jeanie's mother is amazed. "Isn't it something how women back then just *plooped* out their babies and went back to work? I was flat on my back for three weeks."

Jeanie puts Rhea in the crib. Calvin wraps his arms around her and kisses her sweaty neck. They stand over their child, swaying back and forth, grinning, giggling, wiping the tears from their eyes, unable to abandon the little life they created together, unable to join the others downstairs for tuna and noodles, even if it is getting cold.

Three

RHEA CASSOWARY SPENDS her first weeks pressed against her mother's steady heart, or cradled in the safe arms of her father, or inside the reassuring bars of her crib. She enjoys her mother's warm nipples and the sweet milk that trickles out of them. She learns to lift her head and roll on her belly. She learns how to wrap her miniature fingers around her father's big fingers. Discovers the joy of kicking empty air.

Her eyes start seeing things more clearly: those marvelous nipples she's been sucking on; the silvery sunlight beaming into her room through the shimmering square in the wall; the curtains alive with wind; the soft motionless creatures that share her crib, that come to life and twist and shake when her father holds them close to her face.

Her ears start hearing things more sharply: the comforting sounds that come out of her mother's mouth; the funny sounds that come out of her father's mouth; the distant *banging-banging-banging* that lasts all day long.

She begins to learn that her new world is actually two worlds: there is the inside world, divided into squares, some bigger and some smaller, some noisy and some quiet, some smelling wonderful, some smelling not so good; there is the outside world, where the sun and wind roam free, where sounds and smells have boundless energy and infinite imaginations, where creatures twist and shake and move about on their own, where the *banging-banging-banging* is louder.

Her carefree acceptance of life gives way to worrying and wondering: why is there an inside world and an outside world? Who are these two people who pick her up and put her down, fill her mouth with mushy substances, wrap and unwrap her, douse her and dry her, jabber away at her, who have the power to make the light come and go by simply slapping the walls? Why is there that constant banging? That *banging-banging-banging*? And why can't these two people put an end to it? Why can't they just slap the wall and make it quiet?

One day the banging does stop and for the first time in her life, Rhea has a restful day.

More restful days follow. The *banging-banging-banging* fades from her thoughts, though some nights the *banging-banging-banging* drifts into her dreams, into that third world she has discovered. Luckily her cries quickly bring her mother, who picks her up and jiggle-dances her around the room and whisper-sings in her ear.

One morning her father takes her outside. They walk a long way, toward a long, low silvery building. He is jibber-jabbering about something nonstop. When they reach the building, and her father pulls the door open, she starts to tremble, knowing from the hollow rumble that this building was the source of that *banging-banging-banging* all those weeks she lay in her crib.

Now they are walking down an endless square tunnel, noisy and smelly and blurry. Her father has raised her up so she can see over his shoulder. She feels as if she is being born again. The tunnel is filled from floor to ceiling with rows of strange white creatures. Their faces come to sharp points. They have wild sideways eyes. Bags of red skin hang from their chins. They are packed so tightly in their cribs—their cages—that it is hard to tell where one creature ends and another begins. They are all afraid, that much is for certain. And they are all crying and begging to be set free. So Rhea cries, too, and begs to be free of this terrible square tunnel. But the tunnel goes on forever, and the air is heavy and wet and hard to breathe, and the dizzying lights hanging overhead are much too bright, and her father's jibber-jabbering and reassuring pats on her wet bottom assure her of nothing. The tunnel just goes on and on. The white creatures just cry and beg and stare at her sideways, necks stretched long through the bars in their crowded cribs.

Calvin Cassowary's father was named Donald. He was fifty-two when he died. He was a farmer. He had milk cows and hogs, sometimes goats or sheep, always that little flock of chickens. He grew corn and baled enough hay to keep his stock fed all winter. He kept a magnificent vegetable garden, producing all the potatoes, tomatoes, squash, sweet corn, green peppers, string beans, beets, carrots, parsnips, cucumbers, and cabbage the family needed. He also grew a bit of garlic and horseradish and asparagus and rhubarb. Every June he covered his blueberry bushes with netting so the robins wouldn't clean them out. Behind the blueberry bushes was a row of grapes for jelly making. Most years he had a bed of strawberries. He also had apple trees and peach trees and pear trees, and there was a tangle of raspberry briars on the north side of the old barn.

Donald Cassowary loved farming. He had an affinity for the soil—just like his father and grandfather and all the Cassowarys back to Henry had an affinity for it. He could tell what kind of fertilizers his fields needed just by sticking his nose in a handful of dirt. He also had an affinity for his animals, and they an affinity for him. They gave him all the milk and eggs he wanted, and when the time came, they gave him their meat, understanding their biblical role as well as their master did. God, after all, had put men like Donald Cassowary in charge of His creation; told them to be fruitful and to multiply and to replenish the earth and to subdue it; gave them dominion over the fish of the sea, and over the fowl of the air, and over the cattle, and over every creeping thing that creepeth.

Donald also was a damn fine carpenter who could build a new corn crib as well as he could repair an old one. He knew the ins and outs of plumbing, welding, and electrical wiring. He could keep his old Ford tractor running no matter what.

He also was good at the nasty parts of farming. He could put a bullet through the head of a favorite cow when it dropped to its knees with some incurable disease. He could walk his gardens at dusk, popping off rabbits and chipmunks and groundhogs with his .22 rifle. He could set out steel-jawed traps for the raccoon when they got into the corn. He could smash potato bugs with his thumb. When one of his favorite hens got too old to lay eggs, he could chop off her head, yank her guts and feathers, have his wife Betsy serve it for Sunday supper. God had given him dominion, and dominion comes at a high price. You do the things you have to do.

Donald had everything it took to be a successful farmer but the money. He just didn't have enough acres. So that meant a job away from the farm. For many years he drove a tow motor at the snack cake plant in Tuttwyler. He always worked second shift, so his daylight hours were free for the farm. When the snack cake plant moved to Tennessee, he drove a school bus for the local district. The money wasn't as good, and it ate up his mornings and afternoons, but it did leave a few more hours each day for farming, and being happy. The egg money was a big help, too.

Donald looked forward to the day when he could retire, and with his Social Security and his little pension from the school district, farm full time for a few years, the way his father and grandfather and great-grandfather did all their lives. But sixteen days after his 52nd birthday, Donald Cassowary's heart stopped beating. He had just come home from driving the high school football team to an away game in Orrville and was using the full moon to toss a wagonload of hay bales into the loft of the old barn. "Everything dies before its time on a farm," his wife Betsy told Helen Abelard at the funeral.

Jeanie Cassowary changes Rhea's diaper and bends her arms and legs into the tiniest pair of bib overalls ever made. She ties a white bonnet around Rhea's face so the sun won't scorch the top of her tender head. She kisses her nose and slips her into the canvas baby carrier she wears on her chest, the one her mother-in-law ordered for her from the JCPenney catalog. "Let's go feed the chickies," she says. She doesn't mean the 60,000 Leghorns stacked in that long silvery laying house—Calvin and his automatic feeding machines feed those chickens—she means Captain Bates and his harem of caramel-red Buff Orpingtons.

The chicken coop is dark and empty and stinks to high heaven. Cobwebs hang from the rafters. Splotches of black and white manure cover the floor. Jeanie takes the lid off the feed drum and digs the metal scoop into the cracked corn. Rhea likes the crunching sound the scoop makes and she kicks her arms and legs playfully.

Now they go into the chicken yard. Captain Bates and his hens cluck and waddle forward on their skinny yellow legs. Jeanie showers them with corn. "Look how hungry the chickies are," Jeanie says to Rhea. "Peck-peck-peck. Peck-peck-peck."

Back inside the dark coop, they move along the double row of nests. All but two nests have a brown egg inside. One nest has a hen. Jeanie talks to the hen the same way she talks to her daughter, calmly, lovingly. She rubs the hen's soft breast and then reaches under her to see if there's an egg yet. The hen is no more frightened or offended by Jeanie's intruding hand than Rhea is when she feels inside her diaper. One by one the eggs go into the pockets of Jeanie's floppy apron.

When Calvin made the decision to go into the egg business with Gallinipper Foods, he and Jeanie discussed whether to keep the Buff Orpingtons and keep selling brown eggs to their neighbors. Calvin said it would be a lot of unnecessary work for only a few extra bucks. "But if you want to take care of them, we'll keep them until they die off," he said. "My mother always enjoyed gabbing with the customers."

Jeanie thought that sounded uncharacteristically sexist for her artist husband: He'll take care of the real egg business, managing that huge layer house with its automatic feeders and waterers and egg-collectors. Wifey can have her little yard of hens, and *gab* all afternoon with the other wifeys when they come for their weekly dozen or two. It worried her that he was becoming too serious, too responsible, too Republican, too much like her father back in Toledo. But then Calvin drew a hilarious charcoal sketch of her, standing among the Buff Orpingtons, scattering cracked corn, while Captain Bates tried to mate with one of the cats. It's framed now, hanging right behind her chair in the breakfast nook.

After putting the eggs in the refrigerator she sits in that chair and guides baby Rhea to her breast. She hears the driveway crackle and pulls back the gingham curtain. The semi has finally arrived to haul away their first load of eggs for Gallinipper Foods. Calvin is standing by his layer house, arms folded proudly around his clipboard. With him is Norman Marek, Gallinipper's Midwest producer relations manager, pecking away at a bright yellow pocket calculator.

Four

NORMAN MAREK GREETS the Cassowarys with that big friendly yank of a handshake he's perfected over the years. "Cal, my man! Jeanie!" He bends low over Rhea, who's holding onto her father's leg as if it was the strong trunk of an oak tree. "Your daddy tells me you're all ready for kindergarten."

Rhea hides her head under the flaps of her father's sport coat.

The maître d' leads them through a maze of round tables to a plush booth under an arbor dripping with plastic grapes. Presello's is the finest Italian restaurant in Wyssock County, the only one with candles on the tables and recorded accordion music floating through the air. Norman orders the chicken parmigiana and a carafe of the house red. Calvin orders linguini and clams. Jeanie gets the ravioli Bolognese. Rhea is talked into ordering the spaghetti and meatballs, and a chocolate milk.

Norman has invited the Cassowarys to Presello's to present Calvin with a five-year pin—it's in the shape of a rooster's head—and a Certificate of Egg-cellence signed personally by Bob Gallinipper, chairman of Gallinipper Foods. He surprises Jeanie with a pewter necklace of interlocking baby chicks. He frightens Rhea with a tin wind-up hen that bangs away at the tabletop with her beak and then poops a rubber egg, which bounces off the table and rolls under a table of men wearing softball uniforms.

The wine and chocolate milk come and Norman offers a toast: "May the next five years be five times better than the first five."

Calvin clinks glasses with him and smiles. But he doesn't feel like smiling. It's only been three weeks since Jeanie learned from the specialist in Wooster that cancer is eating away at her uterus. There'll be no more Cassowary children. Maybe no Jeanie if the surgery scheduled for Tuesday doesn't go well.

The rain doesn't make the drive home any easier. Jeanie hugs Calvin's arm as if it was the strong limb of an oak. Her free hand

25

plays with the baby chick necklace. "I wonder if Bob Gallinipper's wife wears one of these?"

"If she does, you can bet it isn't made out of pewter."

Neither of them like the bitterness in their voices. They smile at each other and tears fill their eyes. Jeanie puts the necklace back in the cardboard box and sticks it in the glove compartment, with the maps and owner's manual and the ketchup packs from McDonald's.

Dr. Mohandas Bandicoot is still wearing his paper slippers when he comes out to tell Calvin how Jeanie's surgery went. "It looks like we got it all."

It is not the reassuring appraisal Calvin hoped for. He studies the doctor's loamy eyes. "Looks like?"

When Calvin calls the farm, his mother puts Rhea on the phone. "Did the doctor fix mommy's tummy?" she asks.

"He sure did."

Calvin stays at the hospital all day, watching Jeanie sleep. He buys her a pot of violets and a Minnie Mouse balloon. He buys a newspaper and reads about President Carter's latest plan for breaking the backs of those twin demons, inflation and high interest rates. "This one better work, Mr. Caw-tuh," he mutters, imitating the new president's Georgia-mush voice. His contract with Gallinipper Foods pays him only three cents per dozen eggs produced. That three cents isn't worth half as much as it was five years ago. To keep their heads above water he's added two new layer houses—layer houses B and C—and 120,000 more hens. In the spring he'll have to go back to First Sovereignty for the capital to build layer houses D and E.

So those interest rates have got to come down—and soon.

Calvin doesn't leave the hospital until ten. He's tired and the highway is one bend after another and he knows he shouldn't drive this fast, but he's got to be home when Phil Bunyip arrives.

Eggs sounded like a good idea after his father died and the farm fell into his hands. "It's a piece of cake," Norman Marek said that evening as they sat at the wobbly table in the breakfast nook, watching the cows graze on the hillside. "Gallinipper furnishes the hens, the feed, the medication to keep them healthy. We even haul off the old hens when they're spent. All you do is furnish the housing and the labor, pay the light bills and clean out the manure. And we protect you with a long contract, a guaranteed price, no matter what."

Later Calvin and Jeanie worked with a pocket calculator, multiplying that guaranteed three-cents-per-dozen by the number of dozens a starter flock of 60,000 Leghorns would lay in a year. They subtracted loan payments they'd have to make on a layer house, as well as insurance and utility costs, and the higher real-estate taxes they'd have to pay on the farm. "Not as lucrative as teaching school," Calvin joked, "but I think we can make it fly."

So Calvin Cassowary signed a contract with Gallinipper Foods, contingent on him getting a loan for the layer house. Ted Rapparee at First Sovereignty Savings Bank took one look at that contract—Gallinipper's was the largest producer of poultry products east of the Mississippi—and gave Calvin all the money he needed. Now they've got three layer houses and 180,000 Leghorns, and a full-time man to help with the feed and manure, and next year this time they'll have five layer houses and 300,000 Leghorns. And tonight Phil Bunyip is coming to cull the spent hens.

The trucks arrive right at midnight. There are three of them, sleek black diesel cabs, tugging low flatbed trailers stacked high with empty cages. Their airbrakes fart as they plow to a stop along-side layer house A, the one built the summer Rhea was born. There are two or three chicken catchers in each cab. They jump to the ground and immediately start smoking cigarettes. When Phil Bunyip walks over to Calvin he not only has a cigarette teetering on his lower lip, he's got a can of Pepsi in his left hand and a cinnamon roll in his right hand. "Your forklift all juiced up?" he asks.

Calvin nods that it is.

Phil expertly removes his cigarette with his Pepsi hand and finishes his roll in two efficient bites. The cigarette goes back on lip and he heads for the forklift. The chicken catchers know it's time to get busy. They grind their own cigarette butts into the driveway gravel and feed their feet into the legs of the heavy paper coveralls they'll wear. They walk their fingers into rubber gloves and pull dust masks down over their backwards baseball hats.

Phil Bunyip maneuvers the forklift to the back of the nearest truck and takes down a rack of empty cages. He backs around and waits for Calvin to slide the layer house door open. He drives in. The catchers follow. They are young, brawny Indiana men, some of them enrolled at the technical college in South Bend, some high school dropouts just getting used to the hard labor they'll be doing all their working lives.

It's dark inside the layer house. And quiet. The ammonia rising from the manure pits stings the catchers' eyes and makes the nerve endings in their noses twitch. Phil lowers the rack of cages and backs out for another one. The chicken catchers go to work.

There are some 50,000 spent Leghorns in the long silvery house. There were 60,000 hens originally, but 10,000 have already died of suffocation or disease. Just eighteen months ago they arrived as young ready-to-lay pullets. For eighteen months they stood wing to wing, six to a twelve by eighteen-inch cage, unable to flap their wings, their aching toes wrapped around the wire bottoms of their cages, their beaks unable to find a bug or a worm in their tasteless mash. For eighteen months they laid two eggs every three days. Now their human master says they're *spent*, though they could go on laying an egg or two a week for a long time yet. But their master keeps very accurate records of their laying, and he has bills to pay, and if a hen can't average those two eggs every three days, well, it's time for a new batch of pullets, whose uteruses are still chock-full of happy ova, who can fulfill their biblical responsibility and keep the Cassowary farm in the Cassowary family for one more generation.

Calvin doesn't want to watch the catchers do their work. But he has to watch. His contract with Gallinipper Foods requires it. It's part of the company's quality control regimen. He stands in the doorway, where the air is only slightly better.

As the catchers file into the dark and quiet throat of the layer house, their paper coveralls and masks make Calvin think of Dr. Mohandas Bandicoot, shuffling out of the operating room in his scrubs to assure him that Jeanie's odds were good. When they reach for the latches on the cage doors he pictures the doctor lowering his scalpel toward Jeanie's belly.

"Let's do it!" one of the chicken catchers yells. The first cage doors bang open. The catchers reach in and start grabbing. The quiet ends. The screeching begins. The futile flapping of wings and snapping of bones begins. The bleeding and befouling and begging for mercy begins.

The catchers grab until they've got the legs of three hens in one hand. Then they twist their backs and reach in with their other hand, and grab the legs of the other three. The six hens are carried, heads flopping, to the transport cages and stuffed inside, like underwear into a dresser drawer. Leg bones and wing bones and neck bones snap. The catchers go back for six more hens.

Phil Bunyip brings another rack of cages and takes the full one to the truck. The hours pass. The catchers cough and sneeze and blame the "friggin' chickens" for their own miserable lives. Calvin watches one catcher, a boy with freckles and a mop of frizzy red hair, who's perhaps a little pudgy for this kind of work, as he chases a squawking Leghorn up the dark center aisle. The hen has a broken wing, but not a broken spirit. She darts left and right, always out of the boy's reach. The hen sees moonlight and freedom. The hen does not see Phil Bunyip driving in with another rack of empty cages. But Phil sees the hen and he darts to his left and crushes it under his front wheel. Phil and the boy give each other thumbs up and go on with their work. Calvin is reviled, but not surprised. Over the years he's seen Phil crush dozens of fleeing hens like that.

Rhea wakes up at about two. Immediately she remembers that her mother is in the hospital and her Columbus grandmother—her Gammy Betz—is downstairs sleeping on the sofa. A faint stench is slithering through the screen in her window. She slides out of bed and wraps her blanky around her head, a magic cape that will render her invisible to any monsters hiding in the hallway. She shuffles to her parents' room. She feels the edge of the bed and leans over it. "Wake up, Daddy. Something stinks."

But her father's side of the bed is as empty as her mother's side. She hurries to the stairway and hurries down. The blue-gray light of the television illuminates her grandmother's waxy face. "Something stinks, Gammy Betz."

Three times Rhea tells her this, but her grandmother's snoring and the middle-of-the-night jibber-jabber on the television soaks up her tiny voice. She pulls her magic cape tighter and shuffles to the kitchen. Both cats are sleeping illegally on the counter. Biscuit the shaggy sheltie is sleeping on his rug by the porch door, surrounded by his rubber toys. Rhea pets him. Without opening his eyes he licks her hand.

Rhea reaches high and opens the door. She shuffles across the porch. The stench is strong enough out here for her to identify it. It's the feather-and-manure stench of Leghorns. She squints at the layer houses. One of them is surrounded by big trucks. She sees the forklift as it rounds the corner and slips through the open door.

As she shuffles across the wet grass she begins to hear voices: men using bad words, chickens begging. The thin coating of moonlight on the driveway does not protect Rhea's bare feet from the gravel. She silently *ouches* her way across. Soon she is close enough to see her father standing in the doorway. She starts to run toward him, but the rumble of the forklift stops her. She shrinks inside her magic cloak as the forklift backs out with a tall stack of cages, cages crammed with begging hens. There's an old lilac bush on the side of the tractor shed. It's several feet around with a hollow hiding place in the middle. Rhea runs to it. She slips through the spindly limbs and sits like an Indian.

For what seems like hours the man on the forklift takes empty cages in and full cages out. For what seems like hours men shout bad words and chickens beg. For what seems like hours her father stands in the doorway, half in shadow, half in moonlight. For what seems like hours the stench of manure and feathers billows across the yard, seeping through the lilac's spindly limbs, through the holes in Rhea's magic cloak, into Rhea's porous memory.

Suddenly the layer house is quiet. Men pour out and gather in the driveway to light cigarettes. They wiggle out of their coveralls. They walk right past her and wash their hands at the pump by the willow, where her mother gets water for Captain Bates and the Buff Orpingtons.

Her father is still by the open layer house door talking to the man who's just crawled off the forklift. She hears her father use as many bad words as the forklift man does. She has never heard her father use these words before. She pulls the magic cloak down to her chin, wishing it made her not only invisible, but deaf, too. The trucks pull out, the hens stuffed in the cages glistening in the fading moonlight. She watches her father walk to the house. Through the window she can see him knock the cats off the counter with one sweep of his arm.

Suddenly the lilac bush is a scary place—the spindly limbs are dangling snakes and the tickling leaves are spiders. Rhea scrambles out. She takes a few steps toward the porch, then stops and turns toward the empty layer house. She hates the layer houses. The air inside is thick and stinky. The rows of sad chickens give her bad dreams and bad thoughts. Still she is drawn toward the open door and the quiet that's oozing out.

Her magic cloak is Superman's cape now, and she flies to the layer house. She lands in the doorway. The air is gray and as thick as gravy. Feathers float. The hens are gone but not their fear. Rhea can feel it in her nostrils and on her tongue. She starts down the aisle, the empty cages leaning and squeezing.

Then the long silvery building suddenly shudders and the big overhead lights blink on and the big ventilation fans in the ceiling roar. Rhea sees the splotches of blood and runny manure. Sees the flattened chickens on the floor. Sees that some of the empty cages are not empty. She sees torn legs—translucent white bones, dribbles of yellow fat, shreds of white skin, bloody pink meat—fixed to the wire floors by gripping toes. She sees torn wings caught in the wire walls. She sees severed heads, beaks plier-locked on the wire doors, necks like feathery spigots dripping blood.

She hears a throaty plea. In the manure pit beneath the cages she finds a living hen. Its legs and wings and spirit are intact. It wants out. Rhea lays on her stomach and reaches. Her fingers wriggle empty air. So she swings her body and drops feet-first into the pit. The manure mooshes around her ankles. She eases her hands around the hen's throbbing breast, lifts her, and sets her on the floor. The hen springs for the open door. Now Rhea must lift herself out. But her feet are trapped in the slippery manure, and her hands are covered with it, and there is nothing she can do but cry.

Five

IT IS JIMMY Faldstool who rescues Rhea from the manure pit. "Good gravy little girl," he says. "What you doing down there in the chicken shit?"

Jimmy is in his late thirties, but cold beer keeps his mind much younger. He's been working for Calvin Cassowary for three years now, cleaning out the manure pits, spreading it on the fields, burying the dead hens. Despite the cold beer and low esteem, Jimmy is a good man. He always shows up for work on time.

He pulls Rhea out by the arms and carries her to the house. "Your daddy's gonna whoop your little butt," he tells her.

But Rhea doesn't get whooped. Or yelled at. Or hugged. Her father simply has too much on his mind. Instead Gammy Betz gives her a bath and makes her a bowl of Cream of Wheat and calls her Miss Lucky Pants for not drowning in all that chicken poop.

Two days later trucks begin arriving with new pullets for the empty layer house. Each truck carries about 5,000 of the five-month-old hens. The trucks come and go all day. By suppertime layer house A, scrubbed clean of death by Jimmy Faldstool, is filled with 60,000 young, disease-free Leghorns, genetically engineered at Gallinipper's big brooding operation in West Farrago, Illinois, to lay two big grade A eggs every three days for the next eighteen months.

The morning after the pullets arrive Norman Marek calls to make sure the delivery went well. "Everything copacetic?"

"They look good," Calvin reports.

"Didn't lose too many in transport did we?"

"Couple of hundred max."

Norman is pleased. "Is that right? In this heat?" He pauses to make a notation. "And how'd things go with Jeanie? Everything copacetic there, I hope?"

33

Jeanie comes home from the hospital the day before Rhea starts kindergarten. Her legs are weak and she can barely keep from vomiting but she manages to dress her daughter in a new blue corduroy jumper and make sure there are fresh peach slices on her Frosted Flakes. She props herself against the porch post while Calvin walks their daughter to the end of the driveway. The school bus gobbles her up. "Our baby's growing up," Calvin says when he gets back to the porch.

"And I'm dying," Jeanie says.

Calvin presses his lips against her forehead and holds her in his arms. "You're not dying."

She can smell the stale sweat on the collar of his workshirt. She likes the smell. "I'm not exactly living."

"You're going to be fine."

Jeanie closes her eyes, tightly, to keep the tears inside. "Everything's going to be copacetic, is it?"

"Copacetic as hell."

Rhea gets off the bus shortly after noon. Jeanie is waiting for her with a peanut butter and jelly sandwich and a hug. The phone rings shortly after one. It's Rhea's kindergarten teacher. She's mildly concerned. "One of the first things I like to do is have the children draw a picture of themselves. It helps me determine if they view themselves positively. If they're introverted, or extroverted."

"And what did Rhea draw?" Jeanie asks.

"She drew a very pretty picture of herself. I could actually tell it was her."

"Her father's an art major."

"But then she scribbled over her picture with black crayon. She said the scribbles were chicken shit, Mrs. Cassowary. She used those actual words—*chicken shit.*"

The first thing Rhea does after changing her school clothes is run to the chicken coop and dig out a handful of cracked corn from the feed barrel. Then she runs to the old corn crib and crouches until her knees are higher than her ears. The crib sits two feet off the ground on cement block pillars, to keep snakes and rodents from getting in. The ground underneath is a jumble of old lumber, broken baskets, and rusted lawnmowers. The Leghorn she saved from the manure pit has been busy. Though she is closing in on her second birthday, and is officially spent, she does manage one egg every four days. So there are eggs everywhere. Unfortunately the mice and rats and chipmunks and raccoons have been busy, too. Almost all of the eggs have been broken open and their yolks and white sucked dry. "You under there, Miss Lucky Pants?" Rhea asks, giving the hen the name her grandmother gave her.

Every fall, the door to the chicken coop is left open, so Captain Bates and the Buff Orpingtons can range free and feast on bugs and worms and swallow tiny bits of gravel from the driveway to resupply their gizzards with the grit they need to grind and digest their food. They also can scratch and peck to their hearts' content in the vegetable gardens, making quick work of the tomatoes and cucumbers overlooked by their human masters. They can explore the high grass and the shrubbery and hop up on the low branches of the peach and apple trees to look sideways at the endless world and feel the clean fresh breezes. They can pretend to be what nature intended, free birds of the jungle; free to eat and run and sleep; free to lay eggs where and when they want; free to squirt their manure where they won't have to step in it; free to strut as far in any one direction as they wish, without a wall of wire to change their direction; free to risk the hawks in the sky and the fast cats cringing in the shadows.

Yes, when the sun sets they will hurry back to their perches in the coop and their human masters will close and latch the door—after all, they are not truly free birds of the jungle—but at dawn the door will swing open again and another day of sweet pretending can begin.

The white Leghorn looks out from her broken basket beneath the corn crib and sees the Buff Orpingtons scratching in the garden. She sees the magnificent caramel-red rooster with his great red comb and dangling wattles and great curl of black tail feathers and realizes for the first time what this egg laying business is really all about. She scoots out from the dark jumbled safety of the corn crib and nonchalantly pecks her way toward the garden.

Captain Bates sees her among the tomato vines and remembers her from the day she fled past the chicken yard. He calls out his intentions to her. She pecks closer. He fluffs out his neck feathers. She pecks closer. He prances through the tangles of rotting cucumber vines. She coyly trots away. He pursues. True, she is not much to look at. She is small and a good many of her feathers are gone. But Captain Bates knows from her body language what she wants.

And so that afternoon the chromosomes of old Maximo Gomez find their way into the scientifically perfected uterus of a Gallinipper Leghorn. And so it is that Miss Lucky Pants is invited to spend the night on the perches in the coop.

"How in hell did that Leghorn get in with the Orpingtons?" Calvin wonders as he and Jeanie walk with Rhea along the row of grapes Alfred Cassowary planted so many years ago. The grapes are finally sweet enough to eat and they stop every few seconds to pinch one off and suck it out of its purple-blue skin. It's late in the afternoon and a huge flock of starlings is washing back and forth across the empty cow pasture below the layer houses. Captain Bates and his hens are in the garden scratching among the potato vines.

"That's Miss Lucky Pants," Rhea tells him. "I saved her from the chicken shit."

"You shouldn't be using that word," her mother says. "It gets your father and me in trouble with your teacher."

"Okay," says Rhea.

Calvin knows he should go into the chick coop tonight and grab Miss Lucky Pants by the feet and wring its neck and bury it and then make up some story to tell Rhea: "It must have escaped" or "It died of old age." He sure knows he can't keep every damn Leghorn that gets away from Phil Bunyip's chicken catchers. The

Leghorns aren't pets. They're not like the Buff Orpingtons. You don't talk baby talk to them, or sing to them, or give them names. They're not part of the old farm. They're part of the new farm. They're *egg machines*. Yet Calvin knows he can no more wring that hen's neck than he could Rhea's.

Six

TWO DAYS AFTER Thanksgiving Jeanie Cassowary contracts pneumonia. Three days after that she dies.

"Mommy was very sick and God didn't want her to suffer anymore," Calvin tells his daughter as they sit on the edge of her bed. "So He took her to Heaven." The next afternoon they drive to the funeral home in Tuttwyler and Rhea is surprised to see her mother lying in a box. "I thought God took Mommy to Heaven."

"Only her soul," her father explains. "Her body stays down here with us."

That seems fair enough and Rhea has no more questions. Only when they drive her mother's body to the cemetery and lower it into the ground do the peculiarities of death bewilder her again. "Why can't we keep her at home? Where we can look at her sometimes?"

Her father closes his eyes and slowly shakes his head no.

After the funeral everyone gathers at the Cassowary house for a party of sorts. The kitchen counters are covered with casseroles and desserts. The wobbly table in the breakfast nook is covered with stacks of paper plates, towers of Styrofoam cups, pick-up-stick piles of plastic silverware.

Rick Van Varken, balancing a plate of three-bean salad on top of his can of Bud, finds his young widowed neighbor on the porch. In the field beyond the willow and the old chicken coop, two new layer houses sit half built. "They're coming along nice," Rick says. Even with a bath and a spritz of cologne he smells like his hogs.

"They should be finished by now," Calvin says. "Pullets are coming in five weeks."

Rick chases a slippery kidney bean with his plastic fork. "Your father would be proud of you. You've done a fantastic job."

Calvin doesn't answer. He just stares at the half-built layer houses.

"You hear that Dewey Fowler's selling his farm?" Rick asks.

Calvin nods.

"Some developer wants to build two hundred houses on it. Concrete streets and sidewalks and everything."

Calvin nods.

"Lots of families selling off land in that part of the township," Rick says. A cucumber slice slides off his plate and lands in the cuff of his suit pants. "Christ, would you look at that."

Calvin doesn't look. "What if a developer dangled a wheelbarrow full of money in front of you, Rick? Would you sell?"

Rick Van Varken spears the wayward cucumber slice with his plastic fork and eats it. "No way." Having succeeded in getting Calvin's mind off Jeanie for a few minutes, Rick goes inside. He is replaced by Norman Marek, who squeaks across the porch with a small clay pot of scraggly vines. "Sorry I missed the funeral," he says.

"That's okay," Calvin answers.

Norman holds out the pot. He's embarrassed. "Bob Gallinipper made me drive all the way to Indiana for these. He wanted you to have them."

Calvin takes the pot and examines the sick-looking plant inside. "He wanted me to have a strawberry plant?"

"Wild strawberry," says Norman. "Bob wanted me to tell you it's from his grandfather's grave. That he planted them himself when he was a kid. I guess he and his grandfather used to pick strawberries together. Bob's pretty sentimental about family stuff. He says he still goes to the cemetery every spring to eat wild strawberries with his 'grandpop.' Almost makes you want to cry, doesn't it?"

A week later Calvin takes Rhea to the cemetery in Tuttwyler. They take the strawberry plant with them. The grave is still covered with the fancy cut flowers from the funeral home. Calvin pushes them aside and with his bare hands digs a hole in the dirt. He gently removes the strawberry plant from the pot, along with the rich Indiana soil it's nestled in, and puts it in the hole. He rakes Ohio soil around the plant and pats it until it's firm. "Every spring we'll come here and eat strawberries with Mommy," he promises.

"I like strawberries," Rhea says.

Calvin doubts the strawberry plant will live. December in Ohio is no time to plant anything. But it's a good thought, eating strawberries every spring with Jeanie and their Rhea. A good thought.

A memorial stone has been ordered but it won't be delivered until spring, until after the ground thaws and settles. It will be a gray granite stone with Jeanie's name on one side and Calvin's on the other. The date of Calvin's death won't be chiseled in, but the date of Jeanie's will be:

CASSOWARY

JEANETTE	CALVIN
LOVING WIFE	DEVOTED HUSBAND
1950 ~ 1979	1949 ~

It will be one of several gray-granite Cassowary gravestones in the southwest corner of the old cemetery on South Mill, in a neat line just inside the black iron fence, by a bed of myrtle that stays green all winter.

There is the gravestone of Henry and second wife, Camellia:

CASSOWARY

HENRY D.	CAMELLIA E.
BORN MAY 1830	BORN APRIL 1830
DIED SEPT. 1913	DIED JULY 1909
AGED 83 YRS.	AGED 79 YRS.

Safe From the Storms of Life

There is the gravestone of Henry's son, Clyde Willis, and Clyde Willis's first and only wife, the much-suffering Ina May:

CASSOWARY

CLYDE WILLIS
1868 TO 1946

INA MAY

HIS WIFE

1872 TO 1961

There is the gravestone of Clyde's ambitious son, Alfred, and the ambitious woman from Michigan he married, Dorothy Marie Beane:

CASSOWARY

ALFRED E.	DOROTHY M.
Beloved husband & father	*Beloved wife & mother*
1894 TO 1962	1896 TO 1971

PRECIOUS IN THE SIGHT OF THE LORD IS THE DEATH OF HIS SAINTS
Psalms 116:15

There is the gravestone of Alfred's son, Donald. Donald's wife, Betsy, who has remarried and moved to Columbus, may or may not be buried there, too, someday:

CASSOWARY

DONALD	BETSY
SGT. U.S. ARMY WW2	DEVOTED WIFE
1920 • 1972	1923 • 19—

Calvin brushes his dirty hands on his pants and sits back Indian style. He pulls Rhea into his lap and wraps his arms around her. They share a long conversation of silence. Only when Rhea says she has to pee do they leave, driving to the nearest gas station. Then they drive home.

Death and winter are no match for life and business. Layer houses D and E are completed and the trucks arrive from Gallinipper's with 120,000 ready-to-lay Leghorn pullets. Calvin

41

and Jimmy Faldstool work nonstop stuffing the hens in their cages. Calvin now has 300,000 hens squirting two grade A eggs every three days.

Those 300,000 hens also will squirt thirty-six tons of manure a day.

"I don't think I can keep up with the manure much longer," Jimmy warns his boss one Friday afternoon in February as they sit across from each other in the breakfast nook. Calvin has his payroll book in front of him, figuring how much of Jimmy's raise will go for Social Security, how much for state and federal income taxes. Jimmy is sitting in Jeanie's chair. The drawing of Jeanie feeding the Orpingtons is on the wall behind him.

"Too bad Gallinippers can't engineer their hens to crap nickels," Calvin says as his finger works the egg-yolk yellow pocket calculator Norman Marek sent him for Christmas.

"That'd be something," Jimmy says.

Calvin shakes his head at what's left of Jimmy's raise. "I was hoping to hire somebody full time in the spring. But these interest rates—I'll help you with the shoveling until things turn around."

"Good gravy. No need for that."

Calvin looks up at his drawing of Jeanie with the Orpingtons. He bites his lip. He hands Jimmy his check. "Wish it could be more."

Without looking at it, Jimmy folds the check and sticks it in his shirt pocket. His good-natured acceptance of his low-paid life both saddens and embarrasses Calvin.

Jimmy heads for the door, zipping his parka as he walks. "We're almost out of fly strips," he says.

"I'll order some," Calvin says.

Jimmy puts on his gloves, then takes the right one off again, so he can dig his car keys out of his jeans. "Too bad those flies don't crap nickels, too."

No sooner has Jimmy Faldstool's old Chevy slid out of the snow-filled driveway than Marilyn Dickcissel's new Buick slides in. Calvin gets two cartons of brown eggs from the refrigerator and hurries to the porch.

Marilyn has another woman with her today. A young woman.

They walk up the slippery unshoveled sidewalk, like tightrope walkers high over the Niagara Gorge. "I brought you a new customer," Marilyn says.

The new customer is Donna Digamy, who Marilyn has just hired to handle the appointments and billing for her dog grooming business. "Your business isn't the only one growing by leaps and bounds," Marilyn says. Her cigarette smoke is mixing with the frozen air curling out of her nostrils. Donna, it seems, is single, attending the technical college in Wadesburg, working towards an associate degree in accounting. "Pretty, isn't she?" Marilyn says.

Even with the red runny nose and the bright green earmuffs, Calvin can see that this Donna Digamy indeed is pretty. But he is angry that Marilyn Dickcissel would say such a thing to him. Jeanie has been gone only two months.

Donna wipes her nose on the sleeve of her puffy coat. "I only need a dozen."

So Calvin gets another dozen from the refrigerator. He has no time for this damn brown egg business. If it wasn't for Rhea he'd wring the necks of those damn Buff Orpingtons. And just as soon as Marilyn Dickcissel and that runny-nosed girl leave he's going to take down that drawing of Jeanie feeding the chickens. He doesn't need that staring him in the face every damn morning and every damn night. Maybe Jeanie's mother would want it. Maybe he should hide it in the basement, or in the attic. Maybe someday, when time has numbed his anger at God for inventing cancer, he will find the drawing and give it to Rhea.

In April, as the temperature rises and the sweet stench of chicken manure is wiggling from the thawing fields, and flies by the score are staggering out of their hiding places in the window sills, Norman Marek calls. "Calvin, my copacetic amigo," he says, "how's the Egg King of Wyssock County?"

"Tired," Calvin answers. He is boiling spaghetti noodles for supper. Rhea is standing next to him, making finger pictures in the Kraft Parmesan cheese she's shaken out on the counter.

"Not too tired for a little holiday, I hope?"

Calvin is suspicious. He's known Norman too long. "Holiday?"

"Three-day meeting of all our producers and corporate people. The whole shebang is on Bob Gallinipper's dime. And it's a family deal, Cal. You can bring Rhea."

Seven

ON THE FIRST of June, Calvin Cassowary lifts his daughter into the cab of the pickup and helps her buckle her seat belt. They crackle down the driveway, careful not to smash the cats. They pull even with the FRESH EGGS sign. Calvin squints into the still-low morning sun to make sure nobody's coming. Belted in the way she is, little Rhea can't see much more than the latch on the glove compartment. They turn onto the road and head west. Jimmy Fald-stool, atop a tractor, scooping chicken manure into a dump truck, surrounded by a buzzle of flies, waves at them.

Wyssock County is a little bit hilly, but the counties to the west get progressively flatter. They pass field after field of ankle-high corn. Barns and silos sit on the landscape like giant lunchboxes and Thermoses. They reach the Indiana border about the same time as the sun does.

The towns out here are too small for a McDonald's or a Wendy's but they do find a hamburger stand named Sooper's and they sit on a picnic table by a bed of newly planted petunias and share a Big Soopie and fries. Rhea is enchanted by the cardboard tray the fries come in and she wears it on her head like a hat all the way to Illinois. They intersect the interstate and drive north until they are sixty miles south of Chicago. They get off at a great tangle of truck stops, motels, and gas stations. They find the Marriott. The marquee says WELCOME GALLINIPPER FARMS. Calvin doesn't notice that Rhea is still wearing the French-fry hat until they are in the elevator with half a dozen other people. He crumbles it in his hand. "Behave," he whispers.

The room Norman Marek has booked for them is a double and they each get a huge bed. Calvin showers and puts on his suit. He combs the French fry salt out of Rhea's hair and helps her put on her dress. It's the dress Jeanie's mother bought her to wear to the funeral. A serious dress for serious occasions. It's burgundy, made of soft corduroy. It has long sleeves and a row of gold buttons. It's also a short dress, so she has to wear white tights underneath, so no one can see her underwear. Last thing to go on are a pair of shiny, black shoes. "Well, look at you," Calvin says.

They go down to the banquet. A woman at a table by the door gives them name tags. Someone in a chicken suit gives Rhea a bright yellow balloon. The banquet room is dark and there's a woman playing a harp. People are standing in bundles, drinks in their hands. Norman Marek is suddenly in front of them. "Hey! Calvin! Got here safe and sound I see!" He bends over Rhea. "Hey! Look at that balloon!" He promises to steer Bob Gallinipper their way just as soon as he gets a chance. "Bob's looking forward to meeting you," he says.

That's the last they see of Norman Marek all evening. There's a sit-down dinner—baked chicken, wild rice and cold string beans—and then a welcoming speech by Bob Gallinipper himself, while the waitresses plunk down shallow glass bowls filled with balls of lime and raspberry sherbet.

Calvin has never seen Bob Gallinipper in person, though he has seen his smiling face on dozens of brochures and Christmas cards. Bob is older than his pictures. Balder. But the smile is exactly the same in person. It's as wide as a slice of cantaloupe, breaking all the physical laws of distance and perspective, as huge to the people at the back tables as it is to the people sitting up front. "I'm just as happy as the last rooster on earth to see y'all," Bob says. "I look forward to chit-chatting with each and every one of you." He introduces his wife of thirty-three years, his beautiful Bunny. "Without my Bunny, I'd be just another tractor jockey growin' corn and hemorrhoids."

Everybody laughs.

"And God only knows where you'd all be!"

Everybody laughs harder and gives Bunny Gallinipper a standing ovation. Bob kisses her with his cantaloupe smile and then introduces former California Governor Ronald Reagan who says America has to stand tall again and cut taxes and get the government off the people's backs. At the end of his speech, the big chicken appears on the stage and hands him a bobbing bouquet of red, white and blue balloons. Reagan is enthralled by the balloons. When he releases them, and they wiggle like giant sperm toward the fertile chandeliers, the crowd applauds.

Bob Gallinipper steps to the microphone and says, "I think Mr. Reagan is going to be the next president of the United States, don't you?"

When the speeches are finished and the sherbet balls eaten, the tables are cleared and Grand Old Opry regular Louise Peavey bounds on the stage, singing her 1976 hit, "Send Me a Man With Dirty Fingers."

> *"I don't want no man who pushes papers,*
> *Who disco dances and burns the flag.*
> *I want a man who does his duty,*
> *Works hard all day, loves hard all night.*
> *So send me a man with dirty fingers,*
> *A clean-cut man with a dirty mind,*
> *Send me a man with dirty fingers*
> *A real American man for this-here real American girl."*

In the morning there's a big breakfast. While everyone eats their omelets, Wayne Demijohn, Gallinipper's vice president of manure management, speaks about the latest developments in his field. "I know some days it must seem like you're in the manure business, and not the egg business," he begins, "and I'm sure the day will come when the folks in the genetic research department will develop non-defecating hens . . ."

There is a ripple of laughter as the sleepy omelet-eaters try to figure out if he's joking or not.

". . . but until that glorious day comes . . ."

There's a near unanimous agreement that he is indeed joking and the laughter builds.

". . . it's up to guano gurus like *moi* to help you get rid of that awful stuff."

Wayne Demijohn gets serious now. Processes are being developed, he announces, to turn chicken manure into feed for beef cattle. "It's the most exciting development in the poultry industry since the invention of chicken wire," he says. "We predict that within ten short years twenty percent or more of the nation's livestock feed will be comprised of chicken manure."

Omelets eaten, the producers and their families head for the buses. There are five buses, big fancy excursion buses with tinted windows and air conditioning that works and comfortable jet-plane seats that recline with a push of a button. The person in the chicken suit who passed out balloons the night before is standing by the bus door, passing out coloring books and crayons to all the children.

Rhea isn't wearing her somber burgundy dress today. She's wearing a pair of green bib overalls with a bright blue tee shirt underneath. She's got pink tennis shoes on her feet. A fun outfit for a fun day. "We going to go see the chickies hatching now?" Rhea asks her father.

"We sure are," he says.

Bob Gallinipper gets on the same bus with Calvin and Rhea. Calvin prepares to shake hands with him, and thank him for the wild strawberry plant, which, yes, took root and produced a couple of sweet little berries this spring. But Bob doesn't come down the aisle. He just waves at everybody with a single swoop of his arm, then sits in the front seat and reads the *Wall Street Journal.* Calvin thinks about going up and introducing himself. But no one else is doing that. So he rests his forehead against the tinted window and watches the endless corn and soybean fields blur by.

It takes the buses about an hour to reach Gallinipper's hatchery operation outside the university town of Gombeen. It's a big place. The driveway alone is a quarter-mile long, paralleled on both sides by white rail fence. There are about a dozen long buildings, all painted egg-yolk yellow. The buses hiss to a stop and everyone piles out. It's ten o'clock already and the sun is high and bright. Adults squint. The children make awnings out of their coloring books. Everyone is given an opportunity to stretch their legs and use the restrooms. Then the tour begins.

The tour guide for Calvin's group is assistant hatchery manager Ben Hemphill. He's wearing spotless white coveralls and an egg-yolk yellow baseball cap. From the structure of his sentences it's clear he's an educated man. "Gallinipper Foods' Gombeen hatchery operation is the fifth largest in the United States," he begins. "Also one of the most economical. State of the art, start to finish."

Ben Hemphill first takes them into the receiving department where fertilized eggs from the company's eight breeding farms are collected. "On any given day we've got a quarter-million eggs under incubation," he says. He shows them how the incoming eggs are washed and then fumigated with formaldehyde gas to kill any micro-organisms on the shells that could infect the chicks and eventually the humans who eat the eggs those chicks will later produce. "In the hatchery business," Ben Hemphill jokes, "salmonella is a bigger threat than the Ayatollah."

It's a terrible joke. Calvin's mind fills with images of the hostages in Teheran being pushed blindfolded through the chanting, fist-jabbing crowds. But he laughs along with everyone else.

"Follow me," Ben Hemphill says, his arm swooping like John Wayne sending the 7th Cavalry into battle.

In the next room he explains how the eggs are *candled*—shot with beams of light to make sure there's a fertilized embryo inside—then graded to make sure they're the right size and shape to produce a healthy chick. He shows them how the suitable eggs are placed in *setting trays* and put in huge, walk-in incubators, where for the next 19 days they will receive just the right amount of heat and humidity, just as if they were under their mothers. "Just think of these machines as great big loving momma hens," Ben Hemphill says.

In the next room he shows them how the eggs are now placed in *hatching trays* for the final three days of incubation. He opens a deep metal drawer full of hatching chicks. The children are invited to come closer, for a better look. The tiny black laser-beam eyes of the yellow-white chicks scar Rhea's soul. She runs back to her father and hides her face in his belly. "They look just like those packages of marshmallow chicks the Easter Bunny brings, don't they?" Ben Hemphill says to the children.

As they clop down the hallway Ben Hemphill laments that while someday it might be possible through chromosomal manipulation to produce only female chicks, that day has not yet arrived, and that therefore approximately half of all the chicks hatched are males. "Try as he might, a rooster can't lay an egg," he jokes. And that, he says, means the male chicks have to be *culled*.

In the next room that's exactly what's happening. Trays of noisy chicks are lined up on long tables. Workers in white coveralls are checking their genitals. "There are various methods of differentiating male chicks from females," Ben Hemphill says. "Here at Gallinippers we use the *Japanese Method*—that is, we visually identify the rudimentary male sex organs. As you can see, most of our sexors are of Japanese descent, so hence, the Japanese Method. For whatever reason, a number of Japanese-American families have developed a high-degree of skill at chicken sexing. We treasure their expertise and patriotism."

Everyone watches as the sexors peer into the rectums of the chicks.

Rhea notices something else. The Japanese people are putting some of the chicks in blue plastic boxes and tossing others into metal drums. "How come they're throwing those chickies away?" she asks Ben Hemphill.

He answers calmly. "The male chicks are recycled along with other hatchery by-products, into food for doggies and kitty cats."

The tour moves on to the *de-beaking* room. "As you know only too well, chickens like to peck on each other," Ben Hemphill says. "So to prevent future cannibalism in the layer houses, chicks are de-beaked."

"What's de-beaked mean?" Rhea asks her father as they shuffle toward another set of tables stacked high with trays of chicks. Calvin makes a pair of scissors with his fingers and pretends to snip the end of her nose. "They trim the point of the chicks' beaks so they can't peck each other to death."

"Captain Bates and the Orpingtons don't peck each other to death, and they got their beaks," she points out.

Calvin pats her on the head. "That's because they've got a big yard, and lots of other things to peck at. But in the little cages in the layer houses, the hens turn on each other. So, it's to everybody's advantage that they're de-beaked."

Ben Hemphill stands next to a woman in white coveralls and an egg-yolk yellow baseball cap. She has a small gray metal machine in front of her. A thick black electrical cord coils out the back. "Experienced operators like Mindy here can de-beak a chick every three seconds," Ben says. He gives her a squeeze on the neck and asks, "How long you been with us, Mindy?"

"Eight years," she says.

The woman named Mindy can indeed de-beak one chick every three seconds. With her left hand she snatches a chick out of the tray, and bringing her hands together in front of the gray machine, guides the chick's nub of a beak toward a pair of blades *Bzzzzzzp.* The chick sprays the palm of Mindy's hand with watery manure. Mindy's right hand drops the de-beaked chick into a tray of other de-beaked chicks as her left hand snatches another.

"The chicks feel no more pain than you do when you clip your toenails," Ben Hemphill says. "The process scares the little buggers, that's for sure. But it doesn't hurt them."

"If it doesn't hurt, why don't you put *your* nose in there?" Rhea says. Her voice is cold, loud, and startling, as if her little-girl body has been possessed by a demon.

Ben Hemphill laughs and motions for everyone to follow. "Down at this end of the room are the *dubbing* stations—where the chicks' combs are trimmed off.

Rhea holds her hands over her face and watches through the slits in her fingers as women in white coveralls and egg-yolk yellow baseball caps run a pair of curved scissors over the chicks' tiny heads.

Rhea knows all about chicken combs, those zig-zag ridges of red skin on the top of their heads. Captain Bates has a magnificent comb; in the front it flops comically over his right eye and in the back it stands as stiff as a handful of frozen fingers. The Buff Orpington hens have impressive combs, too; from the top of their breaks the fleshy red spears rise like the scallops on the back of a fairy tale dragon. Miss Lucky Pants has no comb to speak of and now Rhea knows why.

"Dubbing increases egg production by one to two percent," Ben Hemphill says. "Floppy combs get in the hens' way when they eat and drink. And they're susceptible to injury from getting them caught in the cage wires. Dubbing also puts the hens on an equal social basis. Confuses the ol' pecking order. Our research shows that chickens recognize each other by their distinctive combs. So if they all look the same, they can't tell who's stronger or weaker, so there's less fighting. Fewer injuries, more eggs."

"A dubbed flock is a happy flock," a wise man in the crowd says.

"Amen," Ben Hemphill says. He starts out the door, then swivels, and gives his arm that John Wayne swoop. "Lunch time, everybody! Hope you like fried chicken!"

Lunch is held in a circus tent, in a grove of maples upwind from the hatchery buildings. Bouquets of yellow balloons bob from the tent poles. The picnic tables inside are covered with red-striped tubs of chicken. A German oompa band wearing green felt hats and lederhosen plays polkas. The guy in the chicken suit dances with Bunny Gallinipper. Rhea Cassowary not only refuses to eat, but climbs up on the tables and runs the full length of the tent, kicking the chicken tubs left and right.

Norman Marek won't let Calvin and Rhea take the bus back to the Marriott with the others. He drives them in a bright yellow company car. He's none too happy. "Bob Gallinipper saw it all, Cal."

"Rhea was just tired," Calvin assures him.

"Then she should have fallen asleep not jumped on the tables and kicked the tubs of fried chicken all over kingdom come."

Rhea is in the back seat, rolled into a ball, hands over her face, wishing she had the magic blanky that makes her invisible. The images of chicks having their beaks and combs sliced off, of boy chicks being tossed into barrels and ground into cans of stinky slop for cats and dogs, are pushing tears out of the corners of her eyes. She's shaking. And itching something awful, on her chest, right between those little red dots her mother used to call her nippie-nips.

"Norman, I'm sorry," Calvin says.

Norman exhales a long gurgle of stale air. "You and Rhea have gone through so much. I realize that. I'm sure Bob realizes it, too. Jeanie was a princess. You met her in college, didn't you?"

"That's right."

"I know what my divorce did to me," Norman says. "So I can imagine how rough it is to lose someone you actually love."

Calvin looks back at Rhea, then out the window. The flat fields are blurring by. "We thought we were going to be teachers. Then my dad died."

"I lost my dad when I was fifteen," Norman says. Afraid that either he or Calvin will start crying, he quickly gets back to the subject. "Gallinipper Foods is a big family. In order to compete and grow, everything's got to be copacetic. Copacetic in the corporate offices. Copacetic at the hatcheries and brooding farms. Copacetic at the layer operations. Copacetic top to bottom. Up and down the line." Now he reaches down and shakes Calvin's knee, demonstrating the depth of his friendship and concern. "Rhea's a sweet girl. But it's obvious everything's not copacetic with her. Ben Hemphill told me she was a brat the entire tour. So it isn't just kicking the chicken tubs, Cal. Maybe Rhea needs help."

"If I thought she needed professional help, I'd take her," Calvin says.

"Maybe I'm way out of line, Cal, but I don't think she likes chickens."

The spot between Rhea's nippie-nips is not only itching, it's burning, as if her heart was lighting matches.

"Just the opposite," Calvin tells Norman Marek. "She loves chickens. Thinks they're all pets. Last summer she rescued one of the spent hens from the manure pits. She calls her Miss Lucky Pants."

Norman's hands are wringing the sweat out of the steering wheel. "Girl thing, I suppose."

Rhea reaches under the bib of her overalls and works her fingers down the front of her blue turtleneck. She scratches the spot between her nippie-nips that's itching and burning. She feels something. At first she's afraid it's a spider. But it's too fuzzy to be a spider. And it's not crawling away. Or biting her fingers. She claws at it. It seems to be stuck right there in her skin. She pinches it. Yanks it. Cries out.

Her father twists. "What'd you do?"

Rhea pulls her hand from her turtleneck and examines the soft and fuzzy thing pinched between her fingers. It's nothing but a tiny white feather. "I had a feather growing between my nippie-nips," she says.

"Behave," her father says.

Eight

THE SAME AFTERNOON they return from Bob Gallinipper's corporate get-together in Gombeen, Calvin Cassowary sits his daughter down on the picnic table in the backyard. "I know the layer houses frighten you," he begins. "They're frightening places—if you let your imagination get in the way."

Rhea has her elbows on her knees and her hands under her chin. She is watching Captain Bates trot after Miss Lucky Pants in the overgrown vegetable garden next to the garage. In the past the little flock wouldn't be allowed to roam free this late in the spring. Once the garden was planted, they'd be confined to their coop and yard to protect the tomatoes, squash, and green beans from their dawn-to-dusk pecking. But with half of her mother in Heaven, and the other half in the Tuttwyler cemetery, her father says there's no time for a garden. So Captain Bates and his hens have all summer to be the free birds of the jungle the Creator intended. "I don't like the cages," she tells her father.

Calvin drags his forearm across his sweaty face. This difficult talk with his daughter reminds him of the difficult talks he used to have with his own father, about things like sex and a young man's responsibility to his family, his country and his God. "I know."

"The chickens don't like them either."

"We can't have 300,000 thousand hens running around loose."

"Why do we have to have 300,000 hens at all?"

"Because we're chicken farmers, Rhea. It's what we do."

"Maybe we should do something else."

Calvin scratches the top of her head. Her hair is the same deep red-brown as Jeanie's now. "When you have a farm, you have to farm." For some reason his mind travels back to the intellectual drivel of his art student days. "It's what the Hindus call karma. It's our destiny. What we are and what we do. Eggs are our karma."

"Chicken jail," Rhea says as Captain Bates hops up on Miss Lucky Pants' back and flaps his wings. "That's what we do. We run a chicken jail."

Calvin stops playing with his daughter's hair, to keep himself from yanking it. "People need eggs. We produce eggs. It's a good thing, Rhea. Something to be proud of."

"I'm proud I saved Miss Lucky Pants from the chicken shit."

Calvin's face needs wiping again. "I'm proud you did, too. But we can't make pets out of all the old hens. We'd lose the farm. So we do what we gotta do, pumpkin seed. You and me."

Rhea scratches between her nippie nips. "You and me, pumpkin seed," she says.

Calvin looks at the empty end of the picnic table. He wants Jeanie to be sitting there, reading a book, eating an apple, curling her hair around her finger, just being alive. "That's right. You and me. And you are going to be six years old in a couple of weeks. Old enough for a few outside chores."

And so Calvin tells Rhea that Captain Bates and the Buff Orpingtons are going to be her responsibility from now on. She's going to start feeding them; gathering the eggs, washing off the poop and putting them in cartons in the refrigerator; making sure the chicken coop door is closed and latched at night. "But remember, Rhea," he says, shaking his finger at her nose, "the Orpingtons are not pets. We take care of them for the eggs and we sell the eggs because we need the money. We don't play with them or give them names."

"Captain Bates has a name," she says. "Miss Lucky Pants has a name."

"It would be better if they didn't." Calvin takes Rhea by the chin and turns her face toward his. She has Jeanie's brown eyes, too, and her always questioning eyebrows. "It's a deal then?"

"Okay," she says, "but if they have chicks I'm not going to cut off their beaks or look up their butts."

Calvin tells her that there won't be any Orpington chicks, that when those hens get old and die off, that's going to be the end of the brown egg business, that the FRESH EGGS sign is coming down for good.

On Saturday they drive to the cemetery in Tuttwyler. They walk across the thick grass to Jeanie's grave. Calvin is still amazed at how well the wild strawberries are doing. He didn't expect that pot of scraggly vines to survive. But the roots took hold and that one plant has turned into three. They find exactly three ripe berries to eat, one for Rhea, one for him, one for Jeanie.

Nine

FLIES ARE ALREADY banging into the window when Rhea wakes. The stench of 300,000 Leghorns is oozing in. Rhea Cassowary stretches and yawns. She pulls up her Holly Hobby nightgown and feels between her nippie nips. There's another feather growing.

She bites down on her tongue and plucks it. And looks at it. White. Silky. Delicate. Sharp as a pin, too. Rolling onto her stomach, Rhea worms her body over the edge of the bed until she can reach the Nestlé's Quik can on her toy shelves. The can already has several of the little feathers in it. She drops the new feather inside and pounds down the lid. Later today she'll be celebrating her sixth birthday. Until then it'll be just another day. She squeaks into the bathroom, pees, and brushes her teeth. She puts on her dirty jeans and a clean tee shirt and goes downstairs. "Daddy? Biscuit?"

Neither answer. Neither are there. Nor are the cats. She plans to have a bowl of Rice Krispies for breakfast but sees the box of Hostess donuts on the table and decides to have one of those instead. When the donut is gone, and the powdered sugar brushed on the floor, she pours an inch of orange juice into a glass and fishes in her bottle of Flintstone vitamins for a Barney. She finds one of her tennis shoes in the box by the refrigerator and one under the table in the dining room. Tonight there'll be a birthday cake on that table and some balloons and crêpe paper dangling from the light fixture. There'll be presents stacked on the buffet. At least that's the way birthdays went before God moved her mother's soul up to heaven.

She puts on the apron her mother used to wear. It's many sizes too big, but Gammy Betz has pinned up the bottom, so it doesn't drag on the ground and make her fall flat on her cute little face. She goes outside to feed Captain Bates and the Buff Orpingtons. And gather their eggs.

As the day drags on Captain Bates and his hens will wander far and wide in their search for bugs and worms. But right now they're gathered by the chicken coop door, waiting for that heaping scoop of cracked corn. Rhea showers them with it, just like her mother used to. "Peck-peck-peck," she says to them, just like her mother used to do. "Peck-peck-peck."

There aren't as many eggs in the nests in the morning as you find in the afternoon, but there are always a few, and you have to collect them, her father says, so no hen gets a notion to *set*. This morning there are five brown eggs waiting in the nests. Rhea gently puts them in the pouch of her apron. Then she hears a frail *cluck-cluck* coming from one of the top nests and she stands on her tip-toes to look inside. "What you doing in there Miss Lucky Pants?" she says.

The white Leghorn pecks sassily at her hand.

"That's not nice," says Rhea. She lovingly scratches the feathers on the hen's breast. The hen softens her mood and purrs something like a kitten. "You got any eggs under there?"

Miss Lucky Pants stands proudly. She has three eggs under her.

It starts to itch between Rhea's nippie nips. She knows she should collect those three white eggs, take them in the house so her father can scramble them for his breakfast. She knows she should obey her father. But Rhea also knows she'd feel terrible stealing those eggs out from under Miss Lucky Pants. She saved that poor Leghorn hen from the manure pit. Gave her a name. How can she now steal her babies away? How can she let her father scramble them?

She pushes on Miss Lucky Pants until she's back on her eggs. The hen kitten-purrs her gratitude.

Rhea takes the other eggs inside. She washes off the manure and puts them in one of the cartons in the refrigerator. She turns on the television and clicks to the Nickelodeon channel and begins the long wait for her birthday.

At noon her father comes in for lunch. "You watch too much television," he yells.

Rhea hears him, but goes on watching. Lassie is telling Timmy about the abandoned puppies she's found. She wonders why

Biscuit isn't that concerned for the plight of others. Biscuit just eats and sleeps and leaves big piles of poop on the lawn.

"Come make yourself a sandwich," her father yells from the kitchen.

"Yuk," she yells back. They've had nothing but sandwiches for lunch since her mother died. Every week they go to the Stop' N Go in Tuttwyler and get lunch meat, bread, and cheese. And it's always the same kind of lunchmeat—pound of Dutchloaf, pound of bologna—and the same kind of cheese—half pound of Swiss—and the same kind of bread—jumbo loaf of wheat. And on Saturday when they have soup with their sandwiches, it's always tomato soup, made Cassowary style, half a can of water, half a can of milk, tablespoon of butter, and a quick shake of pepper. Her father's suppers are better, though just as predictable: hamburgers on Mondays and Saturdays, fried bologna and onions on Tuesdays and Thursdays, spaghetti on Wednesdays, on Sunday rubber pork chops, fried potatoes, and canned peas. Fridays they drive to the Pizza Teepee in Tuttwyler for a pepperoni and mushroom.

Rhea's mother made lunchmeat sandwiches for lunch, too, but not every day. Sometimes she'd make grilled cheese sandwiches. Sometimes tuna on toast sandwiches. Sometimes peanut butter and jelly sandwiches. Sometimes she'd heat up a can of Franco-American spaghetti. There'd always be some kind of fruit, too, a banana or sliced pears or applesauce. On soup days it could be chicken noodle or beef vegetable just as well as tomato. Supper could be meatloaf or fish sticks and Tater Tots or made-from-scratch macaroni and cheese. Carrots or lima beans or asparagus or creamed corn might show up on the table. Some of her mothers choices for supper were uneatable, to be sure. But you never knew what it would be on any given night, except for Fridays, when the three of them would drive to the Pizza Teepee in Tuttwyler.

After Lassie is praised for saving the puppies, Rhea goes to the kitchen for that sandwich.

"What's with Miss Lucky Pants?" her father asks as they sit at the wobbly table. "You haven't brought in any white eggs for a couple days now."

Rhea plays dumb, putting her full concentration on the face she's drawing on her bolonga with the squeeze-jar of mustard. "Maybe she's spent."

"Maybe you're not checking all the nests."

She gives the bologna slice a frown. "Maybe some of the nests are too high for me."

"Then stand on a box."

"I don't have a box."

"I'll get you one."

That night after the spaghetti, Rhea's Toledo grandmother and grandfather arrive. They bring a big cake with them and put it on the dining room table. They put a present on the buffet.

Gammy Betz arrives, too, along with her husband Ben and another present for the buffet. They help her other grandparents hang the balloons and crepe paper.

For some reason, one of their regular brown egg customers shows up for the party. It's Donna Digamy, the one who works at Marilyn Dickcissel's dog grooming business. She sniffles all through the singing of "Happy Birthday."

When it is time to make a secret wish and blow out the candles, Rhea wishes for the same thing she prays for every night—for those little feathers to stop growing between her nippie nips. She knows that people are not supposed to grow feathers there, or anywhere else on their bodies. She knows sooner or later those feathers are going to give her big problems.

The birthday wish doesn't work any better than the prayers. Rhea wakes up itching and plucks another feather from her chest and hides it in the Nestlés Quik can.

Again this morning the house is empty. Again this morning she eats breakfast alone. She finds her tennis shoes, puts on the pinned-up apron, and goes out to feed Captain Bates and the Buff Orpingtons. And gather the eggs.

She finds that her father has kept his word. He's placed a wooden box alongside the nests so she can check the top ones for eggs.

Miss Lucky Pants has another egg under her, and Rhea, though a year older than she was yesterday at this time, faces the same old predicament: Does she listen to her father, or does she listen to her heart? Does she snatch the white eggs out from under Miss Lucky Pants, or does she let her set?

"You're a pain in the butt, Miss Lucky Pants," she growls as she scratches the hen's soft breast.

Miss Lucky Pants tips her head and stares at her with a round, unblinking eye. Rhea leaves her eggs alone.

Only after collecting four brown eggs from the Buff Orpingtons hens does Rhea get a brainstorm. The first thing she must do is make sure her father is busy with something. She finds him in the tractor shed with Jimmy Faldstool, working on the tow motor. Their hands and forearms are covered with grease. Sweat is dripping off their chins. "Are you real busy right now?" she asks.

"Go play," her father says.

"Okay," she says. She runs to the cement block building behind the layer houses. Before going inside she turns and makes sure neither her father nor Mr. Faldstool are watching. This building is the egg house, where the collected eggs are graded and candled and put in heavy cardboard cases for shipping to Gallinipper's. She opens one of the cases and takes out one white egg. She puts it in her apron. Then she takes another egg from another box and another from another.

She goes back to the tractor shed. "I collected Miss Lucky Pants's white eggs today," she tells her father. "Thanks for the box."

"Go play," her father says.

Rhea's deceit lasts only three weeks.

On the same day she and her father are supposed to go to the Wyssock County Fair she discovers that Miss Lucky Pants's eggs have hatched. One chick has already fallen out of the high nest and two of the Orpington hens are fighting over its body. Rhea chases the hens away and puts the mangled chick in the pouch of her apron. She steps on the box and looks in the nest. Miss Lucky Pants proudly rises and spreads her wings. Peeping among the broken egg shells are six healthy chicks.

Rhea breaks the news to her father when they are sitting in bumper-to-bumper traffic outside the fairgrounds. This is the day country singer Louise Peavey performs in the grandstand, right before the demolition derby. So there are lots of cars funneling into the fairgrounds today. For some reason, her father has brought Donna Digamy with them.

"Guess what, Daddy," Rhea says from the back seat.

She has to say it three times before he answers, "What?"

"Miss Lucky Pants has babies."

Donna Digamy rests her chin on the back of her seat and sniffs a trickle of mucus back up her nostril. "Isn't that neat! How many?"

"Seven," Rhea says, "but one fell out of the nest and died already."

"So you've got six?" Donna Digamy asks.

"That's right," says Rhea, "seven minus one is six."

Their day at the fair goes well enough. They eat French fries drenched with vinegar. They eat deep-fried pieces of dough called elephant ears. They walk through all the animal barns. In the cattle barn the cows are standing with their heads facing the wall and their ugly butt-holes facing the people walking along the center aisle. In the pig barn all the pigs are asleep. In the sheep barn all the sheep are asleep. In the goat barn a ram with curly horns bites a button off Rhea's flannel shirt. In the rabbit house the rabbits are asleep.

In the poultry barn the chickens are crowded into cages, just like the Leghorns in the layer houses. The cages are plastered with ribbons, red ones and white ones and blue ones. "What's all those ribbons for?" Rhea asks.

"For first, second and third place," her father explains.

"For running a race?"

"For looking healthy."

Rhea stands on her toes and looks in the cages. Yes, these chickens do look healthy. They have their beaks and their combs. They have all their feathers. They're clean. They're calm. And some are very fancy. "What kind of chickens are these with the feathers on their feet?" Rhea asks her father. There's a big blue ribbon stuck to the cage.

"Chochins."

"How come we don't have any of those?" Rhea asks.

"They're just for show. A lot of food and poop for nothing."

In one cage Rhea sees an enormous black rooster with a white face and huge droopy waddles. "That one looks like Captain Bates."

"That's a Black Spanish," her father says. As they walk down the aisle, he tells Donna Digamy the story about Maximo Gomez, how Chuck Cowrie bought the rooster from a brothel owner in Cuba, during the Spanish-American War. No matter how fancy the chickens are, they all make Donna Digamy sneeze. So they leave the chicken barn and go to the midway and ride the belly churning tilt-the-whirl and pay fifty cents each to see the world's smallest horse.

"You should get one of these for Rhea," Donna Digamy says to Calvin, who's holding Rhea up so she can scratch the tiny horse's big head.

Rhea sees the anxiety on her father's face and answers for him. "A lot of food and poop for nothing," she says.

That night Calvin goes with Rhea to the chicken coop. While she feeds the Buff Orpingtons, he places Miss Lucky Pants and her six chicks in a cardboard box. "This never should have happened," he says.

"But it did," Rhea says, shrugging the way her mother used to shrug.

"And now we've got all these worthless chicks."

"You're not going to make them live in that box, are you?"

"We're going to make a pen for them in the old cow barn—until they're big enough to join the others."

Worry wrinkles Rhea's face.

"Not with the Leghorns," he says. "In here with your grandmother's Buffs. We can't send Gallinippers any of the eggs from these little half-breed buggers."

"We can't have that," says Rhea.

"No we can't. And we can't have any more of your sneaking and lying either."

"I'm sorry."

"Are you, Rhea? If you can't live up to your end of the bargain, Captain Bates is Sunday dinner."

Her father carries the box to the cow barn. The cows have been gone for years but the barn still smells like cows. Rhea sits on an old bale of straw and watches as her father untangles a roll of rusted chicken wire—fencing with holes so small even tiny chicks can't crawl out—and makes a pen in the corner. He sets the box with Miss Lucky Pants and the chicks inside the pen. He reaches into his pants pocket and takes out his jackknife and cuts a rounded door in one end of the box.

"Is that their little house?" Rhea asks.

"Uh huh. That's their little house." Calvin scoops Rhea off the bale and makes a swing out of his arms. "Now you've got to understand, some of your chicks are probably going to die. Some always do. But if you keep them fed and watered, most will grow up fine. And then we'll have a few more worthless chickens. Okay, pumpkin seed?"

Rhea swings back and forth in her father's arms. Her chest is itching, but she doesn't dare reach down her shirt and pluck the little feather that's surely growing there. "Okay, pumpkin seed," she says.

And so Rhea begins taking care of Miss Lucky Pants and her six chicks.

Unlike the chicks stuffed in the trays at the hatchery they visited in Gombeen, these chicks have room to run around. And they do. They run and hop and peck at everything. Miss Lucky Pants teaches them how to drink water from the shallow clay bowl and how to peck at the mash in the metal tray. She also teaches them how to *preen*—clean and smooth their tiny feathers with their tiny beaks.

Although she was born in a metal hatching drawer, Miss Lucky Pants is a wise and attentive mother. When her chicks peep that they're getting cold, she spreads her wings and lets them scramble under her.

One of the chicks dies—Rhea's father said that might happen—but the other five keep eating and growing. Rhea spends as much time as she can in the old cowless cow barn, squatting outside the chicken-wire pen, watching and worrying. The chicks lose their silky yellow feathers and start growing stiff white adult feathers. They start to grow their own wings and pretty soon they are too big to fit under Miss Lucky Pants.

Rhea knows she shouldn't name the chicks. Or make pets out of them. Her father has laid the law down about that. But they are so cute.

So the three female chicks she names Nancy, Mary Mary Bo Berry, and Half Pint— Nancy after President Reagan's skinny wife; Mary Mary Bo Berry after a funny song her mother used to sing to her; Half Pint after the nickname Pa Ingles calls Laura on *Little House on the Prairie*. Despite the clever names she gives them, the female chicks prove to be three boring bumps-on-a-log.

They look alike and act alike. Try as Rhea might to coax them out their sameness, to get them to play and squabble and show a little personality, they just eat and poop and grow white feathers. "Egg machines," Rhea complains, "that's all you're ever going to be. Three dumb Gallinipper egg machines."

The two male chicks have too much personality. The nasty, strutty one with a full spray of black tail feathers she names Black-butt. The scrawny, nervous one with the lopsided wattles and the single black feather curling from its rump like a question mark, she

66

names Mr. Shakyshiver. Blackbutt does everything he possibly can to make Mr. Shakyshiver sorry he was born.

On Thanksgiving Day, Rhea's father takes Miss Lucky Pants and her now-grown family out of the cow barn and puts them in the coop with Captain Bates and the Buff Orpingtons. Immediately the Captain gives Blackbutt a taste of his own medicine, pecking him hard on the toes and chasing him into the corner. Mr. Shakyshiver immediately retreats to another corner on his own. That out of the way, the Captain hops on the backs of the three young white hens, one right after the other.

Ten

THREE DAYS BEFORE Christmas, Calvin Cassowary decides to propose marriage to Donna Digamy. They've been dating for seven months now. Sleeping together for five.

He is surprised by his decision.

Jeanie has been dead for only 13 months. They'd been, as his roommate at Kent State, Dave D'Hoy, once said, "Two peas in a pod, man." Calvin was a daydreamy art major then, Jeanie a daydreamy English major. He could sit on Blanket Hill and make charcoal sketches all afternoon. She could read all night. They shared the same bewildered view of the world as it *was*—the wars and the racism and the pollution and the sexism and the preoccupation with making money—and the same optimistic view of what the world *could* be if people just let other people do their own thing.

Calvin met Jeanie at Boinky's Pizza, just off the campus. She was waitressing and he was eating. It was the fall after the Ohio National Guard went berserk and killed four students during a protest over Nixon's invasion of Cambodia. So Peace and Love and Tragedy was still in the air and when Jeanie brought Calvin his pepperoni pizza, the pepperonis were lined up in the shape of a peace symbol. She did this, she later told him, because she liked his blue-gray eyes and his fu-manchu mustache.

Calvin liked Jeanie's brown eyes and the dimples on her chin, not to mention the braless breasts inside her tee shirt and the smiling cheeks inside her bellbottoms. He came to Boinky's for pizza every night for a week, and each time was served a peace symbol pizza from the waitress with the brown eyes and dimpled chin. Calvin was the shy artist type, but one night summoned the balls to say, "Instead of a peace symbol, why don't you spell out you name?"

When she brought out the pizza it said J E A N I E.

And now, just thirteen months after Jeanie's death, Calvin has decided to propose to Donna Digamy. He doesn't love her the way he still loves Jeanie. Doesn't love her soul. But he sure loves her body and her resolve to work hard and get somewhere. He loves the way she marvels at his plans to be the largest egg producer in the state of Ohio. He loves her selective Catholicism, her ability to have guiltless sex outside marriage while still trusting God to look out for her.

"I think we should get married," Calvin says the night before Christmas Eve as they lay naked and spent in her apartment.

She takes a corner of the sheet and wipes a dribble of cold sperm off her leg. "I think so, too."

The artist in Calvin tells him that he will never love Donna Digamy the way he still loves Jeanie Marabout. But a man needs a woman, and a farmer needs a wife, and hi-o-the derrio and e-i-e-i-o, and what the hell, the sex is so good, and she's getting that associate's degree in accounting, and she can handle the books while he handles the Leghorns. And Rhea does need a mom.

The only downside to Donna Digamy, as far as Calvin Cassowary can see, is her constant sniffing and sneezing. The first time he saw her, when she came with Marilyn Dickcissel for brown eggs, he figured it was a winter cold. But she still had it two weeks later when she came for brown eggs by herself. "That's some cold," he said then. And she said, "I wish it was a cold. It's all that dog hair and the shampoo Marilyn uses."

And so Calvin found out about her allergies. Dog hair and shampoo weren't the only things that made Donna Digamy sniff and sneeze: Cats did. Perfumes did. Dry-cleaning fluid did. The feces of dust mites did. Even chicken feathers did. "I'm afraid I'm allergic to life," she sneezed and coughed to Calvin one May day when they went walking and got too close to a blooming lilac.

On Christmas Eve Calvin takes Donna to J.W. Dangle's Jewelry in Wooster to buy a diamond. He hadn't given Jeanie a diamond. How could an art major afford a diamond? What he could do was make a ring. It came out magnificently. Three delicate bands of braided silver. Now it's in the box of Jeanie's stuff he plans to give Rhea someday.

"I can only spend a thousand bucks," he tells Donna before going into Dangle's.

She dabs her nose with her handkerchief and smiles under-standingly. She has already seen the books and knows how tight things are on the farm. Inside she picks out an $880 ring. The jeweler's aftershave makes her sneeze.

Once they're married—they've agreed on a June wedding—Calvin will take her to an allergist. He's already checked his policy and his health insurance will cover eighty percent of the office calls and all of the prescriptions.

"We're going to have a good life together," he tells Donna as they trot through the icy rain to the car. In the middle of the town square there's a Christmas tree covered with white lights and huge red bows.

She kisses his cheek as they trot, her smile assuring him that a good life will be good enough.

And so the winter passes and the spring passes and the day of their wedding comes. It is a grand Roman Catholic wedding in a grand Roman Catholic church in an old Cleveland neighborhood. Donna Digamy's Catholic relatives are unabashedly ebullient, as if en masse they've died and gone to Heaven. Calvin Cassowary's Protestant relatives are reserved and nervous, as if they've landed unexpectedly in that place Catholics call Purgatory. While the organist prepares them for the sacrament ahead, Calvin's relatives try to name the garishly painted statues ringing the walls. "Is that supposed to be Joseph or John the Baptist?" Calvin's aunt from Penfield whispers.

"Beats me," his uncle whispers back.

The ceremony finally begins. From the length of the bulletin, it looks like it's going to be a long ceremony, with lots of strange things that never take place in a Protestant wedding. Donna's rela-tives know exactly when to cross themselves and exactly when to kneel. Calvin's relatives, of course, know they mustn't cross them-selves. But the kneeling? What about all this kneeling? And now they're going to celebrate communion? Right in the middle of a wedding? "What are the Methodist rules on this?" Calvin's aunt from Beebetown wonders.

When Donna puts a bouquet of flowers at the feet of the Virgin

Mary's statue, Calvin's aunt from Walnut Creek clutches her fake pearls, as if witnessing a Satanic ritual involving goats and naked children.

Yes, this big, splashy and incredibly long Catholic wedding is tough on the Cassowary clan. No matter how hard they try to relax and enjoy the experience, they just can't stop feeling guilty. Feeling like they're betraying the Reformation. Feeling like an angry God is going to send a semi crashing into them on the long drive home.

Weddings are a time for feelings.

For his part, Calvin feels surprisingly free of the guilt he figured he'd feel. He feels Jeanie's presence, telling him it's okay for him to remarry, as long as he doesn't confuse his earthly love for this new woman with his eternal love for her. As long as he's certain this new woman will be a good mother for their Rhea.

Donna feels the inside of her nose tingling, possibly from the priest's cologne, possibly from her own eyeliner.

Calvin's mother, who gave her body to Ben Betz so soon after first husband Donald's death, feels the sweat on her neck as the priest reads from First Corinthians: *The body is not for immorality; it is for the Lord.*

Donna's mother feels relief that her daughter made it to the altar before the sperm of some man wiggled into one of her eggs. She's been worrying about that since Donna was fifteen, and went to Homecoming with Robby Kolicki, who was a good-looking boy but dumb as a post.

Rhea can't see very much of the ceremony over the back of the pew. But she can see the giant Jesus looking down from his cross. She can see from the expression on his face that he does not like being frozen for all eternity in that contorted position. She can see that Jesus feels like tearing his arms and legs free; that he feels like going up to Heaven; that he feels like curling up in Jeanie Cassowary's lap and having her read *Green Eggs and Ham* to him.

The last place on earth Norman Marek wants to be today is at a *business wedding*. Still he can't help but feel a certain amount of satisfaction. This Donna Digamy seems to be a bright, determined young woman, not hampered by the dreamy idealism that plagued Jeanie. And that associate's degree in accounting she's getting. Big, big asset. Best of all, there'll be someone to ride herd on Rhea. So all in all, everything's copacetic.

Calvin and Donna will be leaving for the Poconos tonight. They've reserved a sexy honeymoon cottage with a heart-shaped waterbed and a bathtub in the shape of a champagne glass. But before they can leave for the airport, Calvin has to take Rhea to the cemetery in Tuttwyler to eat wild strawberries with Jeanie.

That single plant of Bob Gallinipper's has multiplied into a dozen or more.

"Daddy married Donna Digamy," Rhea tells her mother. She's only eaten three little berries so far, but already her fingertips are stained red and there's a dribble of pink juice down the front of the lacy dress she wore to the wedding.

"I already told her," Calvin says.

"Did she say it was okay?" Rhea wonders.

"Of course she said it was okay."

Rhea counts the unripe berries on the vines, then says, "Maybe momma's got remarried, too. Maybe she married Jesus."

Calvin cries for six minutes, then says, "When Donna and I get back I'll erect a little fence around the berries—a little white picket fence, I've seen them at the garden center—so the caretakers can't mow them over. Good idea, huh pumpkin seed?"

PART II

"These signs of martyrdom did not arouse horror in the minds of those who looked upon them, but they gave his body much beauty and grace, just as little black stones do when they are set in white pavement."

Brother Thomas of Caleno
First Life of St. Francis, c. 1230

Eleven

BLACKBUTT LOOKS DOWN from the top perch. Dawn is sprinkling through the cob-webbed windows. The big rooster rises on his golden legs and flaps the dust out of his wings. He stretches his neck into a long and impressive S and lets go with his first crow of the new day: *RRRrrrRRRrrrRRRrrrrrrrrrrr!*

His hens *bruck-buck-buck* and go back to sleep.

His brother, Mr. Shakyshiver, wedged between the last two old hens on the bottom perch, offers a timid and submissive *rrRrr.*

Blackbutt has been The Rooster for three years now, since old Captain Bates died of bumblefoot. Now Blackbutt can crow as loud and as early as he wants. Now Blackbutt can ride the hens.

And there are quite a few hens to ride these days. Three times now the girl named Rhea has slipped up and allowed one of the hens to hatch a new brood. Three times now there has been a noisy and frightening scene in the backyard, Rhea's father threatening to get a hatchet and cut off their heads, Rhea crying and promising it will never happen again. But after a year or so of tranquillity Rhea lets it happen again.

And so now there are plenty of hens for Blackbutt to ride, some of them slender and white like a Leghorn, some of them plump and brown like a Buff Orpington, some with exotic black tail feathers like Captain Bates and the legendary Maximo Gomez.

Before Captain Bates died, Blackbutt's life was as miserable as his brother's still is. No hen-riding whatsoever. Humiliation at every turn. Anytime Captain Bates felt like yanking a feather out of his behind he had to stand there and take it. But then the old captain got the bumblefoot, and one night while trying to hop up to his usual roost on the high perch, he slipped and fell head first into the water crock. And now Blackbutt is The Rooster. And dawn is sprinkling across the floor. *RRRrrrRRRrrrRRRrrrrrrrrrrr!*

Blackbutt is impatient. He wants this day to get under way. It's finally spring, after all. The chicken coop door is swung wide open.

He can lead his flock anywhere on the Cassowary farm he wants—into the overgrown gardens, down the gravel driveway, across the wide lawns. He and his flock can be the birds of the jungle they were meant to be. If only the others would wake up. *RRRrrrRRRrrr-RRRrrrrrrrrrrr!*

It was a long winter. The sunlight straining through the coop's cob-webbed windows had kept them alive, but not particularly warm. Every day the air had grow dustier. Every day he'd found more mites and lice under his feathers. Every day the manure had piled higher and every day the cracked corn Rhea brought them tasted worse. Yes, it was a very long winter. Three of the old Buff Orpingtons dropped over dead. Even one of his own sisters died—the one Rhea had named Half Pint back when they were chicks living in that happy cardboard box in the old cow barn. But now! Spring! *RRRrrrRRRrrrRRRrrrrrrrrrrr!*

Finally the hens start jumping off their perches, making their way toward the open door. Blackbutt waits until they are all outside then hops down the empty perches until he is standing next to his trembling brother. He pecks him hard on the toe and then trots out.

The air is still gray and hazy. The ground is soaked with dew. Blackbutt leads his hens into the abandoned asparagus garden just south of the coop. The hens jump into the high weeds and spread out, feasting on worms and grubs and scattered seeds. Then there is a horrifying *Gauk-bwauk!* The weeds start thrashing.

Blackbutt charges in. His hens are flying out. Everyone of them wild-eyed and *gauk-bwauking.*

Blackbutt expects the worse and finds it. A long-snouted creature that looks a lot like the Cassowary's dog has one of his three remaining sisters, the one named Nancy, pinned under its front paws. The creature is yanking out Nancy's beautiful feathers in bunches.

Blackbutt wants to flee. But he's The Rooster. So he clucks defiantly, *Y'auk-auk-auk-auk Y'auk-aul-auk-auk,* and struts on his muscular drumsticks, displays his hackles—his impressive Spanish neck feathers—and demands that the creature lets Nancy go.

But the creature keeps yanking feathers.

So Blackbutt attacks.

Biscuit is on the porch smelling the manure on his master's rubber boots when he hears the *gauk-bwauking*. He leaps to the lawn and barks his way to the chicken coop. Frenzied hens flee past him. His snout sucks in a foreign scent. Understanding his duty to the farm, he lunges into the weeds. He finds himself face to face with a creature not unlike himself. Its face is stuck with blood and feathers, yet it is not a menacing or unfriendly face. It is a timid face. Biscuit is not sure what to do. This creature is doing something he understands very well. Eating.

However, this creature also is doing something that's absolutely prohibited on the Cassowary farm. Eating chickens. So Biscuit spreads his front legs and lowers his ears and barks: *Not permitted! Not permitted!*

But the creature keeps eating. Either it is ignorant of the rules or too hungry to care. Biscuit can sympathize with both possibilities. He, too, is often ignorant of the rules. He, too, is often too hungry to care. Still, if he's learned anything from his human masters, it's that neither ignorance nor instinctual behavior are acceptable excuses. So he opens his farm-dog smile and displays the wolf teeth hidden inside. He attacks, chasing off the skittish creature with nothing more than the earnestness of his bark.

Twenty minutes before the school bus comes, Rhea goes out to feed her chickens. Biscuit goes to the coop with her, and shows her the chewed and bloody bodies of Nancy and Blackbutt in the overgrown garden.

Rhea is twelve now. She has been feeding the little flock of chickens for six years. Twice every day she throws a scoop of cracked corn in their direction and makes sure they have water and that the calcium dish is always full, so their eggshells will be good and hard. When she sees Blackbutt and Nancy, she curls up on the wet ground and cries, and claws at the feathers growing between her tiny Hershey Kiss breasts.

Biscuit licks her face until she gets up. Makes sure she finds her way back to the house. Donna and her father are sitting in the breakfast nook. He's drinking coffee. She's drinking ice water. "Something killed two of my chickens," Rhea says. Her dress is as wet as her eyes.

Donna's nose started to plug up and tickle the second Rhea came into the kitchen. "Go change that dress before the bus comes," she says.

As soon as Rhea is on the bus, Calvin Cassowary finds Jimmy Faldstool and goes to the chicken coop. Biscuit shows them the bodies in the garden. "You're lucky it only got the two," Jimmy says.

"Somebody's dog you think?" Calvin asks. Biscuit is standing next to him, brown eyes full of worry.

"I'm thinking coyote," Jimmy says. He uses the cowboy pronunciation, *kigh-oat.*

Calvin pronounces it the non-cowboy way. "Coyote?

"Dog or coyote. Either way you got a chicken eater."

"Think I should call the dog warden?"

"Good gravy, I would."

So that's what Calvin Cassowary does, calls county dog warden Wally Barghest, who spends twenty minutes examining the chicken carcasses and the footprints in the dirt before offering his expertise. "That old pup of yours wouldn't do anything like this, would he?" He points straight at Biscuit.

Calvin scratches Biscuit's ears. "This guy wouldn't hurt a flea."

Wally Barghest reaches out and pats Biscuit's wet nose. "Then I'd say more than likely it was a coyote." Like Jimmy Faldstool, he says it the cowboy way. "They've been migrating east last ten years or so. They got big trouble with them in the southern part of the state. Chewing up sheep and hogs pretty bad down there. So I wouldn't be surprised. Those layer houses of yours throw quite a tempting stink. You're lucky it ain't happened before now."

The easiest thing would be to have Jimmy throw the carcasses into the dumpster with the dead hens from the layer houses. Dozens go in the dumpster every day. But these are Rhea's chickens. They have names. A piece of her heart. And Rhea has a piece of Calvin's heart. He leaves Blackbutt and Nancy in the garden until Rhea gets home from school. Covers them with empty feed bags so nothing chews them up worse than they already are.

Blackbutt and Nancy are buried on the slope south of the old cow barn. For generations the Cassowarys have been burying their dogs and cats here. Captain Bates and Half Pint are buried here, too.

Calvin watches his daughter dig the hole. "That's deep enough," he says.

Rhea puts one of the feed bags in the hole, spreading it out like a blanket at the beach. She puts Blackbutt in first, then Nancy. She makes sure their floppy heads are touching. She places the other feed bag on top of them and tucks it in. She doesn't shovel the dirt over them, but uses her hands, gently hiding them from the cruel world, handful by handful by handful. The tears she fought off all day at school bubble in her eyes.

"We're going to have to keep your chickens in the chicken yard from now on," her father tells her.

Rhea doesn't answer. She's thinking about the first year she entered Blackbutt in the Wyssock County Fair. She was sure he'd win a blue ribbon. He was so big and fancy. But he didn't win a blue ribbon, not even a red or white ribbon. The judge—a woman with a very wide hind end—said it was because he was a *mongrel*, part Leghorn, part Black Spanish, part who knows what. "Honey," she said, "there's only two things you can do with a rooster like this—roast him or fry him." The next year Rhea entered him again, hoping there might be a different judge. But it was the same woman with the same wide hind end and the same reason for not giving Blackbutt a ribbon. "You going to be the judge next year?" Rhea asked her.

"Honey," the woman said, "I'm the judge every year." So the next year, she was ready. While the woman was standing in front of Blackbutt's cage shaking her head, Rhea crept up behind her and pinned the BEST OF SHOW ribbon she stole from the hog barn on the back of her enormous pants.

So now while tears bubble in her eyes, Rhea is able to laugh. As they walk back toward the house, they see Mr. Shakyshiver confidently riding one of the young hens. "He's the boss now," her father says.

After supper, Calvin calls Rick Van Varken. If a coyote is stalking their chickens, Rick's piglets could be in danger, too.

"I'm glad you called," Rick Van Varken says. "I need to talk to you about something. You and Donna want to come over for some pie and ice cream?"

Calvin doesn't like the way the phone call ended. Doesn't like the sound of *need* to talk to you about *something*. He and Rick have always gotten along fine. As boys they camped out in the woods and swam naked in the deep holes on Three Fish Creek. They were in the Boy Scouts together. For a few years there, when Calvin was protected by his student deferment and Rick was sweating out the draft lottery, they kept their distance. But that's all water under the bridge now.

Dawn and Donna are another matter. Part of the problem is that Dawn and Jeanie were pretty close. They gabbed on the phone and went shopping together. Dawn drove Jeanie to the hospital when her water broke with Rhea. Another part of the problem is that Donna is so damn young. Her body so damn perfect. Dawn's not so young any more and the five boys she bore to carry on the Van Varken name have wreaked havoc with her stomach muscles and the veins in her legs.

While Calvin and Rick talk about the coyote incident in the living room, Donna helps Dawn with the elderberry pie and vanilla ice cream in the kitchen. Everybody's having ice cream except the lactose-intolerant Donna. "I see Rhea's starting to blossom," Dawn says, getting down her best dessert plates from the hard-to-reach cupboard above the sink. "How old is she now?"

"Twelve," Donna says.

Donna's uncomfortable smile doesn't deter Dawn one bit. "Jeanie's boobs were quite big—not Dolly Parton or anything—but I think you and Cal are going to have some serious boy trouble down the road. You get Rhea a training bra yet?"

As soon as they deliver the pie and ice cream to their husbands the talk turns from training bras and coyotes to the real reason for the get-together. "Our families have been living side by side for a hundred years," Rick Van Varken begins. "So I wanted you to know about this first."

It's good pie. Sweet sugary crust. Tangy filling. Calvin stops chewing. "Good lord, Rick. You're not sick are you?"

Rick shakes his head and bites his bottom lip. "I've sold the farm."

While Calvin's wedge of pie goes uneaten, while his ice cream melts, Rick tells him about the financial pinch he's in. Tells him about the five sons he's got to think about. "Hogs aren't like chickens. I can't stack 'em five high in cages. Even if pork prices got up to where they should be, I just don't have enough land here. And you know what the taxes are like in this damn county now."

Calvin sees the tears running down Donna's face, knowing it's not sympathy but the spicy air freshener Dawn sprayed to kill the smell of pig that's soaked into the house. "Good Lord. Where you moving to?"

"South Carolina," Dawn says. "The weather is wonderful!"

"Good climate for hogs, both politically and economically," Rick says, enjoying his own joke. "Cheap labor. Low taxes. Southern politicians don't worry about manure they way they do up here." He drops his head and plays with his pie. He's got more bad news for his neighbor. "The thing is—I sold the farm to the Gumboro Brothers."

"Those bastards building all those big houses north of Tuttwyler? Son of a bitch, Rick."

"I'm not the first farmer selling out to developers and I'm not going to be the last."

"I don't want to hear this, Rick."

"I just wanted you to know first."

"So I could sell out, too?"

"The climate in South Carolina is also good for chickens."

Calvin puts his uneaten pie on the coffee table. "I'm not moving to fucking South Carolina."

So the Cassowarys drive home. And while Donna is upstairs deciding which of her allergy tablets will counteract Dawn Van Varken's air freshener best, Calvin sits on the porch, scratching Biscuit's rump, and thinking about the two new layer houses Norman Marek is bugging him to build, F and G. Thinking about the people houses the Gumboro Brothers soon will be building on the Van Varken farm.

When Donna comes out, Biscuit and the cats dutifully jump off the porch and disappear into the night. "Dawn thinks Rhea should start wearing a training bra," she says.

"I hope those coyotes kill every pig that bastard's got over there," Calvin answers.

Rhea doesn't want to feed her chickens this morning. But she knows she has to. Her chickens are counting on her. So she goes. Feeds them. Gives them fresh water. Makes sure the calcium dish is filled. Each time she goes in and out of the coop she sees the bloody grass and the feathers still scattered about. She loved Blackbutt and Nancy.

When she's finished with her chores she goes to that horrible spot, squats and wraps her arms around her knees, and gathers up the feathers. She puts the feathers in her Nestlé's Quik can, with her own feathers. She snaps the lid in place and reaches for the blue jumper hanging on the doorknob.

Twelve

RHEA CASSOWARY HOPS off the bus and runs up the driveway, using her social studies book as an umbrella. The fat drops on the metal roofs of the layer houses sound like a thousand machine guns. Biscuit is waiting on the porch, wet and stinky. Rhea scratches his happy ears.

She pries her feet out of her shoes and goes in. She can smell the macaroni baking in the oven, hear Donna sniffling in the living room.

"That you, Rhea?"

Rhea, wet shoes in one hand, slippery social studies book in the other, takes just one step into the room.

"I bought you something today," Donna says. She's curled on the sofa with the farm books, her calculator, and a box of tissues. "It's on your bed, big girl."

Rhea has had a difficult day at school. Jennifer Babirusa intentionally bumped into her with her trombone case again, and she got seven of ten problems wrong on the math quiz. So she doesn't need Donna buying her things—it's always something ugly—and she sure doesn't need that condescending *big girl* crap. She goes upstairs without saying thanks.

The bag on her bed is from Kmart. That means Donna was in Akron today, seeing either her allergist or her dermatologist. It's not a particularly big bag and it's not very full. So at least it's not another dumb shapeless jumper. She shakes the bag onto the bedspread. It's a bra.

"Try it on for me," Donna calls up the stairs.

Rhea takes off her blouse and undershirt. She looks at herself in the dresser mirror for as long as she dares, then slips her arms through the bra straps and fastens it.

"Can I come up now?" Donna asks.

Before Rhea can answer that there's no need for her to come up, she can hear the steps squeaking. She quickly puts on a baggy, everyday flannel shirt and sits on her bed, up by the pillows.

Donna comes in and sits on the edge of the bed, blocked from any physical contact by Rhea's stiff outstretched legs. "Does it fit okay?"

"Sure."

"You hooked it okay? Sometimes that can be trouble."

"I didn't have any trouble."

Donna is having trouble keeping her smile up. "Why don't you let me see if it fits right. I've had lots of experience with those suckers."

"It fits."

"I know it's embarrassing—"

"I'm not embarrassed."

"I think you should let me see it, Rhea. You're starting puberty. You're going to need my help on lots of personal things."

Rhea squeezes against the headboard. She could have showed her mother. Her mother, after all, was her mother. Her mother would have understood. "It fits okay and I put it on right."

Donna looks around for a Kleenex box. Not finding one, she wipes her nose with the back of her hand, then reaches toward the buttons on Rhea's shirt. "I want to see it."

Rhea barricades herself behind her knees. "No."

Donna sneezes loudly and pushes Rhea's legs aside. She slides forward. Her fingers hook around Rhea's collar. She starts thumbing the buttons. "Sit still!"

Rhea wants to fight her off. But her arms suddenly feel like they're nailed to the headboard. She squeezes her eyelids. This day had come.

Donna does five of the six buttons and pushes the shirt off Rhea's shoulders. She finds more than the tiny breasts she expected. "What is this?"

She means, of course, the patch of small white feathers that stretches from the center of Rhea's chest to her collar bones. They fluff up around the bra's padded cups like delicate lace.

"Those are my feathers," Rhea says.

"Why did you glue feathers to your boobs?"

"They're not glued," Rhea says. She is breathing as if her lungs are filled with pudding.

Donna's patience is gone. She takes a pinch of feathers and pulls. "You're too old for silly stuff like this." The feathers don't budge.

Rhea tells her again, "They just grow."

Donna pulls harder. Rhea's skin resists, pulling away from her chest like rubber. "You're the most stubborn girl I ever saw in my life."

One of Rhea's arms becomes unnailed and she slaps her father's wife hard across the face.

Her father's wife slaps her back, screams "Damn you!" and, with her angry strength, rips out a handful of feathers. There is blood on the quills.

Rhea collapses on her pillows.

Donna jumps off the bed and backs into the dresser. She is quivering like a sparrow in the mouth of a cat. She is staring through cloudy eyes at the feathers and drops of blood in her hand.

Suddenly she has Rhea by the arm, pulling her down the stairs, through the kitchen, across the lawn toward the layer houses. She is yelling, "Calvin! Calvin!"

Rhea is yelling, "Daddy! Daddy!" Her free hand is trying to rebutton her shirt. She can see her father running toward them. Hear him yelling, "Hold on! Hold on!"

When he is only a few yards away, Rhea yanks her arm free. She runs to him and throws her arms around his waist. She feels his arms wrap around her back. Feels his prickly chin on her neck. "What's wrong, pumpkin seed?" he asks.

Donna pulls her away from her father and holds her tightly by the arms. "She's got feathers, Calvin! Like some goddamn chicken!" She shows him the tiny white feathers in her hand. Shows him the blood. She tears open Rhea's shirt and shows him that the feathers on her chest aren't glued on, but growing there. "I've tried to be a good mother to her, Calvin, but she just fights me every step of the way."

Rhea struggles into her father's arms again. "They just grow, Daddy. I don't want them to."

Her father drops to his knees. His right hand holds her by the belt buckle. His left hand, fingers shaking, strokes the patch of feathers between the flat cups of her new bra. "They're growing there?"

"I can't help it, Daddy."

Rhea sees the worry in her father's eyes. Waits for him to hug her and kiss her forehead. Tell her everything will be all right. Instead she feels him rip a feather from her chest. Feels the electric-shock of it. The lingering toothache-pain of it.

Donna is screeching. "See? See?"

Now Rhea sees panic in her father's eyes. She feels his fingers dig into her feathers. Feels the fire as he rips them out. She does not look down at her chest, but straight into his eyes. He rips. He rips. His fingers claw at the hollow of her neck, at the thin tender skin beneath her collar bones. His fingers invade the cups of her bra, finding each tiny feather in the soft swollen skin.

When at last he finishes and slumps back, she can see the bloody feathers in his palms. "They just grow," she says.

Sometime in the early morning Rhea gets out of bed and gets the Nestlé's Quik can from the shelf. She goes down to the kitchen, stepping on the least-squeaky parts of the steps. She gets the flashlight from the drawer by the sink and sits on the edge of the porch for a while, scratching Biscuit's ears, crying into his shaggy mane. Then she follows the flashlight's amber beam across the wet grass until she sees her feathers. They're scattered in little lumps, like Blackbutt's and Nancy's after that coyote chewed them up. She puts them in the can.

For years she's been plucking the little feathers and hiding them in that can. But they just grow back, each time, it seems, a little bigger and a little stiffer. And each time it hurts a little more, too. Not just on her skin, but deep in her heart.

Now her father knows. Now her father has ripped them from her chest. Why did he do that to her? How could he do that to her? Would he tear out her hair? Her fingernails or toenails? Her teeth? Her eyes? Why her feathers? Because a girl is not supposed to have feathers. That's why he did that. But she does have feathers—

the same as she has hair and teeth and eyes and fingernails and toenails.

The school year ends. The first Saturday of June arrives. Rhea waits for her father to say, "Come on, pumpkin seed, let's go to the cemetery for our strawberries with Mom."

But this year he doesn't say it.

They have been going to the cemetery for strawberries on the first Saturday in June since Rhea was six. The wild strawberry plants have spread completely around the gravestone and sent out runners to some of the other Cassowary graves. Last year the three of them had at least twenty-five berries apiece to eat.

When the first week of June turns into the third week of June, Rhea knows she'll have to take matters into her own hands. All morning she practices marching up to her father and asking, "Daddy, why aren't we going to the cemetery for strawberries this year?" But when he comes in for lunch she can't make herself do it. She is too afraid of him. She has been afraid of him since that day he plucked her feathers. Since that day they've said hardly anything to each other. Their eyes have rolled away from each other. Their feet have kept each other in separate rooms of the house.

After her father goes back out to the layer houses, Rhea rounds up Biscuit and walks down the fields toward the creek, and in the high grass by the rock pile she kneels by the wild strawberries that grow there. The berries are overripe, brownish and mushy, but she picks a handful and nibbles them anyway. "Hi, Momma," she says as Biscuit sniffs the rocks for garter snakes. "It doesn't look like we're coming to the cemetery this year. So I hope this will do."

Thirteen

THE BULLDOZERS ARE already rumbling when Rhea Cassowary wakes up. She goes to her window and looks across the valley. The maples are red and the oaks are yellow. It's October.

There are several bulldozers on the old Van Varken farm, pushing over the hog barns, rearranging the hills to accommodate the one hundred and seven big homes the Gumboro Brothers plan to build. There's also a bulldozer on the Cassowary farm, leveling ground for layer houses F and G.

Rhea gets ready for school. She can hear Donna and her father downstairs, walking nervously from room to room, whispering. She goes down. The bus will be there in ten minutes. Just enough time for her to have a bowl of cereal over the sink.

Her father surprises her. He's wearing a pair of his Sunday slacks and a new shirt. "We're keeping you home from school today," he says.

Donna is wearing a dress. "We're taking you to see Dr. Hauberk," she says.

Rhea knows who Dr. Hauberk is: Donna's dermatologist. "I don't have pimples," she says. "I have feathers."

They wait for Rhea to eat her cereal, then go out to the car. They crackle down the driveway. Turn left toward Tuttwyler and the highway that meanders east to Akron.

Her father hasn't mentioned the feather incident since it occurred. He hasn't said much to her at all. He has barely looked at her. Now he won't shut up. "I know what I did was wrong, pumpkin seed. I didn't mean to hurt you. You know that, don't you? I just wigged out. I was scared."

"So was I," Rhea says from the back seat.

"Dr. Hauberk is really good," Donna says. She's sniffling, as she always does in the car. She's allergic to the fabric on the seats. The drive takes a long hour.

Dr. Hauberk's nurse takes Rhea into an examining room.

Gives her a gown to put on. "You can leave your panties on," the nurse says, "but everything else has to go."

Dr. Hauberk comes in twenty minutes later. Rhea is relieved. Dr. Hauberk is a woman. She's got freckles and long hair the same orange-brown as Biscuit's. She is very nervous for a doctor. "I have to confess, I've never had a patient with feathers. I don't think anyone else has either." She smiles bravely. "But we'll see what we can do. Okay?"

Dr. Hauberk removes Rhea's gown. She studies the feathers on her chest: they're growing over her collar bones and her nipples now, right down her ribs to her belly button. She studies the feathers on Rhea's back: they extend from her shoulder blades to her tailbone dimples. She slowly pulls Rhea's panties down and studies the feathers covering her vulva and her thighs. She lets Rhea pull up her panties and put the gown back on. "They started growing when?" she asks.

"I think I was five."

"About the time your mother died?"

"Uh-huh."

"You miss your mother?"

"Uh-huh."

"I miss my mother."

"Is she dead, too?"

"She lives in Arizona. But my dad's dead. I miss him like you miss your mother." Dr. Hauberk frowns. "Your father has a lot of chickens."

"Pretty soon he's going to have a million."

"That's a lot of chickens."

Dr. Hauberk takes a syringe from the pocket of her white coat. "I'm not sure what I can do for you, Rhea. I'm pretty good at rashes—like the one's your stepmother gets—but this feather thing is a new one on me. But I'm going to take a blood sample, just to make sure everything else is okay." She spreads the feathers just below Rhea's elbow. The needle slides in. "First try—how about that?" The blood leaks into the syringe. "Have you started having your periods yet?"

"Since July."

The doctor scrunches her nose. "Fun, aren't they?"

"They're okay."

The syringe is full. Dr. Hauberk pulls it out and wedges an alcohol-soaked cotton ball between her ruffled feathers. "I know you're getting more and more feathers all the time, but are they getting bigger, too?"

"They're a lot bigger."

"Your father told me he lost his head and pulled a lot of them out."

"Uh-huh."

"About a month ago?"

"Uh-huh."

"He hasn't done it since?"

"No."

"It probably wasn't such a good idea for him to do that, was it?"

"No."

"What about you, Rhea, do you pull them out?"

"I used to."

"But not any more?"

"It hurts too much now."

They do not drive home as Rhea expects. They drive to another office building in another part of Akron. "We're going to have Donna's allergist look at you," her father says.

The news doesn't make Rhea very happy. "Does Dr. Hauberk know that?"

"She suggested it," Donna says. "You'll like Dr. Paillard."

Donna Cassowary has been seeing Drs. Hauberk and Paillard since marrying Calvin. As his wife she qualifies for coverage under his health insurance policy, a godsend after a lifetime of suffering.

Though neither doctor has cured her of her allergies, they have made life infinitely more tolerable for her.

Donna, it seems, suffers not only from the usual allergies—pollen, animals, dairy products, mold, and the feces of dust mites—but also from the modern world. She suffers, Drs. Hauberk and Paillard concur, from MCS, Multiple Chemical Sensitivity. So many things can start her coughing or sneezing. So many things plug her nose shut or make it drain like a faucet. So many things give her headaches, make her dizzy, listless, and nauseous. So many things give her bladder infections. So many things give her rashes, make her eyes swell and itch. Synthetic clothing and carpeting can do it. Food preservatives can do it. Detergents and deodorizers can do it. Cigarette smoke. Cosmetics. Paint. Perfumes. Paper. Central heating. Air conditioning. Easter egg dye.

Dr. Hauberk and Dr. Paillard consult regularly about Donna's allergies, to make sure the pills and ointments they prescribe don't interact negatively. Dr. Hauberk thinks Donna's biggest problem is her own imagination. "Physiological problems can have psychological origins," she tells Dr. Paillard. "I think that deep down Donna may not think she deserves her good looks."

Dr. Paillard doesn't reject the dermatologist's suspicions out of hand—he's read enough psychology to know that the division between body and mind is foggy to say the least—but he suspects Donna is genetically predisposed to her sensitivities. "You could lay her on the couch and make her talk all day about her terrible childhood, and she'd still be allergic to the imitation leather," he once told Dr. Hauberk.

"What do you say we take a little blood?" Dr. Paillard says to Rhea.

"That other doctor already took my blood," Rhea says.

"Well, I need some, too." He sits on a stool with wheels and scoots toward her, syringe in one hand, cotton ball of alcohol in the other.

Rhea holds her arm still while the doctor takes her blood. She liked the woman doctor better. This doctor is old and bald and a man. He tugs on her feathers as if they're made out of plastic.

91

"Do they make you sneeze?" Dr. Paillard asks.

Rhea shakes her head no.

"They itch?"

"Sometimes."

"What about the feathers on your father's chickens? They make you sneeze or itch?"

Rhea shakes her head no.

"You get the girl's blood back yet?" Dr. Paillard asks Dr. Hauberk on the phone a few days later.

"Yeah. Everything's normal."

"My sample, too."

"Find anything in your literature?" asks the dermatologist.

The allergist chuckles. "Like breaking out in feathers from eating too many kumquats? No history of that. As far as I can tell, feathers are symptomatic of only two conditions—either you're a bird or an Indian chief."

Now the dermatologist chuckles. "I didn't find anything either."

"What about electrolysis?"

"I thought about it—for three seconds. If you remember your college biology, feathers in birds are not homologous with hair in mammals. They're entirely different structures, more like the scales on a fish. There's no way I'm going to start zapping that girl with electricity. That's what got Dr. Frankenstein in trouble, if you remember."

"So a depilatory wouldn't do the trick either?"

"Not unless you soaked her for a month."

Dr. Paillard hears Dr. Hauberk tapping her teeth with her fingernails. "So what are you thinking?" he asks.

"I'm thinking I'm way over my head with this one," the dermatologist says. "I'm thinking that this little girl is in real trouble."

The allergist knows what she's getting at. "And you're thinking you and I will be in real trouble, too, if we try to treat her?"

"To tell you the truth, Dr. Paillard, I'd be afraid to send in an insurance form on this one."

One morning in November Rhea wakes up with a feather on her neck. She refuses to pluck it. Donna refuses to pluck it. Calvin wants to pluck it, but each time he reaches for his daughter's neck, his hand starts shaking and his guilt prevents it.

So Rhea stays home from school and Donna goes shopping for turtlenecks. By Christmas Rhea's neck is covered with feathers, by Valentine's Day her arms and legs, too. Drs. Hauberk and Paillard won't see her again, nor will fifteen other specialists who've taken Rhea's blood, read their literature, and considered their careers. They know how to treat dermatitis, psoriasis, dysplastic nevi, and dermatofibromas. They can treat the cancerous melanomas of sun worshippers, remove warts and moles and cherry spots. They can treat allergies, acne, and athlete's feet. Birthmarks. Baldness. They can treat dandruff, hives, and poison ivy. They can treat so many conditions. But none of them has ever seen anyone with feathers.

In January, Calvin spots a tiny feather growing on Rhea's chin and makes an appointment with her teacher and the school principal. "Rhea is developing a skin condition," he tells them, watching the snow fall on the empty playground equipment outside the office window.

"I wondered about the turtlenecks," the teacher says.

"Nothing contagious?" the principal asks.

Calvin shakes his head. "But it's spreading to her face. It's not very pretty. I'm thinking about home schooling."

"Very dangerous," the teacher says.

"I have a degree in art education," Calvin says. "My wife has an associate's degree in accounting."

"Socialization is as important as academic work, especially at Rhea's age," the teacher says. "Cutting her off from other children could be more devastating than whatever teasing she might encounter."

"You sure this skin condition isn't contagious?" the principal asks. "We have seven hundred boys and girls to worry about here."

Calvin can see that the principal is a farmer at heart, that, like himself, he understands that the survival of the flock takes precedent over the problems of a single hen. So Calvin hems and haws and says, "We're pretty sure it isn't."

The hemming and hawing alarms the principal. "Pretty sure?"

Calvin shrugs and the school agrees to help Calvin and Donna homeschool Rhea.

By May, Rhea's entire face is covered with feathers. So are her hands, right down to the middle row of knuckles. She keeps up with her English and science and social studies work just fine, but her math suffers. Donna simply sneezes too much for either of them to concentrate on the problems.

By the Fourth of July, layer houses F and G are finished. They are longer and wider than A, B, C, D, and E. They have automated manure accumulators that eliminate the need for shoveling. Jimmy Faldstool can't remember being happier. "You mean I can just stand here and punch these red buttons?" he asks Wayne Demijohn, Gallinipper's top manure man, who has showed up for the christening of the state-of-the-art system.

"That's pretty much it," Demijohn says. He shows Calvin and Jimmy how the manure will drop out of the hens' rectums onto conveyor belts located under their cages, and how those belts will take it to a big drive-in pit at the end of the building, where Jimmy can charge right in with his front-end loader and fill the trucks without ever wielding a shovel.

"You should install these in the other layer houses," Jimmy says to Calvin. "I'd never have to shovel chicken shit again."

"Maybe someday I will," Calvin says.

The next day a caravan of egg-yolk-yellow trucks arrive from Gallinipper Foods with 200,000 noisy young pullets. Calvin Cassowary now has a million Leghorns. He is also a million dollars in debt. To celebrate his accomplishment Bob Gallinipper sends a case of Indiana wine and a mahogany plaque with a brass plate that reads:

The truck drivers bringing the 200,000 pullets for the new layer houses don't see Rhea. Calvin has seen to it that no one sees her. Rhea has been instructed to go to her room when someone comes. If she's caught outside when the gravel in the driveway starts to crackle, she can hide in the chicken coop. "Your little problem isn't anybody's business but ours," he tells her.

Only Jimmy Faldstool has seen Rhea since the feathers grew on her face and hands, and he has promised to keep his mouth shut. "It's more than just me knowing where my bread's buttered," he tells Calvin. "You Cassowarys are like family to me. I'd no more blab about Rhea's feathers than I'd blab about my being born with only one testicle."

"You've only got one testicle?" Calvin asks.

"Maybe I do and maybe I don't," answers Jimmy.

So the family secret is safe with Jimmy Faldstool. And Rhea runs and hides whenever someone drives in. She feeds her chickens and gathers their eggs and does her homework and stands naked in front of the full-length mirror on the back of the bathroom door. Other than the palms of her hands and the bottoms of her feet, she has very little bare skin left. Just a little bit around her elbows and knees.

Late in August a cold front sweeps across the Midwest. Hail stones as big as glass eyes mutilate corn crops from Nebraska to Pennsylvania. Several inches of rain swell the rivers and creeks and flood soybean fields as far south as Tennessee. Winds topple trees like so many toothpicks. Phil Bunyip, taking a load of Calvin Cassowary's spent Leghorn hens to a pet food plant in Fort Wayne, almost gets himself killed when he loses control of his rig on the Ohio Turnpike.

Rhea sees it on the six o'clock news. It seems that Phil Bunyip, rolling along through the rain and hail, swerved to miss a stalled Winnebago. His rig jackknifed and toppled over, just thirty yards shy of the Maumee River bridge.

"There are just thousands of chickens everywhere," the on-the-scene television reporter is telling the wig-wearing anchorman back in Cleveland. The cameraman pans so people watching at home can see the hens darting in and out of traffic, many getting smashed, but many surviving, dashing into the fields and woods along the highway.

"A very bad day for Gallinipper Foods," the reporter says, "but a good day for a lot of these chickens."

The feathers under Rhea's eyes are wet with tears as she goes upstairs. She curls up on her bed and tries to read one of her Judy Blume novels. She loves Judy Blume. But tonight the words that usually make her feel like a normal girl dash across the page like those loose hens on the turnpike.

Those hens had been doomed. Their final resting place in squat tin cans of food for cats and dogs predetermined. Now some are running free. It seems that Nature intervened. It seems that Nature sent wind and rain and hail, sent Phil Bunyip's big rig skidding.

A few minutes after two, Nature wakes Rhea from her sleep. Sends her downstairs to the kitchen, to the keys hanging on the wall above the wobbly table in the breakfast nook. Nature calls Rhea to the porch and then leads her across the wet grass to the layer house with the lock that matches the key in her hand. Nature sends Rhea inside.

It is not dark inside. The lights in the layer houses are on sixteen hours a day, to trick the Leghorns into thinking it's day, so they lay and lay.

Nature tells Rhea to start opening cages. Start coaxing the hens inside to jump free. "Don't be afraid," Rhea says each time her feathered hand wraps softly around the bottom of a clucking hen.

And the hens are not afraid. The big creature setting them free looks just like them. Has their same gentle way.

There is not time for Nature and Rhea to pardon all 100,000 hens in the building. But by the time Jimmy Faldstool shows up to begin his long shift, hundreds of the young pullets are spread across the empty, moonlit fields where previous generations of Cassowarys used to pasture cows and grow corn and wheat and vegetables for the table. "Egads and little fishes," he says when he finds Rhea in the layer house, "what have you done to complicate my life now?"

Fourteen

RHEA CASSOWARY HAS been sitting in this huge over-stuffed green chair for ten minutes. Except for the Van Gogh posters on the walls, she is alone. But now the door opens and a man comes in. He has a trim white beard. Curly white hair surrounds the brim of his black velvet hat. A red flower droops from the lapel of his suit-coat. His eyes are the same size and color of the chocolate-covered cherries her Toledo grandmother eats. His skin is the same light caramel of a Buff Orpington. He is carrying a tiny cup of coffee on a tiny saucer.

At first Rhea worries that this man may be the Santa Claus God she no longer believes in, come to punish her for her lack of faith. As soon as he opens his mouth she is relieved. He is not God. He is merely a man with an accent.

"Do you like my chapeau?" he asks. His words are thick and musical. His chocolate-cherry eyes are fixed on her.

"What's a chapeau?"

"My new hat. I paid a hundred dollars for it."

"It's a pretty hat."

The man tilts his head sheepishly. He smiles. "You are very pretty, too. You look like a beautiful swan." He takes a sip from his tiny cup. "You don't want an espresso, do you?"

Rhea is tickled by the unfamiliar words this man uses. "What's an espresso?"

"This very strong coffee I drink too much of."

"I don't like coffee."

The man puts his tiny cup and saucer on the corner of his desk. He sits in the other huge green chair. "I am Dr. Pirooz Aram," he says. "Your parents think you need my help."

The feathers on Rhea's neck puff out. "You're a psychiatrist."

He pushes back his velvet hat to scratch the top of his balding head. "That is one of the things I am. But I am also many others things."

Already Rhea is feeling comfortable with him. She can see right through his playful, phony baloney exterior. See that his interior is serious and sincere. "Like what for example?"

Dr. Pirooz Aram's eyes melt wide. "For one thing, I am also a Persian. For another thing, I am an American. I am a fine dancer and an even better chess player. I am a pretty good cook. I am an expert on the ancient poets of my homeland. I am also full of hot air much of the time, and more often than not, helplessly confused by modern machinery."

"I'm lots of things, too," Rhea says.

"Besides a beautiful swan, you mean?"

"Besides a freak," she answers.

Dr. Pirooz angers. "You are not a freak. You are a swan. You must never forget that, Rhea. You are a swan!" He calms himself and folds his hands across his chest, as if he is about to pray. "So, you do not like having feathers?"

"Of course not."

The fingers on his folded hands rise like little cobras and play with his beard. "I want you to think harder about your answer," he says. "Do you really not like having feathers, or is it the way people treat you for having feathers that makes you not like your feathers?"

This question bewilders Rhea. "Huh?"

Dr. Aram laughs with his entire face. "I feel very comfortable with my accent—proud that I am able to pronounce any English words at all—but when I see other people screwing up their faces trying to figure out what I'm saying, I feel ashamed, and sometimes angry. Maybe this is how you feel about your feathers?"

"I never thought about it that way," Rhea confesses.

Dr. Aram takes off his hat. Leaning forward as far as he can, he places it on Rhea's head. "Of course you've never thought of it that way! If you had, I'd be sitting where you're sitting, and you'd be sitting here, asking me about *my* problems. Which would fill a good-sized kettle, by the way."

The next week when Rhea comes for her session, Dr. Pirooz Aram is wearing a bright yellow beret. "Do you like it?" he asks.

"My wife says it makes me look like a dandelion." He puts it on Rhea's head. "I know she doesn't mean it as a compliment, but I pretend she does. 'Thank you,' I say."

The little story makes Rhea laugh.

And Rhea's laugh makes Dr. Aram laugh. "So, tell me Rhea Cassowary, are you sorry you let your father's chickens loose?"

"I only let a couple hundred loose."

"A couple hundred is a lot."

"Not when you have a million."

"Your father has a million chickens?"

Rhea nods.

"And you wish he didn't have so many chickens?"

"I don't care how many chickens he has. It's the cages."

"Ah, the cages! You hate the cages!"

"I guess."

Dr. Aram angrily snatches his beret from Rhea's head. "I do not allow guessing. Either you hate the cages or you don't hate the cages."

"Sorry."

Dr. Aram grins and winks. "You are sorry that you break my rules but not so sorry that you let your father's chickens go free?"

Two days later Dr. Pirooz Aram summons Calvin and Donna Cassowary to his office. The first question the doctor asks Calvin is this: "Why do you keep all those chickens of yours in cages?"

Calvin explains that the cages increase efficiency. "Eggs are a high-volume, low-profit business," he says.

Dr. Aram chuckles. "Fortunately for me, the psychiatry business is exactly the opposite. Very few patients and lots of fancy vacations." Seeing that neither Cassowary is amused by his honesty, he removes the Greek fisherman's cap he's wearing today, sits up straight, and begins to act like the professional they're paying for. "It is going to take a long time to make Rhea a happy person. But I thought I might give you my initial impressions."

100

Donna Cassowary wipes her nose and picks suspiciously at the fabric of the arm of her chair. "We'd appreciate that."

And so Dr. Aram begins: "No one really knows what the mind is—except that it is as distinct from our brains as a bucket from the water it carries. But we do know that the thoughts and images our minds create can have physical effects. Fear gives us goosebumps. We get red in the face. We go white with worry. Our flesh is a mirror of our minds. You are following me? Sometimes my ideas are as confusing as my accent."

Calvin reassures him. "I think I know what you're getting at."

Dr. Aram is surprised. "You do? I'm not so sure I know what I'm getting at myself. I'm a student of the thinking-out-loud school, I'm afraid."

Checking his watch—there's a shipment of replacement pullets coming at two o'clock—Calvin tells the doctor what he thinks he was getting at: "You're saying Rhea's feathers are a psychological reaction to the way I treat my chickens—which is a lot of bullshit."

"You think so?"

"I think so."

Apparently Donna thinks it's bullshit, too. "There's a big difference between getting goosebumps and growing feathers," she says into her soggy handkerchief.

Dr. Aram is nodding. "You are right, of course. Rhea's feathers could be caused by a defective chromosome. But am I safe in guessing, Mr. Cassowary, that there are no other people in your family with feathers? An uncle or a distant cousin? A great-great-grandmother who looked like a turkey?"

"Of course not," Calvin says.

"Then," says Dr. Aram, "you have to admit that Rhea's feathers could have something to do with the way you treat your million chickens?"

The doctor's accusation makes Calvin's face redden. "I don't treat my chickens any differently than any other large operator."

"Do any of your fellow chicken farmers have children with feathers?"

"Not that I'm aware of."

Dr. Aram sees that Donna is getting ready to explode. He hands her the handkerchief from his coat pocket. "Sneeze into this."

She thanks him and does.

The doctor continues, "I was raised a Moslem, but like any good Moslem, I am very familiar with the Christian religion—did you know that Moslems consider your Jesus a great prophet? Anyway, Rhea's feathers reminded me of what happened to Saint Francis of Assisi."

Again Calvin checks his watch. "And just what happened to Saint Francis of Assisi?"

Dr. Aram reaches for the book on his desk. "Let me read this to you: 'It was wonderful to see in the middle of his hands and feet, not indeed the holes made by the nails, but the nails themselves formed out of his flesh, and retaining the blackness of iron, and his right side was red with blood. These signs of martyrdom did not arouse horror in the minds of those who looked upon them, but they gave his body much beauty and grace.'"

He puts the book back on his desk. "It was written in the 1200s, the first account of what today we call *stigmata*, people who feel Jesus's suffering on the cross so deeply that his wounds appear on their skin, too."

Calvin is offended. "So Rhea's feathers will disappear if I get rid of my chickens?"

"Not necessarily," Dr. Aram says. "St. Francis got his wounds twelve hundred years after Jesus's suffering ended. If Rhea's feathers are a reaction to the way you treat your chickens, getting rid of your chickens now might not have any effect on her. Her mind would still picture the suffering she saw."

"There's nothing wrong with the way I treat my chickens," Calvin growls.

"Rhea apparently does not agree," the doctor growls back.

Calvin pulls Donna from her chair. "We're not paying you eighty bucks an hour to tell us why Rhea has feathers. We're paying you to make her behave like a normal human being."

Dr. Aram finds this funny, and wants to laugh. But he knows he mustn't. Not if he is going to help Rhea. "There is a great debate in modern psychiatry, Mr. Cassowary—we call it, 'Which came first—the chicken or the egg?'"

"That's hilarious," Calvin says, pulling Donna toward the door.

Dr. Aram springs in front of him. "Not hilarious at all. It's a very serious question. Very serious. I'm not telling you to get rid of your chickens. All I am suggesting—and I am *suggesting* and nothing else—that Rhea's feathers may be a physical manifestation of her sorrow for the way your chickens are treated. Your chickens. Everybody's chickens. And if she feels that deeply about it—well—is it so surprising she would try to set them free? You can deal with your daughter in one of two ways. You can lock her in a cage like your chickens, so she doesn't do any more harm. Or you can set her free."

Donna backs away from the doctor's aftershave. "We want what's best for her, of course."

The doctor puckers his lips sympathetically. "We do not want to change her mind about things. Or change her heart. What we need to change is her behavior. Transform her destructive impulses into constructive ones."

"And we do that how?" Calvin asks.

"By helping her accept herself," says Dr. Pirooz Aram. "By helping her enjoy having feathers."

Asks Donna, "Who would enjoy having feathers?"

Answers Dr. Pirooz Aram, "How about a swan?"

The next day the receptionist puts down her tea and answers the phone. "Dr. Aram's office—"

"This is Rhea Cassowary's father."

"Yes, Mr. Cassowary—"

"Rhea won't be needing any more sessions."

"Don't you want to discuss this with Dr. Aram?"

"No, I do not."

Fifteen

AT DAWN CALVIN Cassowary sits in the weather-worn rocker on the porch and pulls on his work boots. The lawn is white with frost. So are the roofs of the layer houses. So are the roofs of the new, unfinished people houses on the old Van Varken farm. It is October again.

Calvin crunches down the driveway. First he takes the newspaper from the plastic tube nailed below his mailbox and wedges it into his back pocket. Then he hops across the ditch, to the FRESH EGGS sign his grandfather Alfred put up in 1928. He takes it in his shaking hands and lifts it off its rusty iron hooks. He tucks it under his arm and walks to the garage. The smart thing, he thinks, would be to smash it into pieces with a sledgehammer, and then burn those pieces, so the sign would simply disappear. The respectful thing, he knows, would be to hang it in a prominent place, in the living room, or the kitchen breakfast nook, or even give it to Rhea to hang in her bedroom. But he is too filled with remorse to do either the smart thing or the respectful thing. He gets the stepladder and, climbing to the top step, slides it onto the pile of old dust-covered lumber resting across the rafters. Rhea will never find it up there. Then he goes in for breakfast.

Donna is sniffling about the kitchen, mooshing frozen orange juice concentrate in a Rubbermaid pitcher. She's still wearing the cotton nightgown Calvin pushed up over her thighs the night before. "Rhea hasn't come down yet, has she?" he asks.

"You should have talked to her about it first," Donna says.

Calvin pours his own coffee and sits down at the table. It wobbles under his elbows. "Either way I'd get a fight. This way it's done."

The upstairs toilet flushes and the steps start squeaking. Rhea pads into the kitchen. "Morning, pumpkin seed," Calvin says.

Rhea doesn't answer him. She goes to the cupboard where the cereal boxes are kept. She chooses the Honey Nut Cheerios.

Rhea is wearing her baggy blue bathrobe. She wears it almost every day now. Whether she is wearing anything underneath, Calvin and Donna don't know, but probably she isn't. Her feathers cover her entire body now and they know pants or a tee shirt or even underpants would be uncomfortable for her. Her hair is gone now, replaced by a cap of small, frizzy feathers that layer down across her ears and jaws like shingles on a roof.

When the Cheerios are drowned in milk, Rhea squeezes around the back of the table, to her place in front of the window. No chance anyone will see her, though. The venetian blinds her father installed in July are closed tight.

"I've got something to tell you," Calvin begins. "You won't like it."

Rhea says nothing. Her eyes are fixed on her bowl of cereal. After only a few spoonfuls, the feathers on her chin are dripping with beads of milk.

"We're not going to sell brown eggs anymore," Calvin says.

Rhea says nothing.

"We're only getting—what—three dozen a week?" Calvin says. "And we're down to Marilyn Dicsissel and Mrs. Baleen."

"And Beth Craddock," Donna says.

Calvin doesn't appreciate her help. "And Beth Craddock," he repeats.

Now Rhea says something. "Which makes three. Which is more than a couple."

Calvin shifts his elbows. The table wobbles. "The point is this: Donna is busy with the house and the bookwork and taking care of you. She can't drop everything every time somebody drives in for a dozen brown eggs."

"I could do the selling," Rhea says.

Calvin's frustration is bubbling. "You don't need everyone gawking at you."

"You mean you don't need it," Rhea says.

"Your father and I are not ashamed of you," Donna says.

"Then let me do the selling."

"We are not going to bother with three dozen eggs a week," Calvin says. "I've already taken down the sign."

Rhea pries open the blinds. "You really took it down—daddy?"

Calvin checks his watch, kisses his wife, and pats his daughter's feathery head. "And it's going to stay down." He runs to the garage, backs the pickup out, and beeps the horn. Jimmy Faldstool comes trotting. He's dressed a bit better today, clean pair of jeans and a flannel shirt without any holes.

"Ready to rock-and-roll?" Calvin asks as Jimmy hops in.

"That I am," says Jimmy.

Calvin can tell by the way Jimmy's cheek muscles are twitching that he wants to ask him something important. But after that business over the FRESH EGGS sign, he is in no mood for an important question. So he lets Jimmy's cheek twitch and crunches the pickup down the driveway and heads toward Tuttwyler.

On Townline Road they pass the Chervil's place. The field east of the house is littered with rusted farm equipment. There are dozens of old tractors and an uncountable collection of disks, plows, cultivators, combines, balers, and manure spreaders. Every one of them is busted and rusted, held to the ground by tangles of high grass and blackberry briars. This is how the Chervil brothers, Doug and Dale, scrape out a living, specializing in hard-to-find parts for old farm equipment. D&D Tractor Sales, they call their business. They supplement their income by selling pumpkins at Halloween. As Calvin and Jimmy drive by, Dale is busy unloading a trailer of them on the front lawn.

"We'll stop on the way back and get a pumpkin for Rhea," Calvin says.

"That'll be nice," Jimmy says, cheek muscles twitching again. "My boy's outgrown having a pumpkin."

Calvin smiles at him and quickly turns his attention back to the road. He knows Jimmy Faldstool like the back of his hand. Whatever Jimmy wants to ask him has something to do with his boy.

In Tuttwyler they find a place to park on the square. Calvin heads for First Sovereignty Bank. Jimmy heads to the hardware store for fly strips. They'll meet at the Pile Inn for a quick coffee and a donut before driving over to Mueller Auto Parts to buy that new battery for the tow motor.

Ted Rapparee greets Calvin with a big grin and an even bigger handshake. "I know it's not a pleasant thought, Cal, stringing out your loan," he says, dropping into his swivel chair, "but we're here for you, buddy."

"The papers are ready?"

"All they need is your John Hancock," Ted says. He opens the folder in front of him and spreads out the forms like a magician splaying a deck of trick cards. He pushes a silver pen across the desk.

Calvin bends over the forms. "The interest rate is locked in?"

Even though the forms are upside-down for him, Ted knows exactly where to point. "Tight as a drum."

"Good," Calvin says, though there's nothing good about it at all. Stretching out that loan another ten years will cost him an additional hundred thousand in interest. And unless Gallinipper's new contract ups its per-dozen price another penny, he'll be extending his other loans, too.

Ted reaches for the silver pen as soon as Calvin sets it down. "How's the family, Cal? My Amy misses Rhea not being in school anymore."

Calvin stands and wipes the sweat from his palms, eager for the good-bye handshake. He knows why Ted said that. Ted knows about Rhea's feathers. Just like everybody knows.

Calvin trots across the square toward the Pile Inn. Inside he can pick out Jimmy's clean flannel shirt from the eight or nine other shirts hunched over the counter. He also can make out Paul Bilderback's back. He drove a school bus with Paul for several years, and Paul always had a big sweat stain down the back of his blue workshirts, like the stripe of a skunk, even in the cold months.

Calvin starts for the empty stool next to Jimmy when he hears Paul ask, "That true about Cal's girl being covered head to toe with feathers?"

He hears Jimmy answer, "That ain't for me or you to talk about."

107

Hears Paul say, "Then it's true."

Hears Jimmy answer, "That's your conclusion."

Hears Paul say, "Makes you wonder what kind of cock Cal's first wife was fooling with."

Hears the other men hunched over the counter laugh like hyenas. Hears Jimmy say, "I think you better shut up."

Hears Paul say, "Now Jimmy, don't get your feathers ruffled."

Sees Jimmy push Paul off his stool and pelt him with donuts and pieces of pie from the dessert rack. Hears himself say, "Ready to go, Jimmy?"

The laugher collapses and the men swivel back to the counter. Jimmy's eyes are hot with anger.

Paul Bilderback crawls to his stool. His face is covered with powdered sugar and pie filling. He cocks his arm to take a swing at Jimmy, but thinks better of it.

Calvin and Jimmy walk to Mueller's Auto Parts and buy the new battery. They head for home. "Ain't we gonna stop for that pumpkin?" Jimmy asks as they drive past the Chervil brothers' place.

"Not today."

"Buy 'em too early, they'll just rot," Jimmy says, adding, "It's the same with Christmas trees. Too early, the needles fall off."

"That's right," Calvin agrees. He reaches out and squeezes Jimmy's shoulder. "Thanks."

Jimmy smiles, knowing his boss isn't thanking him for his advice on pumpkins and Christmas trees. "I hear cracks about Rhea all the time like that."

"I suppose you do."

Jimmy's cheeks start to twitch again and after taking a deep breath asks the question he's been wanting to ask all morning: "My boy's turning sixteen next month and I wonder if you wouldn't have a job for him? Just part-time."

Calvin thinks about his loans and his exploding costs, about the wages and benefits for the three full-time men he's had to hire since ascending to the million-Leghorn level. "Sure," he tells Jimmy.

Three days after his sixteenth birthday, the very Saturday he takes and flunks his temporary driver's license exam, Joon Faldstool comes to work at the Cassowary farm. His father drives him, and stays with him all morning, showing him how to shovel out the manure pits in the older layer houses. How to hose down the concrete floors without making a mess. Where to wash up before going home.

"Washing up is the key to this job," his father says. He shows him how much liquid soap to squirt on his palms. He shows him where the clean towels are kept.

Calvin makes Rhea go upstairs when he sees Norman Marek's car coming up the driveway. He gathers the homeschooling workbooks off the table and gets out the farm ledgers. He also gets out two of the better coffee cups. Saucers, too.

Norman is as friendly as ever. But he's also a bit nervous and he puts more sugar in his coffee than usual. "Cal," he says, "let me get right to the skinny. All this crap about cholesterol is taking a toll on egg consumption. Now we know this health and fitness stuff is just a fad—a five-minute Hoola Hoop thing—but until the industry can wind up its PR machinery, well, we've got an egg glut."

Calvin may have majored in art, but he understands the laws of supply and demand as well as anybody. "My contract locks me in at three cents a dozen."

Norman splays his fingers and calms the air between Calvin and him. "Of course your contract locks you in. Nobody's gonna dick with that. But still the pain has got to be spread around somehow, doesn't it?"

"Meaning what?"

Norman Marek sips and puckers and plays with the button on his ballpoint. *Click-click. Click-click. Click-click.* "What it means," he finally says, "is that Bob's asking all the producers to take ten percent of their hens out of production—for the time being."

"That's a hundred thousand hens. That's a lot of money out of my pocket."

"Out of my pocket, too," Norman Marek says. "Everybody at corporate has been asked to take a temporary ten percent cut in pay. Everybody tithes ten percent to the god of over-production and before you know it prices have re-couped and everything's copacetic—"

Calvin takes Norman's half-full coffee cup away from him. "Copacetic, my ass."

Norman cranes his neck to see if Calvin is refilling the cup or putting it in the sink. He's relieved when he sees it's a refill. "It's only a matter of time before people come to their senses and start eating eggs for breakfast again, instead of those damn rice cakes. So I'm counseling patience, Cal. P-a-t-i-e-n-c-e."

"I can't lose this farm, Norman."

"We'll work with you, Cal. Bob loves you like a son."

"The Bob I've never met?"

"I keep him apprised."

The refilled cup lands hard on the table. "Apprise Bob of this—at his urging I've grown my flock to a million hens, taken on a million dollars in debt. I've got manure and flies up the wazoo. I've got a daughter who hates my guts and breaks out in feathers the way other kids break out in pimples. I've got—"

Norman stops spooning sugar. "Then all that feather stuff is true?"

Calvin throws Norman's coffee cup against the wall.

Sixteen

DONNA CASSOWARY PUTS on her parka, knit cap and gloves, and skates down the icy driveway to the mailbox. Stuffed in the box with the bills and Christmas catalogs is a thick brown envelope. It is addressed to Rhea. There is no return address in the corner except for the word GRANDMA! The flap is heavily Scotch-taped. There also is a row of staples.

Donna hurries back inside where she has left herself a hot cup of tea. "Rhea!" she yells, loud enough for her voice to carry up the stairs, "your grandma sent you a package."

The steps squeak and Rhea pops into the kitchen. "Which grandma?"

Donna shrugs and holds it out for her. "Feels like a book."

Rhea looks at the single word and exclamation mark in the corner. "Probably Gammy Betz." She squeaks back upstairs and flops on her bed. It takes a couple minutes for her to dig off the tape and pry off the staples. Finally the flap is open and she shakes out the book. A note is taped to the cover:

Dear Rhea,

This is not a package from your grandma as the wrapper says. It is from me, Dr. Pirooz Aram.

It is very unprofessional of me to send you this book. For some reason your father does not want you to see me. Which is his right. But I never had a patient with feathers before!

So if I cannot be your doctor may I be your friend? A friend you cannot see but is always thinking of you?

If you do accept my friendship, Rhea, then also please accept this little book. It is called Manteq at-Tair. In English it is called *The Conference of the Birds*. It was written 800 years ago by a man from my homeland named Farid ud-Din Attar.

111

The book is about a journey. And I hope that you will find the time to read it during your own journey.

Never forget, Rhea, you are a swan! Do you hear me? A swan!

Best wishes,
Pirooz Aram

p.s. In case your parents have opened this package instead of you, let me say Mr. and Mrs. Cassowary that I apologize for meddling, and that if you wish to sue me for malpractice, I understand fully and promise I will not try to defend myself.

Rhea studies the cover. Below the title is a wonderful painting of a large tree with star-shaped leaves. Gathered under the tree are many types of birds. There are peacocks and roosters and ducks, cranes and doves and woodpeckers, white birds and black birds and red birds and blue birds.

The book begins with a long introduction, apparently explaining why it is such an important book. The print is very small and the words very big. Rhea reads only a few lines before putting the book under her mattress. She smoothes the feathers on her face and lowers herself to her pillow. She wants to nap but the birds on the book's cover are fluttering on the insides of her eyelids. The funny man who sent her the book is dancing in her mind, waving that fancy hat he called his chapeau. She pulls out the book and leafs through the introduction until she finds the first chapter. The page surprises her. It is a poem. She flips further. The entire book is a poem. She turns back to the beginning and reads:

"Dear Hoopoe, welcome! You will be our guide;
It was on you King Solomon relied
To carry secret messages between
His court and distant Sheba's lovely queen."

She reads no more than that when Donna appears in the doorway, a wadded tissue in each hand. "So which grandma is it from?"

112

"Gammy Betz," Rhea lies, "like I figured."

"What's it about?"

"Birds."

Donna winces. "Birds?"

"I think. I haven't read very much yet."

Donna dabs her nostrils with one tissue and then the other. "I'm sure your grandma means well. But you are not a bird."

Rhea knows what's coming next, the you're-a-normal-human-being speech. "What would you do if I laid an egg?" she asks her stepmother.

"You are not going to lay a egg."

"And how do you know that?"

"Because you don't have an egg thing inside."

"All females have an egg thing inside."

"You know what I mean. You don't have a bird egg thing."

Rhea tells her that a bird's egg thing is called an oviduct.

Donna is not impressed with her knowledge of bird anatomy. "Well, you don't have one of those. You've just got feathers. Which one of these days will fall out and you'll be normal again."

Rhea closes her book. "You don't know that. For all you know I'll have these feathers forever. For all you know I'll start clucking and lay a big egg."

"You are not—"

Rhea start clucking. Bends her arms into wings and starts flapping. Starts grunting. Rolls over and looks at the indent her butt made in the mattress. She pretends to pout. "Maybe next time."

"This is difficult enough for us—you don't have to add to it with a shitty attitude."

Rhea duckwalks across the bed. "Wouldn't it be terrible if my feathers were contagious? Some morning you'll wake up with feathers between your boobs. Just like I did."

Donna retreats to the hallway. "It is not contagious."

Rhea stands up at the bottom of the bed and, flapping furiously, leaps to the floor. "Maybe you'll start laying eggs, too. Ooooh, the stretch marks! Ooooh, the stretch marks!"

Seventeen

JOON FALDSTOOL LIKES working at the Cassowary farm. It gives him something to do while other boys his age are playing sports, talking sports, or pursuing their first sexual experiences. Joon doesn't have any real friends. Doesn't have any real talents. Doesn't have a chance in hell of ever having sex with anyone but himself.

He works every weekday from 3:30 to 6:00. And until he gets his driver's license—which could be quite a while, given that he still hasn't passed the test for his temporary—he will continue to have the school bus drop him off.

No, it isn't easy being a Faldstool. First, the Faldstools are short—no Faldstool male has ever topped five-four. Secondly, the Faldstools are not very bright—no Faldstool male has ever possessed the capacity for anything but the most mundane and monotonous work. Remarkably, in the three centuries since the first Faldstool arrived in the New World from England as an indentured servant, no Faldstool male has been able to elevate the family's physical, mental or economic stature by breeding with a woman of superior strain. His own father's choice of a mate— Eileen Aspergres—not only failed to move the family forward economically, but saddled future generations with a third inhibiting trait: big ears.

Yes, Joon Faldstool has the Aspergres ears. Big, thin, red ears that look like someone held him down and flattened them with a mallet. When the sun's behind him they glow.

So Joon Faldstool is short. So Joon Faldstool is dumb. So Joon Faldstool has big ears. So Joon Faldstool works every day after school at the Cassowary egg farm shoveling manure. And he likes it just fine.

Yesterday was the last Sunday in October. In Ohio, that means the end of Daylight Savings Time, that extra hour of sunlight giving people another hour to be productive. Today it will get dark an hour earlier than yesterday. People will drive home from work in the dark. Eat their supper with the kitchen light on for the first time since March.

For a not-too-smart sixteen-year-old, Joon knows quite a bit about Daylight Savings Time. He learned it from his big-eared grandfather, Hap Aspergres. Hap, who lives in self-imposed squalor in an ancient silver housetrailer in Acorn County, decades ago forsook the accumulation of money for the accumulation of useless knowledge.

Joon made the mistake of asking Hap about Daylight Savings Time when he was nine or ten, after his father and mother had argued for several hours one April night about whether they were supposed to move the hour hand on the kitchen clock ahead an hour, or back an hour. Joon's father said it should be moved back. His mother insisted ahead.

Hap shook his head sadly. "Your mother's right. In the spring you move the hour hand ahead one hour, so that when it's nine o'clock at night and still light out, it's because it's really only eight o'clock."

"I think I understand that," said Joon.

"Just remember, in spring you spring forward and in the fall you fall back." Hap went on to tell him more about Daylight Savings Time than he or anyone needed to know. "It's said Benjamin Franklin came up with the idea, way back in the 1780s, as a way to save on candle wax. Idea didn't get very far. Wasn't until World War I, when every last drop of oil and spurt of electricity was needed for the war machine, that politicians took the idea seriously. Congress adopted it in 1917, the year I was born. Farmers hated it, though, and after the war Daylight Savings Time was repealed. Came back during World War II and stayed. It's all a bunch of nonsense as far as I'm concerned. Like God doesn't know what he's doing. But it's to be expected, Joonbug. Mankind jiggles with everything the Almighty took sixteen billion years to perfect."

115

Joon gets off the bus and runs up the Cassowary's driveway. In the employee locker room he puts on his overalls and rubber boots. He goes to Layer House D, to being shoveling.

Man—Calvin Cassowary in particular—has jiggled with time inside the layer houses, too. In the layer houses it is high noon sixteen hours a day. That's how many hours a day the ceiling lights are kept on—sixteen hours on, eight hours off—so the Leghorns lay extra eggs. Joon's father explained it to him on his first day there. It was, Joon thought, an impressive explanation for a man who couldn't figure out when to spring forward or fall back.

"In order to get 250 eggs a year out of these ladies," his father said as they walked the length of a layer house, "you got to keep their ovaries pumping. Keeping the layer houses lit sixteen hours rain or shine does just that. It ain't easy on their assholes, but a hen's got to pay for her keep like anybody else."

Joon shovels manure for two hours. He knows it's getting dark outside. But inside the layer house it's high noon and the hens are squirting eggs. Those eggs are rolling forward across the wire floors of their cages to a conveyor belt that takes them right to the shipping room.

At a quarter to six Joon hurries to the locker room and slips out of his boots and overalls and washes. He spritzes himself with Old Spice, gathers up his books and gym bag, and goes outside. It is already dark. He sits on the bench by the door and waits. Sometimes his father comes out right away. Sometimes it's not for a half hour.

From the bench Joon can see the light on in the Cassowary kitchen, see Calvin Cassowary's wife, Donna, fixing supper. She has an electric mixer in one hand and a Kleenex in the other. His father has told him that she sneezes a lot. Maybe so, Joon thinks, but she is nothing to sneeze at. He feels himself getting an erection and forces his eyes away from the kitchen window. He sees the dim light inside the little chicken coop where the scraggly little flock is kept. He knows that the Cassowarys are pinching every penny these days. Knows the coop should be dark. Knows that the hens in there are allowed to lay when they feel like it. He can make points with the Cassowarys, and his father, he thinks, if he turns that light out. "By the way," he could tell Mr. Cassowary the next time he sees him, "I turned off the light in the little coop for you the other day."

"Thanks," Mr. Cassowary will say.

So Joon puts down his books and duffel bag and walks across the lawn to the chicken coop. He looks in the dirty window. The light is not coming from the light bulb in the ceiling, but from a flashlight. He presses his face against the glass and squints. He sees the Cassowary's daughter, Rhea, sitting on the bottom perch, surrounded by chickens. The beam of the flashlight is bouncing off an open book cradled in her lap.

In the pink glow of the flashlight's red cap, he can see the feathers covering her face. She looks like a giant owl sitting there, deep-set eyes blinking, stiff neck turning from side to side. When he squints he can see that her lips are moving, just slightly. *Whoa! Look at that! She is reading to her chickens!* He runs back to the bench. In a few minutes the light in the chicken coop goes out and the door bumps open. He sees Rhea running across the dark lawn to the house. He sees the blinds in the breakfast nook go down.

The next afternoon Joon can't wait for the sun to go down. He washes and rushes outside to see if there's a light in the chicken coop. There is a light. He goes to the window and watches Rhea read to her chickens. Very weird, he thinks. It's the kind of thing he might do himself, he thinks, if he were covered with feathers.

All weekend Joon thinks about Rhea reading to her chickens, especially when he is raking the wet leaves that are ankle-deep all over the backyard.

Over the years his father has told him quite a bit about the girl and her chickens: about the Leghorn she rescued from the manure pit; about the name she gave the fortunate hen, Miss Lucky Pants; about how she let her set and have a brood of chicks; about how her father had a fit; about how the rooster she named Blackbutt was killed by a coyote.

117

His father talked about darker things, too: about Rhea's mother dying; about Rhea one night trying to free an entire layer house of hens; about the time he came out of layer house B and saw Mr. Cassowary yanking fistfuls of feathers from Rhea's naked chest.

On Monday Joon doesn't work until six as usual. He stops at a quarter after five and, after giving himself an extra spritz of Old Spice, sneaks to the chicken coop. He doesn't go to the window. He goes to the door. He opens it gently, not to sneak in, but so he doesn't startle Rhea or the chickens. "I'm Joon Faldstool," he says. "Jimmy Faldstool Jr."

Rhea swings the flashlight beam into his eyes. "Tired of watching through the window?"

Joon shuffles across the floor and kneels by the perches. Rhea is sitting on the first perch, slightly above him. The chickens, huddled on the ascending perches like people at a football game, *cluck* and *bruck* a little, but quickly accept him. "I know about your feathers," he says.

"I know about your ears," she says.

Joon wishes that his head would shrivel up and drop inside his shirt collar. "They're gigundo, aren't they?"

"Not as gigundo as my father said."

Joon changes the subject. "Do the chickens understand what you're reading?"

The feathers around Rhea's eyes stick out a bit, as if she's snickering underneath. "Duh? They're chickens!" Her feathers smooth and her eyes soften. "But I think they like hearing my voice. I know I like hearing it. That's why I read to them, I guess. To hear my own voice."

"Like the sound of your own voice, do you?"

"Not especially. But I don't get to hear it much in the house. Nobody talks to me unless they're yelling. Which means I'm always yelling, too. So it's nice to hear myself talking calmly once in a while."

Joon wants to know all about her feathers—how she got them, what it's like to have them, how she goes to the bathroom, the whole shebang—but he decides it'll be smarter to talk about something else. "What's the book about?"

Rhea picks up a long tail feather from the floor and uses it as a bookmark. "It's a poem. But it's pretty neat. There's this one kind of bird, called a *Hoopoe* or something, that wants to take a bunch of other birds to see the king of birds, the *Simorgh* or something. They all have an excuse why they can't go. But the Hoopoe tells each of them a story and they feel guilty and go along. That's as far as I've gotten."

Joon finds it bizarre that a girl covered with feathers is reading a story about birds to a coop full of chickens. He also finds it sweet and kind and mystical and incredibly feminine. "Your parents don't mind you reading to them?"

Rhea ignores the question. "This psychiatrist I used to see sent me the book. He thinks it'll help me adjust to having feathers."

"You think it will?"

Rhea eases herself off the perch and goes to the window. She cups her hand around her eyes and peers into the kitchen. Her stepmother has a meat fork in one hand and a Kleenex in the other. "He was really strange. Always wearing these funny hats. But he didn't think my feathers were *my* problem. He thought they were everybody else's problem. Like your gigundo ears aren't *your* problem. But the problem of the people who think you look goofy. You know?"

"So you don't go to the funny hat doctor anymore?"

"My father wants my feathers to be *my* problem. I better go in."

Joon follows her outside. She's wearing a baggy coat, so he can't tell for sure, but she doesn't appear to have poofy butt feathers like real chickens do. "Can I listen to you read tomorrow?"

"No way," Rhea says. "We'd get caught and then I couldn't come out here anymore. I don't even want you looking through the window. You saw me and heard me talk. You know I don't cluck or tweet or have a beak. And if you're wondering, I don't lay eggs."

They teeter on the chicken coop step trying not to look at each other. It's getting colder and there's a drizzle. "I suppose I'll see you around," Joon finally says.

Rhea runs to the house.

119

As Joon walks back to the bench there is a sudden halo of light around his head. Rhea must be shining her flashlight at him. His huge Aspergres ears must be glowing red.

Eighteen

"WHAT'S YOUR ROOSTER'S name again?" Gammy Betz asks Rhea.

"Mr. Shakyshiver."

They are sitting at the long table in the dining room, in the cold northwest corner of the old farmhouse. Thanksgiving dinner has been over for an hour. The table has been cleared, the dishes washed. The others are in the living room—Donna and Rhea's father, her grandmother's husband Ben, her uncle Dan and the Latino woman he brought with him from San Diego.

"And the one the coyote killed?" Gammy Betz asks.

"That was Blackbutt," says Rhea. "He looked a lot more like Captain Bates than Mr. Shakyshiver does."

Rhea's grandmother pushes up her sagging cheeks with the heels of her hands. "Oh, I liked that Captain Bates."

Rhea knows she is in for a treat now, a rambling, wistful soliloquy on her grandmother's old rooster. Woven in this story about Captain Bates will be the story about Maximo Gomez, Alfred making that FRESH EGGS sign, the story about her father being afraid to reach under the pecking hens for eggs when he was a little boy, so many wonderful Cassowary stories.

Instead Rhea's grandmother starts to tell a new story, about the giant she named her rooster after. "Did I ever tell you about the real Captain Bates?" she begins.

"Only that you once tried on his big boots," Rhea says. "And that they came up to your rear end."

Her grandmother laughs and begins, telling her that Martin VanBuren Bates was born in eastern Kentucky in 1845; that he joined the Confederate army when he was sixteen; that he was a big boy when he joined and kept growing right through the war, to seven feet, eight inches and 470 pounds; that by the end of the war he had risen to the rank of captain.

 (She does not tell Rhea that after the Civil War, Americans developed a huge interest in human oddities—giants and midgets

121

and women with beards, people who could swallow swords or twist themselves into pretzels, dark thick-lipped people said to be cannibals from faraway islands.)

She tells Rhea that a man who puts on shows—an *impresario*—lured Bates into show business with promises of fame and fortune; that during a tour of Europe, Captain Bates met and fell in love with a woman even bigger than he was; that her name was Anna Swan and that she was from Nova Scotia and that she was seven feet, eleven inches; that when they were married Queen Victoria gave them expensive wedding presents.

She tells her that after years of traveling the world, the captain and Anna bought a farm in Seville, which, as Rhea knows, is only a few miles north of Tuttwyler; that the house they built had big doors and big windows and fourteen-foot ceilings.

She tells her that despite their height, despite the fact that people were always gawking at them, despite their fame, Captain Bates and Anna considered themselves normal people who deserved a normal life.

(She does not tell her that while living in that big house in Seville, Anna, after gushing six gallons of embryonic fluid from her uterus, gave birth to the largest baby known to medical history, a twenty-three and three-quarter-pound boy thirty inches long, with a head nineteen inches in diameter; and that he lived less than a day.)

She does tell her that many of the friends they'd made while touring came to visit them at their farm: midgets and Siamese twins and a man with very little meat on his bones who billed himself as a living skeleton; that these people, like the Captain and Anna, despite the way people gawked at them, were ordinary everyday people, like everybody else.

(She does not tell her about the time the floor beneath Anna and the captain collapsed while they were dancing at a neighbor's house; about the captain being a sour and angry man always coming to blows with smaller men; that when Anna died, the coffin-maker thought the dimensions the captain sent him were a mistake, and so when Anna's coffin arrived, it was much too small for her; that the funeral had to be delayed until a new coffin could be built; that to avoid the same humiliating mix-up when he died, he had his own coffin made and kept it in his barn for thirty years.)

Rhea loves her grandmother too much to tell her she already knows all those stories, both the good ones she's telling and the bad ones she's leaving out. She knows them because a month ago her father went to the library in Tuttwyler to get books for her homeschooling and came home with one on Captain Bates and Anna. It was called *There Were Giants on the Earth*. Rhea also knows why Gammy Betz is telling her only the good stories. It's because Gammy wants her to think of herself as normal. Instead of the human oddity she is.

"For years and years they put his huge boots on display at the fair and let people try them on," her grandmother says. "And yes, Rhea,. they came right up to my rear end. I couldn't have been more than five or six."

Rhea finishes the story for her. "And years later when your new rooster kept growing and growing, and strutting liked he owned the world, you thought of Captain Bates and those big boots."

"That's right," her grandmother says.

Rhea loves her Gammy Betz more than anything. During dinner, she was the only person who didn't try to force a piece of turkey on her. Even the Latino woman had tried that. "Come on!" she said, her eyes looking everywhere but at Rhea's feathers. "Everybody eats the big bird on Thanksgiving! What kind of American are you?"

Gammy Betz hadn't said anything like that. She just made sure she ate her mashed potatoes and a slice of cranberry sauce and one of the rolls while they were still warm.

Nineteen

THE ACCIDENT ON the Ohio turnpike cost Phil Bunyip his left eye, but it has not affected his punctuality. As always he arrives right at midnight. As always he jumps out of his truck drinking a Pepsi, smoking a cigarette, and eating cheap pastry. "That forklift of yours all juiced up?" he asks.

Calvin Cassowary gives him an exaggerated nod, one that can be seen in the dark.

Phil signals to his chicken catchers and they start putting on their paper overalls, rubber gloves and masks.

Calvin can see the wrinkles of concern around Phil's eyes. "Anything wrong?"

Phil draws on his cigarette and licks the icing off his little finger. "I just hope the boys don't let their emotions get in the way with this load."

"Know what you mean," Calvin says. And he does know what Phil means. Tonight's work will be different than usual. The hundred thousand Leghorns they'll be ripping from their cages tonight aren't spent. They're year-old hens at the peak of their laying, two eggs every three days. Ordinarily they'd have another six months of laying before being trucked to the pet food plant. But these are the 100,000 hens Calvin has to cut from his flock.

"It's not like chickens have souls or anything," Phil Bunyip says. "But you do catch yourself feeling a little funny snuffing out these young hens before their time."

Calvin does not stand in the doorway to the layer house and watch the culling, as his contract with Gallinipper Foods requires him to do. Instead he goes back to the house and climbs the stairs to his bedroom and closes the door behind him.

"You coming to bed already?" Donna asks with sleepy surprise.

Calvin takes off his pants and sits on the edge of the bed. He peels back the allergen-free cotton blankets and puts his hand

124

under her allergen-free cotton nightgown. Calvin has no reason to feel guilty in the bedroom. Donna is always receptive to unplanned sex. The endorphins her brain releases numb her ever-present itch to sneeze.

So Calvin just goes ahead and enjoys himself—enjoys the way his own endorphins numb his many problems—his life without Jeanie, his daughter with the feathers, his bills and bank loans, his need to husband the Cassowary family farm through one more generation, his young wife's inability to conceive.

Donna has been to a doctor. Calvin, too. There's no reason in the world why she can't conceive. She just doesn't.

After the sex Calvin and Donna squeeze their pillows together. "Tilt your butt so it doesn't run out," Calvin whispers.

Donna tilts, as instructed. "I don't know why you're so antsy about me getting pregnant. I'm young. We'll have babies."

"We've been screwing for seven years."

"And enjoying it. Yes?"

"Of course."

"Then let's just keep enjoying it, okay?"

"It's psychological, Donna. Your subconscious doesn't want you to give birth to a baby with feathers."

Donna raps him on the forehead with the flat of her hand, the same way she does when he's snoring. "Rhea is the one with the problem, Cal. Not me. One of these mornings I'll roll over and puke on your face and we'll know I'm pregnant."

"This isn't something to joke about."

"Isn't it? When you think I'm subconsciously telling myself not to conceive? Like that would be possible?"

"Mind over matter."

"Not the way I orgasm."

"What do your orgasms have to do with it?"

"They've done research on this. Orgasms aren't just for fun. They have a reproductive purpose. The muscle spasms in my uterus throw your sperm toward my Fallopian tubes, where the egg is waiting. So, if I didn't want your baby, I wouldn't come so easy."

Calvin surrenders. His voice softens into a playful tease. "Smart women turn me on."

Donna kisses the spot where she rapped him. "Then how about another ride, rooster boy? I feel a sneeze coming."

Donna looks at the clock on the dresser. It's 5:30. Calvin's side of the bed is empty. Outside, Phil Bunyip's trucks are revving up. Mr. Shakyshiver is crowing for the sun to rise. Biscuit is barking just for the sake of barking. Donna sniffs back the mucus in her nostrils. Coughs. Sneezes. Exchanges her hot pillows for the cool ones on Calvin's side. Tries to sleep. But can't.

She has been unfaithful to her husband. Unfaithful to him with her half-truths. She wants to have children with him, yes. He is a magnificent man. But he is a man with a daughter with feathers. Yes, she opens her womb to him. Allows him to spend as much time in there as he wants. She loves their sex. Her orgasms are for real. She tells herself not to be silly. Or afraid. Calvin's sperm is normal, she tells herself. It has been tested and retested. No one in Calvin's or Jeanie's family had ever grown feathers before. There are no records of it. Or rumors of it.

Donna knows that she is a smart woman, just as Calvin said. With her intellect and her sensuality, she is able to override her silliness and her fears and copulate joyfully. But is he right about her subconscious fears? Have they, like dutiful medieval defenders, erected a castle wall around her eggs? Do they pour cauldrons of boiling oil onto his advancing spermatozoa?

It may not just be Rhea's feathers that keep her from getting pregnant. It also may be Calvin's lingering love for Jeanie Marabout. She knows that their marriage is founded on practicality. The need for fantastic, mind-numbing sex. The need for a business partner good in math. The need for a mother.

She knows, too, that Calvin's and Jeanie's marriage was founded on something more fundamental than practicality. It was founded on love. She has no way of knowing whether the sex between Calvin and Jeanie was better or worse than the sex between Calvin and her. But surely their *lovemaking* was better.

Maybe Calvin's subconscious is the problem. Maybe despite his eagerness for a son he doesn't want her to have equal status with the great Jeanie Marabout. Share the great Jeanie Marabout's high and heavenly pedestal.

Donna pulls the cotton sheet over her head and remembers the afternoon, just six weeks after they were married, when she explored the fruit cellar in the basement. It was a dark and musty little room that made her sneeze something terrible.

The walls were lined ceiling-to-floor with wide wooden shelves. There were maybe a hundred glass jars on those shelves, jars of tomatoes and pickles and rhubarb and green beans and beets and apples and pears, grape and raspberry jelly. Bundles of garlic and onions hung from the ceiling. There was a huge bin of wrinkled potatoes. There were webs of dust and webs made by spiders. There were mousetraps loaded with chunks of moldy cheese. And there was something else. Stuck behind the jugs of homemade wine was a small picture frame. Donna pulled it out and saw the drawing of Jeanie feeding chickens. When she saw the rooster trying to screw the cat, she laughed out loud. The drawing made her think of the empty rectangle on the wall above the table in the breakfast nook—the wallpaper inside that rectangle lighter than the rest—and she knew that this drawing once hung there. She wondered how long it would be before Calvin drew a picture of her? A drawing she could frame and hang on the wall.

Eight years have passed. Calvin has not drawn a picture of her. Calvin has not drawn a picture of anything. Jeanie Marabout was married to an artist. She is married to a man with a million chickens.

She can hear Phil Bunyip's trucks pulling onto the road, heading west toward a pet food plant somewhere in Indiana. Now she is married to a man with 900,000 chickens.

.

Rhea follows the flashlight beam to the chicken coop. This second week of December is unseasonably cold. The kind of cold that makes the tips of your ears ache and your breath smolder. The kind of cold that makes a door slam louder. The chickens, already settled on their perches, *gauk-bwauk* for mercy, then, seeing that the sudden intruder is only their mistress, and not a coyote or that jumpy old dog who lives on the porch, cluck until everybody's calm again.

Rhea sits on the bottom perch and opens the book Dr. Pirooz Aram sent her. "If you remember," she says to the chickens, "the birds are finally on their way to find their king. But now they're flying over spooky and empty lands." The chickens cackle deep in their throats. She begins to read:

> *"One of the birds lets out a helpless squeak:*
> *'I can't go on this journey, I'm too weak.*
> *Dear guide, I know I can't fly anymore;*
> *I've never tried a feat like this before . . ."*

After these few lines Rhea hears the coop door squeak open. "Hi," a voice says.

She knows who the voice belongs to, but aims her flashlight anyway. "Didn't we agree you wouldn't come anymore?"

Joon Faldstool shuffles forward like a toy robot with weak batteries. "I just wanted to tell you I got my temporary."

Rhea lets the flashlight beam burn into his eyes for several seconds—punishment for disobeying her—then lowers it to her book. "Big deal," she says.

"It was my fourth try," Joon says. "I'm really not that dumb. I just panic on tests."

Rhea's voice softens. "My father says you should go with the first answer that pops in your head. 'Trust your synapses,' he says."

Joon kneels by her feet, as if she was a queen or a goddess or a great philosopher. "Synapses?"

Rhea pretends she knows what she's talking about. "They're the microscopic thingamabobs that pass information between your brain cells. They only let you down if you think too hard and short-circuit yourself."

"Your father teaches you at home, huh?"

"He was going to be a teacher until he inherited the farm."

"But he teaches you at home because of your feathers, right?"

"He figured everybody would make fun of me."

"They would, too. Everybody makes fun of my ears."

"I can see why."

Now they laugh. Not just giggle in a nervous way. But *laugh*. It frightens the chickens.

"When are you going to get your real license?" Rhea asks.

Dread wrinkles Joon's face. "I'll still be taking that test when I'm fifty."

"Not if you trust your synapses."

They laugh again. Frighten the chickens again.

When there is silence again, Joon says to Rhea, "You have a good attitude about things."

"For someone with feathers?"

"I mean for anybody."

Rhea bites down on her lip, suppressing a pang of self-pity. "That's not what you meant. But that's okay. Actually I have a shitty attitude."

"Not as shitty as mine."

"We're not going to play 'My Attitude Is Shittier Than Yours,' are we?"

He shakes his head no and she continues reading:

> *"Your heart's congealed like ice;*
> *when will you free yourself from cowardice?"*

The next night Joon shovels manure furiously so he can sneak away to the coop and listen to Rhea read to her chickens. "You want to take a walk?" Rhea asks him when he slips through the door.

They sneak around the side of the coop and Rhea whisper-yells for Biscuit. The old dog comes loping. They head down the hill toward Three Fish Creek, their breath smoldering around their heads.

"Don't tell your father," Rhea says, "but I sneak out at night all the time and walk in the woods."

"Faldstools don't blab," Joon insists.

"Everybody blabs," Rhea says.

They follow the creek until they find a spot where the ice looks thick enough to hold them. They slide to the other side and wind their way through the huge naked maples. Biscuit sniffs in circles, stopping often to raise his hind leg.

"My great-grandfather used to tap these trees to make syrup," Rhea says. "We had a real farm then. Cows and pigs and maple syrup and brown eggs laid by hens who ran around free and ate bugs. Now we run a concentration camp."

They head up the slope toward the Van Varken farm, where huge homes now grow. "My father told me about the time you set a bunch of them free," Joon says.

Rhea slaps him hard on the chest. "I thought Faldstools didn't blab?"

He rubs the spot. "I thought what you did was pretty cool."

PART III

"God the Most High created the angels and placed within them the intellect, He created the beasts and placed within them sensuality, He created the children of Adam and placed within them both intellect and sensuality. So he whose intellect dominates his sensuality is higher than the angels, and he whose sensuality dominates his intellect is lower than the beasts."

Jalaluddin Rumi
The Mathnawi, c. 1260

Twenty

IT'S 5:30 A.M. It's March. It's raining. Calvin Cassowary sees the headlights of Helen Abelard's car. It's amazing how many years that woman has been delivering the *Wyssock County Gazette*.

He puts on his poncho and boots and heads for the mailbox. Rivulets of gray water are zig-zagging down the driveway, collecting in a muddy pool by the road. If the FRESH EGGS sign was still up, it would be swaying and shimmering.

He watches the tail lights of Helen's car as it rolls up the hill toward Maple Creek Estates, the housing development being built on the Van Varken's old hog farm. At least fifty homes are up already, half already occupied. None of the quarter-acre *estates* that comprise Maple Creek have either maple trees or a creek. The creek and the maples are all on the Cassowary estate.

As Calvin pulls the paper from the tube he sees another pair of headlights coming. They are low and close together. A Saab or a BMW, Calvin figures. The car is moving fast but when its lights hit him, it decelerates and stops. The window zips halfway. A pair of gold-framed glasses appear. They are attached to a melon-shaped head. An impatient "Hey!" comes out of the head.

Calvin makes sure no other car is coming—these days you have to worry about that sort of thing—and walks to the car, which he can now see is a small Mercedes coupe. In order to be some-what even with the melon-shaped head inside, he has to bend. "Hello," he says.

"You work here, do you?" the head says.

"Every day," Calvin says. "It's my place."

"Even better," says the head. "What's with the smell?"

Calvin knows the man in the Mercedes is not talking abut the way he smells personally. He knows it's about the chicken manure. It's especially ripe this morning, given that it's finally spring, given that it's raining and the wind is blowing. "You're one of the new Maple Creek people, I gather?"

"Correct!"

"Well," says Calvin, consciously giving himself the slow, stereotypical, by-crackie voice of a farmer, "this is a chicken farm, so the smell would be that of chickens."

The head is not amused. "Not acceptable."

"Not acceptable? Don't think I get your drift."

"This is the country, pal—clean fresh air."

Calvin grins and squats and rests his forearms on the car door, so his face is only inches away from the head. It is obvious that this man is not aware of Calvin's loans, or his bills or his taxes, or that he has a daughter covered with feathers, or that his wife can't seem to get pregnant. "That's why you moved out here, isn't it? The clean fresh air. And the big red barns and the rolling fields and the romping horsies as far as you can see."

"You getting smart with me?"

Calvin chuckles. No, this guy doesn't know anything about his problems. "You see, there is lots of clean fresh air in the country. But there's also lots of shit. Chicken shit and cow shit and pig shit. And shit stinks."

"You're spreading it on your fields," the head points out.

"I've thought about installing a million little flush toilets. But I'm not sure the chickens would use them even if I did."

"The stench comes right inside my house."

"Mine, too," Calvin says.

"Completely unacceptable."

Daylight is spreading and cars are beginning to pull out of Maple Creek Estates. Calvin stands. He no longer speaks in his by-crackie voice. "The truth is, you haven't smelled anything yet. Wait until the summer months."

The head studies his rearview mirror, frowns at the cars snaking toward them. "I'm going to call a meeting of the home-owners' association. We know our rights." He pulls a business card from his coat pocket and thrusts it into Calvin's hand, the way in an earlier time a man of honor might drop a gauntlet.

Calvin reads the card. The man is the financial vice president of a company called AdvenTec. "Well, Mr. F. Douglas Remora, it's always good to know the name of a man who knows his rights. I'm Calvin Cassowary."

"Totally unacceptable," the head says, as the window zips shut and the Mercedes coupe breezes away.

Calvin shouts after him, "Eat more eggs! I'm dying here!"

Only now does Calvin unroll the newspaper and read the top headline:

COUNTY TAX HIKE WILL BE SHOCKER

As he walks up the driveway, Calvin wonders how long it will be before it reads:

HOMEOWNERS SUE OVER FOWL SMELL

And so he is not surprised three weeks later when two registered letters arrive on the same day. One is from the melon-shaped head in the Mercedes coupe, Mr. F. Douglas Remora, advising him that the Maple Creek Homeowners' Association has indeed met and has retained the services of attorney D. William Aitchbone. The second letter is from D. William Aitchbone himself, advising him that a lawsuit will be filed unless "proactive steps are taken immediately to abate the offensive odors emanating from your place of business."

The letters arrive on the same day Norman Marek calls to inform Calvin that things are less than copacetic at Gallinipper Foods. "Bob wants producers to cull another ten percent," he says.

That night when Calvin is lying in bed watching *The Tonight Show*, Donna walks naked from the bathroom and straddles his hips. She runs her hands up under his tee shirt. She Groucho-Marxes her eyebrows.

He starts to work her nipples, then drops his hands. "We're in big trouble, aren't we?" he asks.

Donna rolls off and burrows under the sheet. She reaches for her box of Kleenex. "Basically, we're broke."

135

"Broke?" The word explodes from his lips like the belch of a bullfrog.

"I've been putting our groceries on VISA for three months."

"We've got 900,000 chickens and we're borrowing money at eighteen percent to eat?"

Two weeks later Phil Bunyip and his catchers arrive and haul away another 90,000 Leghorns. Now Calvin Cassowary has 810,000 chickens. A week after that a letter arrives from Dewlap & Snood announcing a regrettable six percent hike in feed prices. That letter is followed by a phone call from Della Osprey, midwestern sales manager for Myco-Med, advising him of the regrettable eight percent increase in the vaccines and antibiotics he uses to prevent his egg machines from contracting unproductive diseases. One day a story in the *Gazette* reports that Ohio Edison Company is seeking state approval for an increase in electricity rates. Another day the *Gazette* reports that growing tensions in the Persian Gulf will result in a doubling of heating oil prices in the fall. Donna comes home from shopping in tears. "What's wrong, babe?" asks Calvin.

"Look at the price on these bananas," she answers.

This is how Calvin Cassowary's spring goes. On a sunny day in May he calls Paul Bilderback. "How about meeting me for coffee at the Pile Inn this afternoon," he says. "Just you and me."

Calvin and Paul haven't talked since the day Jimmy Faldstool pushed him off his stool and pelted him with donuts and slices of pie. At first Calvin and Paul cannot talk about anything but the weather and the lousy start the Cleveland Indians are off to. Then Paul stretches his arms along the back of the booth and says, "Cal, I'm really sorry about all that other garbage."

"Paul," Calvin confesses, "I think I'll have to drive school bus again in the fall."

Paul leans over his coffee cup. "Drive bus? You've got a million chickens."

Calvin tells him it's now only 810,000. Tells him about the skyrocketing feed and medicine prices. The taxes he has to pay. The unreasonable insurance policies he has to carry.

"Holy Toledo," Paul moans. "I figured you were the richest sonofabitch in the county."

"So you think they'll need drivers in the fall?"

Paul Bilderback scratches his eyebrows. "The school board always needs drivers but—I'll just say it, Cal—you're sitting on a goldmine out there."

Calvin's head starts shaking from side to side. "Sell the farm to developers? Like Rick Van Varken? I'll never do that."

Paul's head starts shaking, too. "I'm not talking about selling your farm. That's chicken feed. I'm talking about your daughter."

"My daughter?"

"You've got the only human being in the world covered with feathers—and you hide her away like she's a freak."

Calvin's hisses like the fuse on a lighted stick of dynamite. "She is not a freak."

"Of course she's not a freak. Not a bad freak, anyway."

"What the hell does that mean?"

"Lots of people are freaks of nature. Kareem Abdul Jabbar. Elvis. Albert Einstein. Dolly Parton. That giant who used to live right up the road here in Seville—"

"Captain Bates."

"Every one of those people was born a freak, Cal. Born with special gifts they could cash in on. And you've got that sexy little girl up there covered with feathers."

Calvin drives his fist square into the flat expanse between Paul Bilderback's wild eyes.

That same afternoon Calvin carefully opens a certified letter with his swollen hand. It's from Pauline R. Plover. Pauline graduated from West Wyssock High School the same year he did. They were in several classes together, including art class. She was the only one who could draw or paint better than him. Now Pauline is administrative clerk of the Wyssock County Common Pleas Court and it is her duty to notify him that the Maple Creek Estates Homeowners' Association has filed a lawsuit against him, demanding that he immediately stop exposing the families of

Maple Creek to the deleterious effects of his chicken manure. They also want $1.3 million in cash.

Calvin sits at the wobbly table in the breakfast nook and empties a mug of black coffee, one small noisy sip at a time. Then he calls Norman Marek. He leaves this message on his answering machine: "Hi, Norman. This is Calvin Cassowary. I'm being sued. Call me as soon as you can. Okay?"

It's nine that night before Norman calls back. He tells Calvin not to worry. "You're not the first to be sued over this, and you won't be the last. Get a good night's sleep and in the morning hire the best lawyer in town."

"The best lawyer in town has already been hired by the home-owners' association," Calvin informs him.

"Then hire the second best. And put him in touch with us. Our legal beagles have all the ammunition you'll need to blow those bunny hugging pukes to kingdom come."

Calvin has the phone cord stretched as far as it will go. His forehead is pressed against the cold glass on the porch door. His layer houses lay side by side like a row of huge coffins shipped back from some little war. "Is this going to be expensive, Norman?"

"Just remember you've got Bob Gallinipper on your side," Norman says. He promises to FedEx a Manure Management Lawsuit Kit first thing in the morning. He promises that everything will be copacetic.

At 11:30 Calvin curls up on the living room sofa like a fetal giraffe and clicks on *The Tonight Show*. He hears the laughter but not Johnny Carson's jokes. Sometime after three he squeaks upstairs. Shortly before five he squeaks back down and puts on the coffee. For an hour he busies himself preparing Rhea's lessons. Given her feather problem, he wishes she had a greater enthusiasm for learning, a love for art or science, a knack for music or mathe-matics, something that would demonstrate God's fairness. But Rhea is just an average student. She just plods competently along.

By the time Jimmy Faldstool pulls in, Calvin has finished three cups of coffee and soaked up the acid puddled in his stomach with four slices of unbuttered toast. He rushes out to the layer houses, not because Jimmy has to be told what to do—Jimmy knows the routine better than he does—but because it's been a long and brutal night and he needs a friendly face.

Jimmy gives him the smile he needs, then says, "You look like crud, Cal. Didn't you sleep?"

Calvin holds up his thumb and index finger, showing Jimmy he only slept about an inch. He follows Jimmy inside to the employee locker room.

While Jimmy nervously changes into his overalls and rubber boots, Calvin nervously makes a pot of coffee. Only when the Mr. Coffee is dripping and puffing does he fold his arms tight around his ribs and say, "Jimmy, things aren't going very well."

Jimmy leans against the wall and searches his chin for a spot that needs itching. "Cal, you just say the word and I'll quit. I'll have Joon quit, too."

"Jimmy, Jesus. That's not what I'm saying. You and Joon would have to quit eight or nine thousand times to put the farm back in the black."

"Sorry we don't make more," Jimmy says. He gets two paper cups from the cupboard and sets them side by side on the table. Then he says, "You're the best boss I've ever had."

Calvin fills the cups. "And you're the best employee I've ever had. In fact—"

Calvin stops talking and takes a long sip of coffee. That *in fact* that just tumbled out of his mouth was completely unexpected, a decision made by his subconscious, against the better judgment of his conscious self. "In fact, Jimmy, I'm promoting you to manager."

The cup in Jimmy Faldstool's hands is quivering like a volcano about ready to blow. "Good gravy, I ain't smart enough to manage this place."

"You're already managing it," Calvin says, "and if you're smart enough to manage it when I'm here, then you're sure-as-hell smart enough to manage it when I'm not here."

"When you're not here? Good gravy!"

139

Having been forced by his subconscious into a decision, Calvin feels relaxed, even sleepy. He goes to the house. Goes to the desk in the dining room and searches the drawers for a pad of typing paper. He finds the sharpest pencil he can. Donna is just squeaking down the stairs when he's heading out the door. "I'll be back in a couple hours," he says.

Donna sneezes and waves good-bye.

It is still early. No more than seven. The sun, although bright, has not yet floated free of the trees on the eastern horizon. Mr. Shakyshiver is crowing with confidence.

Calvin looks for Biscuit, hoping the dog will follow him into the woods, the way farm dogs are supposed to follow their masters. But Biscuit is off on some adventure of his own, it seems; either that or he's still curled up in the back of his dog house. So Calvin heads for the woods alone.

The fields below the layer houses are slippery with mud. The fields stink, too. The chicken manure spread just before Thanksgiving is just now thawing. In the weeks to come it will seep deep into the soil, fortifying the roots of a hundred varieties of weeds. For generations these fields were filled with neat rows of corn or soy, hay or wheat. Now they are filled with weeds.

He descends the fields all the way to Three Fish Creek. On the barren hill above him sit the dozens of big houses that comprise the outpost of urban-sprawl erroneously known as Maple Creek Estates. Some of the houses are supposed to be Victorians, some Tudors, some Georgians, some New England saltboxes. But beneath their brick and vinyl facades, beneath their gingerbready affectations, they are all of the same style, Reaganesque: huge empty boxes of plywood and particle board, held together with glue and staples and adjustable mortgages; temples of two-income opulence which their owners will be forced to sell the instant they're downsized and/or divorced.

Calvin has not been inside any of the houses himself, but Donna has. She went snooping with Marilyn Dickcissel when the first two models were opened to the public. "The kitchens are absolutely gorgeous," she reported. "They have these little garages, with these little slide-up doors, where you can park your toaster and your coffeemaker."

Marilyn had been impressed with the bathrooms. "You've never seen such big bathtubs in your life. Especially the ones in the owner's suites. You could bathe a bull."

Calvin had laughed at that, and pictured a huge grinning Hereford luxuriating on his back in a sea of suds, while Marilyn scrubbed its huge balls with a floor brush. "And just what is an owner's suite?"

"What we hicks call the master bedroom," Donna said, letting him know she was well satisfied with the old Cassowary farmhouse.

Despite the lawsuit he faces, Calvin is glad that the stench of his 810,000 Leghorns is rolling up that hill.

He follows the creek upstream. The water is still clear and shallow, speeding noisily over the gray-blue shale bottom. In a week or two, when the spring rains begin in earnest, the water will boil deep and brown, uprooting small trees, and rearranging rocks. As he walks he looks for minnows in the deeper holes, but doesn't see any.

Three Fish Creek twists between high shale walls for a half-mile or so. Then the banks fade away and the surrounding land flattens out. He is on Andy Abram's dairy farm now. Andy must be getting up there, Calvin thinks. How long before these fields and pastures are covered with Reaganesque mansions, their huge bathtubs filled with luxuriating bulls?

He follows the creek into a marsh. It covers several acres. The spring growth hasn't started yet, so the marsh is brown and barren. The old deer path is still here and as he walks it, he expects any second to scare out a doe or two.

When he was a kid he came here all the time to sketch. There were always wonderful things to draw in the marsh: the cattails and the floppy burdock, the sparrows in the scrub apple, the blue heron and the spider webs, the toads and turtles that sat still just as long as you wanted.

The favorite thing Calvin liked to draw here was the quiet. No matter what he drew he was really drawing the quiet.

And so Calvin leans his back against the trunk of a shaggy hickory and opens his pad and presses his cold fingers around the pointy end of his pencil. And he draws. But he doesn't draw the weeds or the trees, or the birds, or the quiet. He draws the shameful idea that has been banging around in his head since that afternoon at the Pile Inn, when he drove his fist square into Paul Bilderback's face.

Sometime around noon he starts for home. He doesn't follow the creek back, but takes the high fields. In the mud and melting snow he sees the tracks of deer and rabbits and crows and feral cats. He sees big dog-like tracks that—unlike the unruly meandering tracks a real dog makes—are perfectly spaced in a straight line. Coyote tracks, that's what they are.

He's going to talk to Rhea about his idea right after lunch. Maybe tomorrow, after supper.

Twenty-one

RHEA CASSOWARY IS supposed to be working on her report on Galileo Galilei, the Italian astronomer who got himself into big trouble with the pope for suggesting that the earth was not the center of the universe. Instead she is reading about the weird ancient Chinese practice of binding girls' feet. Strips of cloth were wrapped so tightly around their feet, that their arches broke, leaving them crippled for life. Apparently rich Chinese men found their wincing and hobbling sexually stimulating.

She's had this problem before: starting out to learn what she's been assigned to learn, then getting lost in the pages of her encyclopedias and learning other stuff. Just last week when her father told her to read about the French impressionists, she ended up learning about a black cowboy named Deadwood Dick.

Rhea puts down her encyclopedia when she hears the gravel in the driveway crackle. It's 3:30. She bounces off the bed and slides to the window. Yes, that crackle belongs to Joon Faldstool, who passed his driver's test on the first try, and today is driving to work completely by himself. She watches Joon park the rusted, pea-green AMC Gremlin his father helped him buy. She watches him get out and stretch. He's staring straight at her window. She sees his quick timid wave and wonders if he can see her, or whether he's just hoping she's there. She waves back.

The days are getting longer now that spring's beginning. That makes it harder for Joon to sneak to the chicken coop after he's finished with his manure shoveling. Some days he makes it, some days his father, or Rhea's father, or both fathers, are too close by for him to try. She knows that tonight he will try to sneak to the coop no matter what. He will want to show her his driver's license.

Rhea hurriedly reads about Galileo. Scribbles some notes to prove she's been working hard on her report. *Holy cow!* The pope threatened him with torture if he didn't change his mind. Before going down to supper she takes off her bathrobe and puts on a baggy sweatshirt and a pair of fat-man's overalls. A girl with feathers can only dream about jeans and tee shirts, about walking shorts and sleeveless blouses, about backless prom dresses or wedding dresses. A girl with feathers has to be satisfied with bathrobes and baggy sweatshirts and fat-man's overalls.

Strangely, Rhea's father doesn't mention her Galileo report during supper at all. He is eating his ravioli in silence, making eye contact with no one, sipping his ginger ale slowly, nibbling at his bread like a rabbit. Donna isn't saying anything either. Donna isn't even sneezing. Something is up.

Rhea takes a long drink of milk, then says, "Galileo invented the telescope," she says.

Her father awakens from his trance. "After supper—after the dishes—we're going to talk about something important."

Rhea swallows the rubbery pillow of pasta in her mouth after only a few chews. "I have to feed my chickens first," she says.

"Not tonight," her father says.

When the last fork and spoon are dried and put away, the dish towel hung over the back of a chair to dry, Rhea shuffles, heart beating fast, into the living room. Her father is in his chair, hands tucked in his pants. Donna is in her oak rocker, Kleenex box in her lap. The television is off. There are any number of things this important talk could be about. It could be about her schooling. It could be about Joon Faldstool sneaking to the coop. It could be about her feathers, some new medicine or operation to make her normal. It could be about Donna or her father having some fatal disease. Cancer, like her mother had.

Rhea sits on the end of the sofa. She carefully folds her legs under her bottom, so her feathers don't bend. She hears her father say this:

"Well, pumpkin seed, we have some big decisions to make. About the farm. About how to keep it. You know why I specialized in chickens. We've fought enough about it, haven't we? Even though you and I disagree on this, I think you understand that modern farming is just like any other business. That you have to specialize. The days of a few cows and some pigs and a little of

144

this and a little of that are long gone. And I decided to specialize in chickens and eggs. And I hope you can understand that. And respect that. Because I respect your opinions. You know I do. I love you. Donna loves you. Everybody loves you. You're special to us. We're not at all ashamed of you.

"The thing is—we're very lucky to have had this farm all these years. Every generation has had to sacrifice. Life is about sacrifice. And family. I wanted to be an art teacher. I would have been a good one. Then dad died and mom remarried and my responsibilities changed. Understand what I'm saying, pumpkin seed?

"So I couldn't let my dad down. Or my granddad Alfred. Or old Henry or any of them. They didn't go through all the crap they did—all the work and sacrifice—just so I could be an art teacher. Somebody had to run the farm. And that somebody had to be me. And I had to find a way to make the farm work. Pay the taxes and put food on the table. I couldn't worry about teaching other people to think creatively. I had to think creatively myself. Eggs sounded like a good idea.

"And eggs *is* a good idea. But right now, things are really crazy in the economy. The fat's being squeezed out. Some egg producers aren't going to survive. They're going to lose their farms and they're going to—God knows what they're going to do—but I know what we're going to do. We're going to make it.

"So it's time to think creatively again. Time for each member of this family to think about what we can do. What special gifts do we have? How can we use those gifts?

"And you, pumpkin seed, you have a very special gift. For some reason you've got feathers. Nobody knows why you've got them or how you got them. But you've got them."

Rhea watches the tears run down the sides of her father's nose and curl around his nostrils and tumble over his quivering lips. She watches his quivering fingers splayed over his quivering knees.

"The thing is," her father says, "you may be the only hope this family has. Every month we have payments to make to the bank. We have taxes and utilities, feed bills and salaries. And we're being sued over the manure—I haven't told you about that yet—but it's going to get messy.

"But this is going to be your decision, pumpkin seed. We're not going to force you into anything. I didn't have to come back to the farm. Dan wanted to stay in the Navy. That was okay. Your Gammy Betz moved to Columbus. That was okay, too. So you have to think about what the farm means to you."

It's three days before Rhea feels like reading to her chickens again. At supper her father and Donna talk about the weather and how the meatballs taste. They do not ask Rhea what her decision is going to be. It's as if they never had that important talk in the living room.

After the dishes are washed, Rhea heads for the chicken coop with her book and flashlight. The chickens huddle around her. Blinking and clucking, occasionally going after a louse wiggling beneath their feathers, they listen as she tells them about the birds' journey to find the Simorgh, their king.

> "'Before we reach our goal,' the Hoopoe said,
> 'The journey's seven valleys lie ahead;
> How far this is the world has never learned,
> For no one who has gone there has returned.'"

Rhea is just beginning to tell her chickens the names of the seven valleys when Joon Faldstool slips inside the coop. She smiles at him, with her eyes. She feels the skin beneath the feathers on her face warm. "The first valley they enter is the Valley of the Quest," she tells her chickens.

> "When you begin in the Valley of the Quest
> Misfortunes will deprive you of all rest
> Each moment some new trouble terrifies,
> And parrots there are panic-stricken flies."

Rhea reads until she sees that both Joon and her chickens are restless. She tucks the book in her coat pocket. "Walk?" she asks him.

It's still not completely dark outside. But it is cloudy enough for them to sneak down the fields toward the creek and the woods without worrying about being spotted. "I passed my driver's test," Joon says with as much nonchalance as he can muster.

"I saw you drive in. You didn't hit anything."

Joon's ears redden. "Of course I didn't hit anything."

Rhea giggles and, without thinking, slips her arms around his arm.

Three Fish Creek is high. The bank is slippery. They lean against the hollow trunk of a huge old maple that has fallen. "I kept looking for you in the coop," Joon says. "I figured either you got sick of reading to your chickens, or you got sick of me."

Rhea has a smart-alecky answer ready—*Don't be silly, I never get sick of reading to my chickens*—but she's too sad for a smart-alecky answer. She takes off her knit cap, exposing her entire head of feathers. "I've been busy thinking."

Joon has never seen her entire head before. The feathers on the top are as delicate as the feathers on her face. Her ears, like her nose, are bare and pinky-white, and small. "Thinking about what?"

She tells him about the farm's problems, about the bills, and the debts, and the lawsuit by the Maple Creek Homeowners' Association. "What if your father said you were the only person who could save your family from going bankrupt?" she asks.

"I'd know we were in huge trouble."

Rhea slaps him hard on the arm to let him know she's being serious. "What if the only way to save your family was to spend the summer going from one county fair to another, charging people to look at your big ears—would you do that?"

"Who would pay money to look at my ears?"

"What if instead of having big ears you were covered with feathers? Would—"

"Your father's making you do that?"

"He's not making me. He just says it's the best way for us to make a lot of money quick. To save the farm."

"You're not some two-headed calf, Rhea."

"That's the point. People pay to see two-headed calves. Think how many would pay to see a girl with feathers."

"I wouldn't," Joon assures her.

"Yes you would," Rhea says. "I would, too."

"No way."

"It would only be for the summer," says Rhea. "Dad says we could make a lot of money. And as soon as egg prices go up I can stop."

Joon is standing in front of her now, stroking her feathery cheeks with one hand, dabbing the tears from his eyes with the palm of the other. "I can't believe you're seriously considering this!"

"I've already decided to do it."

"You'd let people gawk at you like that?"

"If I wasn't hiding in the house all day, people would be gawking at me already."

"But you wouldn't be charging them. That just seems—"

"If I'm going to live any kind of normal life, I have to get used to people gawking."

Joon is marching back and forth in front of Rhea now, his boots digging an angry ditch in the thawing ground. "I wouldn't do it. No way."

"You had the courage to take your driver's test."

"Being a freak in a sideshow is a little different than taking your driver's test."

"Courage is courage."

"Humiliation is humiliation."

"Shoveling chicken poop isn't humiliating?"

"Not if nobody's watching."

As Joon marches by in his ever-deepening ditch, Rhea grabs his arm and pulls him toward her. "It's all a matter of attitude. If I don't consider myself a freak, other people won't either. If I don't pity myself, others won't."

Joon takes her hands and holds them against his chest. "That all sounds great. But that's not the way people really are. You've been hidden away. You can sit up in your room and daydream about how good and fair people are. Take it from a freak who's been out there. People are turds."

It's completely dark now. They walk back to the chicken coop. They don't say much more to each other.

Rhea goes to bed early, a quarter to ten. Her body wants to sleep. Her mind does not. And so she wraps her blanket around her and twists into a ball, like a chick awaiting birth inside a warm egg. Her mind flickers like a broken lamp:

She thinks about the book Dr. Pirooz Aram gave her . . . . those poor birds following that Hoopoe through those seven dangerous valleys . . . Valley of the Quest . . . Valley of Love . . . Valley of Insight into Misery . . . Valley of Detachment and Serenity . . . Valley of Unity . . . Valley of Awe . . . Valley of Poverty and Nothingness . . .

She thinks about the Leghorns . . . ripped from their cages in the black of night . . . Miss Lucky Pants getting away . . .

She thinks about the giants from Seville . . . Captain Martin VanBuren Bates . . . Anna Swan . . . rubbing elbows with presidents and kings . . . falling through the floor while dancing . . . Dr. Pirooz calling her a swan . . .

She thinks about her father . . . wanting to teach art . . . his own father dropping dead . . . going deep in debt building those layer houses . . . asking her to display herself like a fancy hen . . . to save the family farm . . . like he tried to save it . . . .

Twenty-two

CALVIN CASSOWARY DOESN'T want to get out of bed. It's been a week since Rhea agreed to his plan for saving the family farm. At first her consent relieved him. Made him proud. Confident things were going to work out fine. Now he's not so sure. Relief is turning into anxiety. Pride into shame. Confidence into uncertainty.

"Get up already," Donna says, poking his chest with her elbow. "It's a good idea."

Calvin digs out a handful of Kleenex from the box under the bed table and hands them to his wife. He gets out of bed and puts on the old, knee-ripped Wrangler jeans he laid out the night before. Puts on the old paint-speckled shirt that had been his father's. Squeaks downstairs to make coffee.

When the coffee's made he pours himself half a cup and puts the rest in a Thermos. He slides his sketch pad under his arm, fishes out three thick-leaded carpenter's pencils from the junk drawer by the refrigerator, goes out on the porch, where he stands slowly sipping his coffee, hoping that the chilly morning air will scour his doubt.

He goes to the old cow barn. Slides the doors open, as far as they will go, to let as much sunlight in as possible. The barn has been empty for nearly fifteen years, but the smell of cow lingers. The sight of his father and grandfather pitching bales of hay into the high lofts lingers, too.

This morning's work will be easy.

He rips the six new canvases from their plastic bags, then, after driving spikes into the walls, twelve feet off the floor, exactly twelve feet apart, hangs them like medieval tapestries.

The canvases are gray. They need to be white. He pries open the five-gallon tub of paint he bought at Bittinger's Hardware in Wooster, the same day he bought the canvases, and with a brush as wide as his hand, starts painting. When one side of the six canvases are painted he turns them over and paints the backs. He goes in for lunch.

"Finished yet?" asks Rhea.

"Just getting started, pumpkin seed," he answers. Donna has made grilled cheese sandwiches. He remembers that when Jeanie made grilled cheese sandwiches, she made them with thick slices of real American cheese. Donna uses thin, pale slices of fake cheese, individually wrapped in plastic.

In the afternoon Calvin starts sketching.

That day he hiked up Three Fish Creek to the marsh, he'd drawn Rhea's county fair exhibit from every angle, sketching the words and pictures that would be on every panel of canvas. The six canvases will form an outer wall around a small stage in the middle. This is where Rhea will sit, queen-like, in a golden chair, surrounded with arrangements of silk roses and daisies. She'll be protected from the sun and rain by a canopy, painted white with golden stripes. Silver bunting will drip from the canopy, swirl down the corner posts like frozen lightning.

Rhea will look beautiful sitting there. Music will be tinkling in the background. Exotic Middle Eastern music maybe. Maybe the haunting music made by wooden Incan flutes. Maybe an Appalachian dulcimer gently plinking Pachabel's Canon in D Major. Donna had Pachabel played at their wedding. Everybody loves Pachabel. Even crusty old farmers at county fairs love Pachabel.

Calvin begins to sketch the first canvas. This one will be all lettering. Old-fashioned circusy letters. They will say:

RHEA THE FEATHER GIRL

AMERICA'S TEEN-AGED DOVE

COVERED HEAD TO TOE WITH REAL FEATHERS

Calvin hasn't used his fingers for anything but writing checks for fifteen years. They still have their natural talent, but they are stiff and uncertain and won't move his pencil an inch until so ordered by his equally stiff, equally uncertain brain. "Damn!' Calvin hisses again and again as his lines on the canvas fall short of the perfect lines in his head.

It is midafternoon before the letters are drawn exactly as he wants them. He wants to fill them with paint right away. But he knows Jimmy Faldstool needs help in the layer houses. Rhea's schoolwork needs grading, too.

In the morning Calvin can't wait to get out of bed. To make his Thermos of coffee. Fill in the letters on that first canvas. He does not paint the letters flat, like the letters on old Alfred's FRESH EGGS sign. He gives them depth and roundness. They appear to float on the white canvas. He stands back and, in awe of his own work, says, "Damn!"

He starts the next canvas. It will read:

SHE'S AMAZING!

SHE'S REAL!

SHE'S BEAUTIFUL!

Donna Cassowary always has too much work to do. Cook. Clean. Shop. Manage the books. Manage her MCS, her multiple chemical sensitivities. Now she has to sew Rhea's Feather Girl costume. Calvin wants it finished by the first of next week, so he can paint Rhea's portrait on his canvases.

"Maybe I can get Marilyn to help," she suggests to Calvin. "She does all the dance costumes for the Tuttwyler Tappers."

"I don't want local people knowing about this," Calvin says. "We let Marilyn Dickcissel in on this and we might as well take out an ad in the *Gazette*."

So Donna has to go it alone.

She drives to Freda's Fabric House in New Waterbury. She wishes she could buy polyester. It is so easy to work with. There are so many beautiful textures and prints. But synthetic fabrics are just soaked with formaldehyde. Formaldehyde gives her brain fog. Makes her cuticles itch like poison ivy. Rhea's costume will have to be made of natural fabric.

She sneezes the entire hour she's in Freda's. MCS is a bitch. It turns you into a convulsing zombie, alive but robbed of a full life. "You can't imagine what it's like," she told Calvin on their second date, when they were sitting on a bench atop the dam at Hinckley Lake, watching some old man with a boil on his neck fish for bluegill. "There are chemicals in everything today. Everything we eat. Everything we wear. Take something simple, like going to a restaurant. First, the seat cushions make you itch. Then the ink on the menu makes you sneeze. The waitress's perfume welds your eyes together and the MSG on the lettuce makes you puke. It's like that constantly."

"Can't you get shots or something?" Calvin asked.

She told him that while shots and pills were helpful—and incredibly expensive—there were only three sure-fire ways an MCS sufferer could escape his or her misery. "And only one of them is permanent," she said.

"Death, you mean?"

"Bingo."

"And the two temporary ones?"

Donna hesitated. It was, after all, their second date. "Sleep and sex."

Calvin was intrigued immediately. "Sex?"

"When you get—aroused—your endorphins override everything else that's going on in your body—toothaches, gas, allergies, sore toe, everything, so you can—you know."

Donna watched Calvin's face fill with blood, knowing it wasn't from embarrassment.

"So," he said, "if there's ever anything I can do to help you with this MCS of yours . . . ."

They made love for the first time that night, on an itchy blanket made of synthetic fibers. And now after all these years of marriage they still make love twice a week and her endorphins are

153

still kicking in just fine. But her eggs just won't let his sperm knock down the door.

She's been married to Calvin for nine years and she's only been out to the layer houses two or three times. She's never been out to the old barn at all, all that dust and mold and decaying hay. She's never once scratched the cats under their chins, or dug her fingers into Biscuit's fluffy back. She just stays in the house, doing housework and doing the books. She walks around the lawn a little. Walks in the woods once or twice in the winter when the pollen balls are frozen. She's as much a prisoner as Rhea is. As much a freak. She should have an exhibit on the midway, too:

THE AMAZING DONNA—QUEEN OF KLEENEX

SHE WALKS! SHE TALKS! SHE SNEEZES AND SNEEZES!

SHE CAN'T GET PREGNANT NO MATTER HOW MUCH SHE SCREWS!

Donna buys some cotton, some silk, several yards of flimsy linen gauze, a bag of gold sequins, beads of many colors.

That night she spreads out what she's bought on Rhea's bed. "Any ideas about your costume?"

Rhea shrugs. "I guess it's got to show a lot of my feathers, huh?"

Donna dabs her nose. "Well, yes. But we're not going to make you look like some hoochie koochie dancer."

"Hoochie koochie?" Rhea asks.

"Like a stripper."

Rhea laughs at this. "I could be totally naked. That would make us some money."

"I was thinking maybe something Egyptian," says Donna.

"How about a Grecian goddess?" asks Rhea. She playfully raises her arms as a Grecian goddess might.

"Oooh, that's an idea. How about a fairy tale princess?"

"Or just a fairy," says Rhea. "Sort of a Tinker Bell look, you know?"

"Maybe something Indian," says Donna.

"India Indian or Pocahontas Indian?"

"Pocahontas Indian. Buckskin skirt with fringe. Big headdress maybe."

Rhea's head is shaking no. "I'm already a walking headdress."

Says Donna, "Well, then how about we go with the Egyptian thing?"

When Rhea's costume is finally finished, Calvin sketches her in it. It takes three hours for him to get the sketches he needs. Then he spends the night—from midnight until well after dawn—transferring his best sketch to the remaining canvas in the barn. Then he paints it, his hands shaking the entire time.

He is amazed by the finished portrait. It is beautiful.

Twenty-three

AT DAWN THEY leave for the Burgoo County Fair. It is the first fair of the summer, in Ohio's flat western corner, where the cornfields blend into Indiana without anyone noticing.

Rhea Cassowary is in the pickup with her father. The lunch Donna made them is in a grocery bag on the seat between them. Peanut butter and jelly by the smell. Joon Faldstool is behind them in his Gremlin. Joon has been recruited to sell eggnog-flavored snow cones.

Both Joon and the snow cones were late additions to the county fair idea, both coming from Joon's father about three weeks ago.

"You know what," Jimmy Faldstool said one morning when he and Calvin were having their morning coffee in the locker room. "I was looking through the classifieds in the Cleveland paper the other morning and saw this little snow cone wagon for sale. Completely equipped for $3,200. I says to Joon and the wife, 'Good gravy, everybody likes a snow cone when they go to the fair—know that I do—and wouldn't that be a way to make some extra money. For everybody concerned.'

"'I could buy that snow cone wagon,' I says, 'and set it up there by Rhea's exhibit, and sell snow cones to the people coming out, or just walking by. And I could split my profits fifty-fifty with Cal.'"

Calvin said, "Think you could make it pay? Every county fair I've been to there's a snow cone stand every ten feet."

Jimmy was ready for his boss' skepticism. "You sell cherry and grape and root beer snow cones like everybody else, you might not make much. But if you were selling egg nog snow cones—nobody else would be selling eggnog snow cones. And it would fit right in with Rhea being covered with feathers. And look at all the eggs we got. Good gravy, Cal. We paint up that little

156

wagon fancy like you did those canvases and put it right there by the entrance and we'll make money hand over fist."

Calvin said, "Our eggs belong to Bob Gallinipper."

Jimmy said, "True enough. But our family responsibilities belong to us."

And so Calvin gave Jimmy the green light. It was a cute little wagon with counters and windows on three sides. Jimmy painted it bright yellow with milky white trim. On the sign board on top Calvin lettered:

ICE NOGGIES!

EGGNOG-FLAVORED SNOW CONES

MADE WITH FRESH FARM EGGS

Above all three windows he painted portraits of Rhea, herself enjoying an Ice Noggie.

And that's why Joon is following in his Gremlin, pulling the snow cone wagon. Rhea can see in the pickup's side mirrors that he's sucking on a can of pop.

The pickup itself is pulling a tiny house trailer. It's an old one, a 17-foot sky blue Holly built in the late fifties. It has two beds and a kitchen, but no bathroom. So they'll have to use the public toilets. The bed of the pickup carries the stage and the canvases, a plywood ticket booth, two cases of Rhea the Feathergirl tee shirts, and the high-back Victorian chair that old Henry's second wife, Camellia, bought brand new from the Sears & Roebuck catalog. Calvin has painted the chair gold to look like a throne.

When they get to Tuttwyler, Rhea is surprised when her father turns left and drives towards the town square. "I thought Burgoo County was the other way," she says.

"It is," he answers. He is smiling easily.

This time of the morning there is no one on the sidewalks and only a few cars on the street. Her father circles the square and turns onto South Mill Street. Rhea now knows where they are going. They are going to the cemetery. "Wait here," her father tells Joon after they park.

The grass is still wet. By the time Rhea and her father reach the row of Cassowary graves their feet are soaked. The strawberry plants circling Jeanie's grave are tall and thick and shiny with dew. The berries are red and plump.

It has been three years since Rhea and Calvin were there together, though he has come every year to tell Jeanie about the difficulties between him and their daughter. So Jeanie is up to speed about the feathers and that unfortunate plucking episode.

"As you know," Calvin tells Jeanie, "I've been a real schmuck. But everything's okay now—copacetic as Norman would say. Anyway, things are okay, and Rhea and I are on our way to the Burgoo County Fair, to make the money we need to save the farm. You'd be proud of her."

The three of them can't possibly finish all the berries, so after eating all they can, Rhea leaves a few on the top of all the Cassowary gravestones.

Calvin and Rhea are both crying as they walk back to the truck.

"You miss her, don't you daddy?"

"Sure I do."

"We're going to start coming again every year, aren't we?"

"You bet. I'm sorry I—"

"It's okay, daddy."

Calvin puts his arm around her. "I've never been able to figure that Bob Gallinipper out. He's such a money-grubbing asshole. Yet he gave us that strawberry plant when your mother died. I told you how it was from his own grandfather's grave?"

"Some people are hard to figure," Rhea says, trying to figure her father out.

It's midafternoon when they finally arrive at the Burgoo County fairgrounds. "Soon as we park the trailer, Joon and I will go over to the midway," Rhea's father says. "I think you should stay in the trailer—until we get the lay of the land."

Rhea knows what he's saying. "Until we see if people are going to laugh?"

"Nobody's going to laugh, pumpkin seed. Anybody does, I'll punch them in the nose."

"Get their dollar first," says Rhea. They look at each other and giggle. They feel close. Father and daughter on a great adventure. Saving the farm together.

Her father parks the house trailer in a flat field west of the fairgrounds. There are dozens of trailers and buses and RVs parked here, homes for the vagabond entrepreneurs who'll be selling every imaginable enticement during the week ahead. "Joon and I'll be back soon as we get things set up," her father says. "Five or six probably. I'll make hamburgers."

For hours Rhea sits at the small table in the front of the trailer, peeking through the venetian blinds that cover the window, watching people come and go. There are healthy girls with freckles and ponytails wearing 4-H tee shirts, pulling cross-eyed goats or carrying cages of rabbits. There are mysterious people with dark Gypsy skin, arms wrapped wide around cardboard boxes of stuffed animals. There are bowlegged farmers in bib overalls, arm-in-arm with pudgy women wearing shapeless dresses. There are skinny men balancing huge cowboy hats on their heads, toting toolboxes and long extension cords. When she turns and looks out the side window, she can see the midway rides, sticking above a row of closely planted evergreens. From the little window in the rear, she can see the animal barns, the long roof of the grandstand, the light poles surrounding the racetrack.

She tries to nap but can't. She tries to read from *The Conference of the Birds*. But the poems don't sound the same without Mr. Shakyshiver and the hens there to listen. Without Joon there to listen. Joon and her father do not return until eight.

"Sorry. Took a lot longer than I expected," her father says. His face and hands are dirty. His hair is soaked with sweat.

Joon sits across from Rhea. He doesn't say a word. He is just smiling. Just happy to be there, apparently. He'll eat with them, and work all day at the exhibit, but he'll have to sleep in the back of his Gremlin. That's already been decided.

"Well, let's get those hamburgers fried," her father says. "One or two, Joon?"

"Two if that's okay."

"Two it is. Rhea, find the Fritos, and the paper plates. We'll eat better tomorrow. Open a can of fruit cocktail or something. You like fruit cocktail, don't you Joon?"

"Sure."

"You locked the snow cone wagon, didn't you? We don't want anybody walking off with our eggs."

"It's locked."

"These midway people are pretty spooky. You should see them, Rhea."

"I saw a lot of them from the window."

"You kept the door locked, didn't you?"

Rhea, tearing open the paper plate bag with her teeth, nods.

Her father does a good job frying the hamburgers. The Fritos are a little stale. They watch the sky turn purple-black. Watch the midway lights come on. Listen to the hyena-like laughter seeping through the thin walls of the trailer next to theirs. At ten Joon gets the hint and goes off to sleep in the Gremlin.

"Just remember that I'm proud of you," her father says.

"I will," says Rhea. She puts on the cloak Donna sewed for her, pulls the floppy hood over her head. Donna said the hood was called a cowl. Her father helps her from the trailer. Locks the door. Makes sure it's really locked. Makes sure that the doors on the pickup are locked and really locked. He takes a fat breath of the French fry grease air. "Let's go make some money!" he says.

They enter the midway. The rides are just beginning to crank up. Calliope music is *oop-poo-pooping*. They pass one exhibit where the world's smallest horse can be seen for a dollar. A color-fully painted semitrailer promises the world's largest collection of

160

exotic snakes, featuring Big Liz, a thirty-foot anaconda from the jungles of Brazil. They pass a tiny dark-skinned old woman sitting in a lawn chair, beneath an enormous green-striped umbrella, selling useless carnival junk: tee shirts with cheeky sayings, baseball caps with fake women's breasts on the brim, fuzzy brown monkeys and shiny pink pigs dangling on sticks, Mylar balloons in the shape of Bugs Bunny and Tweetie Bird, Dayglo sunglasses and cheap jewelry.

They reach their exhibit.

"Daddy, your paintings look great," Rhea says. She saw the canvases when they were hanging in the barn a hundred times. But now, here in the sunlight, surrounded by the colors and sounds and smells of the county fair, they look bigger and brighter. She takes a shy look over her shoulder to see if her father's artwork is luring any of the fairgoers. None yet. But a few heads are turning.

They slip under the chain that hangs across the entrance like a smile. Rhea's father turns on the music. *Blimmm. . . Blimmm . . . . Blimmm . . . Blimmm . . . .* the first mournful notes of Pachabel's Canon in D Major. "Donna decided we should try the Pachabel first," her father says, turning up the volume. "We'll go to something peppier if enough people don't come in."

Come in. If enough people don't come in. The reality of what she's agreed to do slides up and down her spine like a pizza-cutter. She feels the feathers on her neck sticking out. In just a few minutes her father is going to remove that chain and people are going to hand him dollar bills. They're going to shuffle around the corner of the canvases and start their gawking and their stupid questions. And this will go on all day, until eleven tonight. And then tomorrow. And then all summer.

"Well, pumpkin seed," her father says, "time to get the show on the road." The wobble in his voice tells her he's feeling the reality of this thing, too.

Rhea throws back her cowl and unties the shoe-knot on her cape.

Joon Faldstool watches the cowl fall away. He focuses on the delicate golden circlet that rests on the back of Rhea's head like a halo. He has seen her bare head before, the tiny white feathers cascading in neat rows toward her neck and shoulders. But he has not seen much else of her. And if the painting on the canvas is correct, then he's about to see quite a bit.

Rhea finishes untying the knot at her throat. She takes a huge breath and lets it motor-boat from her pursed lips. She peels the cape from her shoulders and then swings it around and jumbles it into a ball and hands it to her father.

Though he's standing a good six feet away, Joon's nostrils have captured Rhea's seeping breath. He fills his lungs with it and then lets it escape through his own suddenly rubbery lips. The costume is beautiful. She is beautiful.

Without the baggy sweatshirts and overalls she wears at home, she looks much smaller, thinner, more petite. *Petite.* That's the word. The costume is sort of ancient Egyptian. Sort of Olympic figure-skater. It is made of yellowy gold silk. The neckline is high. A *V* of blue, green, red and silver sequins extends nearly to her waist. Low on her hips is a wide belt of white and gold plastic pearls, clasped by an oval blue stone the size of an Easter egg. The pleated skirt is neither too full nor too snug. It ends just above her knees.

What Joon looks at most are her feathers. The costume is sleeveless. So he can see her plump upper arms. He can follow the feathers down to her narrow elbows, and down her slender forearms to her wrists, where they fray like frilly cuffs. His eyes drop quickly to her legs. The feathers ruffle over her knees, then descend smoothly over her shins and calves to her ankles where, without the slightest ruffle, they disappear into satin ballet slippers.

"Wow," he says without thinking, "you look so cherry."

Rhea, embarrassed, explains to her father that cherry means cool.

"I know what cherry means," Calvin Cassowary says.

Yes, Calvin Cassowary knows what cherry means. Knows that Joon didn't mean cool. Knows that feathers or no feathers, Rhea is a fourteen-year-old girl and Joon, big ears or no big ears, is a sixteen-year-old boy. He remembers the night on Blanket Hill, at Kent State, when he popped Jeanie's cherry, and his cherry, too. And now he's got to deal with a sex-crazed boy selling Ice Noggies just three feet from his half-dressed daughter, twelve hours a day, all summer long. Oh, he knows what cherry means.

Rhea has been sitting in the high-backed Victorian chair for twenty minutes now. The Pachabel has numbed her nearly to sleep. She hears her father nervously cajoling people to buy a ticket. "Covered head to toe with real feathers!" he's barking. "A beautiful quirk of human evolution! A metaphysical marvel!" She also hears Joon's timid plea: "Ice Noggies! Gitch-yer eggnog-flavored snow cones right here!"

Then the head of a man peeks around the canvases. The head has a bright blue Ted's Plumbing & Heating cap pulled tightly over a fringe of curly gray hair. The head smiles sheepishly. It doesn't advance. Nor does it retreat. It just floats there. Rhea now hears the voice of a woman. "Let's just leave, Ronnie. I really don't want—"

The floating head says, "Come on, Louise. We already paid our dollars."

"You're a sucker for every trick that comes along," says Louise.

"She looks real enough. Come on!"

And so Ronnie and Louise slide around the canvases and grin their way towards the stage. "Hi, young lady," Ronnie says. Louise says nothing.

"Hi!" Rhea says. She stands up.

"So you're really covered with feathers?" asks Ronnie. "Like other people are covered with skin?"

"I've got skin, too. Under the feathers."

"The man outside said you started growing them when you was five."

"Just a few at first."

Louise gets up the nerve to ask a question: "Did you want to grow them, or did they just grow?"

"They just grew."

"Well, you're a real pretty girl," Louise says.

Ronnie and Louise gawk for another minute without saying a word, then smile and say good-bye. "Do you think they're really real?" Rhea hears Louise asks from the other side of the canvases.

Hears Ronnie answer, "They're real feathers, but whether they're really hers, who knows."

Hears Louise say, "Then why'd we waste two dollars?"

All in all, Rhea decides, it went pretty well.

Next inside the canvases is a tall, stringy man with black shoulder-length hair and a blue-suede cowboy hat decorated with turkey feathers. His black tee shirt reads: No, I DIDN'T FART—I SMELL LIKE THIS ALL THE TIME! He needs a shave and a tube of Clearasil. His girlfriend needs a bra. Her stomach fat is puffed over her Indian-bead belt like the top crust of a dinner roll.

The first thing the stringy man says is, "Bummer! I thought she'd be naked!"

The girlfriend slaps his butt. "Be nice."

The stringy man presses himself against the stage. "Can you lay eggs?"

Rhea forces a laugh. "No, I don't lay eggs."

"Been plucked yet?" he asks.

It's Rhea's turn to say, "Be nice."

"Can I have a feather?" he asks, reaching.

The girlfriend takes him by the back of his belt and drags him toward the exit. "Come on, let's go see the rabbits."

As they retreat, the stringy man clucks, "Pluck-pluck-pluck!" and thrusts his bony hips toward Rhea. "Pluck-pluck-pluck!"

Rhea can feel the tears trickling through the feathers on her cheeks. This one did not go so well.

The day goes on. They take a break for lunch. Hot dogs, and

fries, watery Cokes. The afternoon lasts forever. They go to the trailer for Cassowary-style tomato soup and that promised can of fruit cocktail. Rhea tries to nap, but cannot. They hurry back to the exhibit. The midway is crowded with people, a goodly portion of them happy to plunk down their dollars to see Rhea the Feather Girl, or to try an Ice Noggie.

Later in the trailer Rhea's father lights the propane stove to make popcorn. On one side of the tiny table Joon counts his snow cone dollars. On the other Rhea counts the dollars she made. When the popping and counting are finished they finally relax, sharing their respective horror stories. They'd been only a few yards from each other all day, but they'd all been so busy. They marvel over how much money they took in.

"Better than I expected for our first day," her father says, his yawns deforming his words into the howl of a hound dog. "Once I get my spiel down, we'll do better yet."

After Joon goes off to sleep in his Gremlin, Rhea and her father change into their pajamas and get into their beds. They leave on the light above the little sink. Both bags of dollars, the snow cone dollars and the Feather Girl dollars, go under Calvin's pillow. So does a loaded .22. First thing in the morning he'll take it to the most honest-looking bank in Burgoo City.

While they were eating popcorn at the table, there had been a lot of laughter as Rhea described the people coming in to gawk. But some of it hadn't been so funny, and Calvin, resting his head on his folded elbows, sends his fatherly voice across the dark trailer, from his bed in the back, to her bed in the front. "Wasn't too tough, was it, pumpkin seed?"

Twenty-four

"Isn't she just darling," says the jowly woman with fox-red hair to her companions. The woman shouldn't be wearing shorts, but she is.

"Thank you," answers Rhea the Feather Girl. It is only a few minutes after ten and these three middle-aged women are the first of the new day to plunk down their dollars. She stands up and takes two steps to the edge of the stage, refreshed and ready for a long day of being gawked at, being asked the same questions over and over.

"Are those feathers really real?" asks the woman with the huge rat's nest of Crayola-yellow hair. She shouldn't be wearing a sleeveless blouse, but she is.

"They're mine," answers Rhea.

The woman with the fox-red hair squints suspiciously. "This hair's mine too, honey, but only 'cause I paid for it."

Her friends laugh. So does Rhea.

"I didn't pay for these," Rhea says.

"Don't they itch?" the third woman wonders. She is wearing both shorts and a sleeveless blouse. Her legs and arms are no bigger around than No. 2 pencils.

"Not really," answers Rhea.

"Or stink?" asks the woman with the fox-red hair.

Rhea struggles to maintain her smile. "Of course not."

Suddenly the Crayola-yellow woman is on the stage, clutching her by the wrist, sniffing along her arm.

"Please," says Rhea, trying to brush away the women's grip.

Now the pencil-limbed woman is on the stage, wiggling her index finger up under the feathers on Rhea's knee. "Leotard. Like I thought."

Rhea tries to move back but the big Victorian chair is blocking her retreat. "Please. That's my real skin."

Suddenly bee-sting pain shoots up Rhea's leg. The pencil-limbed woman is pulling one of her feathers. "Whaddya know about that," she says, twirling the plucked feather in front of her face, "they are real."

"Oh, I want one, too," says the fox-red woman. Her fingers wriggle toward Rhea's neck. The Crayola-yellow woman's fingers are wriggling toward her forehead. Rhea yells "Daddy!" She flings her chair at the women and jumps off the back of the stage.

Her father hurries the indignant women out. When he demands the feather back, the fox-red woman demands her dollar back. The exchange is made. "I just wanted a souvenir," the woman says.

"Then buy a tee shirt," he says.

And so the second day begins. By the time the midway lights go out for the night, several others have tried to pluck a feather. Each time Rhea yelled for her father, and in every instance except that first one, he talked them into buying tee shirts instead.

Early in the morning her father drives into town, finds the hardware store, and buys a roll of chicken wire. When Rhea goes to the midway, she finds a single, two-foot band of the fencing tacked across the front of the stage. She had cried all the way to the midway. Seeing the chicken-wire makes her cry again.

Late in the afternoon it starts to rain and the midway clears. Joon makes use of the lull to mix a fresh batch of nog. Rhea's father trots to the Kiwanis Club tent to buy them some supper. Rhea puts on her cape and pulls the cowl over her head, anxious to explore the exotic entertainments of the midway for herself. "There's that Feather Girl," she hears a girl working in a corn-dog stand whisper to a girl selling saltwater taffy.

Rhea is drawn to the enormous umbrella where the tiny, old dark-skinned woman sells useless carnival junk. Maybe she'll get Joon something. Something goofy.

"Halloo sweetie girl," the woman says from the shadow of her umbrella.

"Hello," answers Rhea. She looks at the rack of personalized key chains, knowing there won't be one that says JOON, or even JUNIOR.

"I fear this rain'll last all night," the umbrella woman says.

"Think so?"

"Know so. I been midwayin' all my life. This rain ain't going away. You watch, sweetie, they'll close the fair early tonight."

Rhea starts fishing through the sunglasses.

The umbrella woman cackles. "With that big floppy hood what you need sunglasses for?"

"I was thinking of getting them for my—for the guy in the Ice Noggie wagon."

"Oh, I had one of them yesterday. Pretty damn good."

Rhea is drawn to a pair of black wraparounds. "I'm Rhea."

"Sure. You're Rhea the Feather Girl. You're making some good money over there."

"Better than we expected." Rhea decides against the sunglasses and looks at the plastic rings.

"You're new at this game, are you?" the umbrella woman asks.

"It's our first fair."

The umbrella woman shakes her head sadly. "I've worked a billion of them."

Rhea sees her father coming with a stack of cardboard food trays. "I better go."

"Sure. If they do shut things down early—which they will— why don't you and the eggnog boy come by? We're just down the row from your trailer. Old blue camper on an even older red truck. Me and Robert Charles see you coming and going every day."

"Maybe we will," Rhea says.

The rain lets up just before six and the midway gets busy. Two boys, their faces just starting to be pimpled by puberty, come in with big cups of vinegar-soaked French fries. They do nothing but giggle. Then the tallest of the two lunges over the chicken wire and yanks a feather from the tender back of Rhea's hand. They run. Her father puts up another layer of chicken wire. Now the fence is nearly as tall as she is.

Just after seven it starts to rain again. And lightning. People run for their cars. The rides shut down, their operators fearing electrocutions and lawsuits. At nine, words spreads down the midway that the fair is shutting down for the night. The umbrella woman knew what she was talking about.

168

"I feel like I'm inside a bongo drum," Joon says, as the rain pounds the trailer's thin metal shell. He's counting the snow cone money. Rhea's father is counting the Feather Girl money. Neither are happy with the take.

Rhea pulls the curtain across the back of the trailer and changes into a sweat shirt and a pair of her overalls. She slides the curtain open, announcing, "Me and Joon are going to visit the lady who sells the carnival junk."

Asks Joon, "We are?"

Says her father, sipping from a can of ginger ale, "It's raining."

Rhea is ready for him. "Her camper's right next door almost."

Says her father, "I still don't want you going out at night."

"Right next door, daddy."

Her father tries honesty this time. "I don't think it's a good idea associating with these people."

Says Rhea, "Daddy, we're these people, too. I'm Rhea the Feather Girl and Joon sells Ice Noggies! You're one of those sleazy midway guys." She imitates him: "'Ladies and gentlemen! Boys and girls! Just inside, Rhea the Feather Girl! The Almighty's most amazing gift to mankind! Covered head to toe with real feathers! A beautiful quirk of human evolution! Put down a dollar! Put a memory in your heart!"

Her father is laughing ginger ale from his nostrils. "Okay. You can go for one hour."

Rhea and Joon dash through the rain to the blue camper on the back of the red pickup truck. Two knocks and the door opens. The dark and tiny umbrella woman puts a hand over her puckered lips and shakes her head, then realizing her visitors are getting soaked, steps back so they can climb in. "I told Robert Charles you'd more than likely be coming by."

The camper's low, noisy ceiling is just an inch above Rhea's head. Joon has to bend his head sideways to fit. The umbrella woman fits just fine. She is well under five feet, much shorter than Rhea expected. Most startling is the woman's head. It is oblong,

169

and not much larger than a turnip. Her nose curls like the beak of a parrot. Her forehead slopes sharply. Her hair, thin and white, is pulled back and tied into a donut.

The umbrella woman introduces her brother, who is sitting on the edge of the bunk bed that extends over the cab of the truck. His head and shoulders are slumped, his legs are dangling. He is even smaller than his sister. His head is smaller, too. He has the same parrot-beak nose and the same sloping forehead. He's as bald as an egg. "This is Robert Charles. He don't walk or think too well. But he's a sweetie. Ain't you Robert Charles?"

"I'm a sweetie," says Robert Charles.

"And I'm Eleanor," she then says, "though everybody including myself has called me Jelly Bean since I was knee-high to a wiener dog."

"I call her Mrs. Roosevelt," says Robert Charles, "'cause Eleanor was Mrs. Roosevelt's name."

Jelly Bean puts her hands on her wide hips and studies her guests. "Now I know you're Rhea the Feather Girl. But this boy I don't know except that he sells those fine snow cones."

"Joon," says Joon. "James Faldstool Jr."

Jelly Bean has them sit at the little table next to the little stove. She goes to the little refrigerator and takes out four cans of root beer. From one of the little cupboards she pulls a jumbo bag of potato chips and rips it open with her teeth. She squeezes in next to Rhea. "So, those feathers are for real, are they?"

Rhea explains how she started growing them when she was five. That nobody knows why. That her father has 810,000 Leghorns. That he once had a million. That they're doing the county fair circuit to save the farm.

"And you don't mind showing yourself off?" Jelly Bean wonders, nibbling on a chip like she's a squirrel.

Rhea takes a while to answer. "It's tougher than I thought."

"Too many assholes," Joon says.

Jelly Bean claps her hands joyfully. "Assholes with money."

Says Robert Charles, "You got that right, Mrs. Roosevelt!"

Jelly Bean leans back and folds her arms and studies Joon.

"Now tell me about those ears. In my day, we'd put you in the freak show as Junior the Elephant Boy. I bet you spin like a top when it's windy."

Rhea knows she's just kidding, trying to make them feel comfortable in front of two tiny people with heads the size of turnips. "What about you and Robert Charles? You've been working the fairs for a long time, I guess."

Jelly Bean's eyes widen white. "Seventy-five years. Fairs and carnivals now, but for a long time we worked the circuses and amusement parks. 'Til the freak shows got closed down by do-gooders. Now instead of selling our little heads, we sell trinkets. Long as I can drive and make change we're fine and dandy."

"Fine and dandy!" says Robert Charles.

Jelly Bean tells them their story: "Starting at five years of age we was put in the freak shows as Jelly Bean and Roo Roo, Lost Children of the Aztecs. As you can see, me and Robert Charles are what they call pinheads. Pinheads was very popular in the freak shows. They dressed us up like Indians, with feathers and zig-zaggy costumes. Even gave Robert Charles a rubber spear. Shaved our heads to make them look even pointier. Oh we worked all the big shows. Jelly Bean and Roo Roo, Lost Children of the Aztecs. But we ain't no Aztecs. We're just two tiny little Negroes from Cincinnati. Black you'd call us today, I guess."

Says Robert Charles, "Black is beautiful."

"What we really are," Jelly Bean continues, "is what they call *microcephalics*. We was born with tiny bodies and even smaller heads, to healthy normal-sized parents, Archibald and Lucille Peele. For some reason Robert Charles was born dumber than a post and me only half-smart. State of Ohio won't give me a driver's license, but I've been driving this and other rust-buckets around the country for forty years, with stolen plates, and I've never once been stopped for anything. The trick is to drive exactly five miles over the speed limit, no matter what the speed limit is. Cops figure anybody driving five over the limit must have a license in their pocket, or they wouldn't be driving five over. And no cop's going to stop you for just five.

"So, for years and years we worked as *human curiosities*. As *atavistic specimens*. Throwbacks to an extinct race. Making money hand over fist until they closed down the freak shows. I'm surprised the fair board let you rent space on the midway. I suppose they figured you was a fake, just like I did. Makin' money as a fake is fine today. Being real ain't allowed.

"Oh yes, we made all kinds of money as Aztec pinheads, when all the time we was Cincinnati Negroes. Now we're selling junk toys and dirty tee shirts—the shirts is clean but the sayings is dirty."

"But we still making some fine money," Robert Charles chimes in.

Jelly Bean chuckles. "Just enough for food and gas and midway space at the next fair. Summers in the North. Winters in the South. Driving and driving. Praying we don't blow a tire."

Says Robert Charles, "Pedal to the metal."

Jelly Bean squirrel-nibbles another chip. "So you don't mind being on display, sweetie girl?"

"A few try to pluck a feather. But it's—"

"Lots of folks used to rap us on the head with their knuckles," Jelly Bean interrupts, "to see if we'd ploonk like a coconut."

"But it's okay," Rhea assures her.

Jelly Bean's head is slowly bobbing. "My daddy said we'd stay in show business just long enough to buy a little filling station. But we pin-headed 'til the day he died, and then carted mama around pin-headin' until she died. Then we pin-headed on by ourselves. 'Til the do-gooders started doing their good."

"We're just doing the county fairs until September," Rhea says. "Then we're going back to the farm."

Jelly Bean goes on with her story, hiding whatever sympathy or suspicions she has. "Oh, there's been lots of famous pinheads over the years: Rosi, Wild Girl of the Yucatans. The Mexican Wild Boy. Tik Tak. Henry Johnson simply went by the name of What Is it? They called us Aztecs because we looked like the slopey-headed Indians on the walls of those old temples down in Mexico. To the last drop we pinheads was all Negroes."

Shouts Robert Charles, "Black is beautiful!"

"Me and Robert Charles never got as famous as some did," Jelly Bean says. "For one thing our heads was bigger than most, and we came along at the ass-end of things when the do-gooders started making people feel sorry for freaks. Midwayin' ain't no life, if you're going to do it all your life."

"We're just doing this until egg prices go up," Rhea promises.

"That's good," Jelly Bean says softly. She gets Joon another root beer. "We worked with all sorts of freaks. Midgets and dwarfs and men who could drive railroad spikes up their noses. Giants and fat ladies. Three-legged men. They'd have a painting outside of a man with three perfectly fine legs, running along or tap dancing. But inside the tent you'd see his third leg was just a little shriveled up thing with only a couple toes. That's why I'm so surprised by you! I saw that painting of you and . . ."

"My father painted it," Rhea says.

". . . and I figured either you was a complete fake or you just had some bad skin disease. But when you come by my stand, and I see all those thick pretty feathers, I didn't know what to think. Did I Robert Charles?"

"You was perplexed, Mrs. Roosevelt!"

"No," Jelly Bean says, "I've seen alligator boys and snake girls and womens with hair on their faces like grizzly bears, but I never heard of a girl with feathers. I wish I was smarter so I knew what made perfectly fine and normal parents give birth to such strange children."

173

Twenty-five

AT EXACTLY ELEVEN the last dandelion head of pyrotechnics explodes over the grandstand. The smoky sky slowly turns black. The Ferris wheel grinds to a stop. People head for their cars. The Burgoo County Fair is over for another year.

Joon and Rhea's father immediately get to work, folding the canvases, rolling up the canopy, rolling up the lengths of chicken wire that protected Rhea from the assholes, packing it all away in the pickup. Rhea takes charge of the snow cone wagon, scrubbing the counters, securing the egg cases for the drive ahead. By the time they hook onto the housetrailer and bump across the empty field toward the highway, it's three in the morning.

"Dinkum County here we come," her father sings.

"Do-dah, do-dah," Rhea sings back.

At six they pull off the highway and stop at a McDonald's for breakfast. Rhea stays in the cab while her father and Joon go inside to order the Egg McMuffins. She watches the normal people eating their breakfast at the tables. She sees her father use the pay telephone. Sees Joon wave at her while he sucks on the straw of a large Coca-Cola.

Joon joins Rhea and her father in the cab. They unwrap and eat, shoulder to shoulder, Rhea in the middle.

"Was that Donna you called?" Rhea asks her father.

He is chewing angrily. "Who else would I call at six in the morning?"

"Everything okay?"

He swallows angrily. "The homeowners' association won't accept our offer."

"And that means what?"

"It means we're going to trial. I don't know what those bastards expect from me."

Joon lets his straw slip free of his puckered lips. He offers a sip to Rhea.

She accepts. As she sucks on the straw she watches her father's disapproving frown. That frown has been there all week, every time she and Joon got within ten feet of each other.

They reach the Dinkum County fairgrounds right at eight. The old man at the gate sphincters his eyes and reads their midway contract. "Weatherman says we're going to have a fine week," he tells them. "Maybe some rain Thursday. Always rains one day."

Rhea spends the day inside their trailer. She tries to read. Tries to nap. Goes from one tiny window to another, trying to spot the blue camper and rusty red truck that belongs to Jelly Bean and Robert Charles. When she finally spots it swaying up the road, she runs to greet them, without her cape and cowl. "Sweetie girl, how you doin' today?" Jelly Bean squeaks at her, as she rolls down her window. "Where's the elephant boy?"

"Helping dad set up."

"Set it up, break it down," Robert Charles says.

The next morning Rhea does put on her cape and cowl, and walks with her father and Joon to the midway. The sky is the color of a nasty bruise and the canvases are flapping. "Looks like our one day of rain is about three days early," Joon says.

"Hope not," Rhea says. But she's lying. She hopes it does rain. Tomorrow, too. All week. All summer. She hopes it rains forever.

"I've made some changes," her father says as they enter the square of canvases that surrounds her stage. "To make it a little easier on you."

Rhea is already untying her cape when she sees them. "Oh, daddy," she says.

Her father is quite happy with his work. He's extended the chicken wire all the way to the top of the canopy. And not only in front of the stage, but on the sides, too. "You'll be safe now," he says. Outside the canvases the rides start to churn. Tinkles of tape-recorded calliope music ride the rolling aromas of French fries and grilling onions. "Let's get to work, pumpkin seed."

And so they do. And despite the bruised sky and the noisy breeze, it does not rain at all. Dinkumites by the score plunk down their dollars. They gather around the chicken wire, gawking and giggling, asking Rhea The Feather Girl again and again if she lays eggs, crowing and clucking as if they were the ones covered with feathers.

The next day the sky is as blue as a Wedgwood vase. The day after that even bluer. In fact there is not a drop of rain all week, despite the gate keeper's wise assertion that it "always rains one day."

It takes all week for Sunday to come. For the pyrotechnic dandelions above the grandstand, for the rides to stop churning. Rhea is inside the snow cone wagon scrubbing when Jelly Bean stops by. They hug. "Where you folks going next, sweetie pie?"

"Abner County. I think."

"Abner County? That shriveled up prune of a fair? Hooo! You should be going up to Wyssock County. Big fair. Make some good money up there."

"We're from Wyssock County."

"I understand," says Jelly Bean.

Jelly Bean makes six trips to the phone booth before getting up the nerve to place her call. She holds the phone book and inch from her Aztec-parrot nose and punches the numbers with her cocoa-colored pinky finger. After only half a ring someone answers: "Wyssock County Children Services."

"Yes ma'am . . . I don't mean to sound like a do-gooder— because I ain't one—but there's this sweet little girl . . . ."

Twenty-six

THERE IS NO easy way to get to Abner County. No interstate comes within seventy miles and the old U.S. routes in this part of the state run east and west, not north and south. So April Poulard, twenty-eight, interim director of the Wyssock County Children Services Board, has to drive the narrow, curvy, pot-holed state routes.

She reaches the Abner County courthouse three hours and seventeen minutes after leaving New Waterbury. She writes down her mileage. "Jeesh!" She hadn't averaged over forty-five miles an hour the entire time. As soon as she's inside the old red-bricked building, a voice echoes down the steep oak-banistered stairway: "That you, April?"

April Poulard's voice echoes up. "Mrs. Pilchard?"

A stocky woman in her sixties is descending the steps. She stops to catch her breath and study her counterpart. "You call me Ruth or I'll throw my shoe at you."

They take Ruth Pilchard's car, a midnight blue Mercury. They reach the fairgrounds in just five minutes. It hasn't rained yet today, but it rained yesterday, and the day before, and the clouds are still low and dirty. "I could flash my ID and get us in free," Ruth Pilchard says as they join the line of people winding toward the ticket booth, "but I don't think it's a good idea to broadcast our business, do you?"

Sam Guss learned about April Poulard's secret trip to Abner County the usual way—late night coffee and donuts with Doris Ackley at Edee's. Doris is always eager to pass on the courthouse gossip to Sam, though Sam knows she would rather it be pillow talk than donut shop talk. Sam has been stringing her along for years like this, hinting at a future romance, digging out juicy stories for the *Wyssock County Gazette*.

177

The Abner County thing is the most bizarre tip Doris ever gave him. Bizarre but believable. Sam first heard rumors about the girl with feathers three, maybe four years ago. But he hadn't tried to dig it out. You don't write stories about strange people unless they do strange things. A story needs a hook. A story needs justification. As Managing Editor Paul Grant likes to say in his best West Virginia French, a *raison d'être*.

Doris was right about one thing: April Poulard is on her way to Abner County. Sam stays as far behind her white Ford Escort as possible.

He slips into an empty parking place across from the courthouse and watches April go inside. He watches her come out with another woman. That must be Ruth Pilchard, the woman Doris said April was going to meet. He follows them to the fairgrounds. So far so good.

Sam Guss hangs back and watches the two women buy their tickets. He could try to get in free with his press pass but decides to go the incognito route, even though he knows he won't be reimbursed. "*Au contraire*," Mr. Grant will twang.

Sam hides behind the public toilets while April and Ruth Pilchard buy cotton candy. He follows them down the midway. Slips the 35mm Canon out of the side pocket of his sportsjacket. Puts his ballpoint pen between his teeth.

Sonofabitch! Doris was right on the button. There, stuffed between two of those three-balls-for-a-buck-win-a-stuffed-animal games, is a flapping canvas with fat circus letters that says:

RHEA THE FEATHER GIRL

And that's Calvin Cassowary, out front in the Styrofoam straw hat beckoning April and Ruth to plunk down their dollars. He knows it's Calvin Cassowary because the *Gazette* has put his photo on page one three times since the Maple Creek Homeowners' Association filed its lawsuit against his chicken farm.

Twenty-seven

WHEN THE TABLE in the breakfast nook wobbles beneath Calvin Cassowary's elbows, he pounds it hard with the flat of his fist. There is still an inch of cold coffee in the mug First Sovereignty Savings Bank gave him when he took out that first quarter-million-dollar loan against the farm.

He heaves the mug against the wall anyway.

Donna finishes blowing her nose and goes back to buttering the toast. "That was real smart," she says.

"We've got a dozen mugs just like it in the cupboard."

"It's not the mugs, Calvin. It's the wallpaper. It's my sanity."

He watches yet another television crew pull up. There are five of them now. It's only 7:30 in the morning. "Fuck the wallpaper."

She sets the toast in front of him. "And fuck my sanity?"

There are more than the five television crews parked in front of the farm this morning. There are a dozen newspaper reporters and maybe three dozen gawkers. There are kids from Maple Creek Estates, weaving their bicycles in and out of the parked cars. There are deputy sheriffs. There are three empty egg-yolk yellow semis from Gallinipper Foods trying to pull in.

The commotion makes Calvin think about that day at Kent State when he was a sophomore—May 4, 1970—and the Ohio National Guard opened fire on protesting students. Those shootings, senseless as they were, at least were understandable, given the madness of those years. President Nixon had invaded Cambodia. Students had burned the ROTC building. The National Guard was sent in, guns loaded. Nine students were wounded and four shot dead.

But why all this commotion now? Why are those two deputies unrolling that yellow crime scene tape? No crime has been committed here. The only thing here is an art major doing everything he can to keep his farm in the family for one more generation. "How long do you think it will be before they send in the

179

National Guard?" he asks Donna, finally taking a bite of toast. It's already cold.

Donna is squatting in front of the stove, picking up the coffee mug shards. "Tomorrow some politician will get caught with his pants down around his ankles and the reporters will go away. Everyone will go away."

"That knucklehead from Children Services won't go away."

The dustpan of shards rattles into the wastebasket. "Everything we did was on the up and up."

"Was it?" Calvin asks as he watches the Maple Creek boys ride chest-high through the yellow crime tape, pretending, he supposes, that they've just won the Tour de France. The *Gazette's* first story on Rhea appeared three days ago, when he and Rhea and Joon were still at the Abner County Fair. Jimmy Faldstool read the story to him over the phone:

"The big black headline across the top of the page says, 'FEATHER GIRL PROBED' and the little headline under that says, 'Children Services fears abuse by desperate father.' And there's this big picture of Rhea staring out through a wall of chicken wire. Good gravy, Cal. She looks pitiful."

And that's how Calvin found out. He ran back to the trailer, where Rhea was watching Joon eat his Rice Krispies, and, not knowing what to say, said only, "We've got to go home right away."

They left Joon at the fair, to keep an eye on the exhibit, to keep selling Ice Noggies, and drove home as fast as the narrow, curvy state routes would allow. When they pulled in, there was a white Ford Escort sitting in the driveway. Inside the house he found that knucklehead from Children Services, April Poulard, asking Donna one question after another. Donna was crying from the questions and sneezing from the young woman's apricot-scented hairspray.

The following day the *Akron Beacon Journal* and the *Cleveland Plain Dealer* and the *Columbus Dispatch* ran their stories. Then the television crews arrived. After the six o'clock news the gawkers started arriving. The deputies. The boys on their bicycles. And now this morning the yellow crime tape.

At 9:30 the lawyer Calvin hired to handle his squabble with the Maple Creek Homeowners' Association arrives. Donna opens the door just wide enough to let him in.

"Morning all," says Michael Rood III. Remembering Donna's allergic reaction to nearly everything, he plucks the war club-sized briar pipe from his stained teeth and slips it, still billowing, into the side pocket of his seersucker sports coat. Instead of a briefcase, he carries his important papers in a replica Pony Express saddlebag. He slides into the chair across from Calvin. "Worry not, my friend. I think we can get this 'ol bag of donuts behind us pretty quick."

"You said that about the homeowners' lawsuit," Calvin reminds him.

Michael Rood III admits his earlier mistake with a long hard nod. "Right-e-o. I said it would never get to trial and I was wrong. But it won't be a long trial. No jury in Wyssock County is going to find against the smell of a man's manure."

"Let's hope," Calvin says.

"Any-hoo, that 'ol bag of donuts is down the road. Today we've got another problem, don't we?"

Donna brings him a mug of coffee. "They're threatening to put Rhea in a foster home."

"They always threaten that. SBB. Standard bureaucratic bluff. Where is our sweet little chickadee, anyway?"

"In her room," says Donna.

Michael Rood III approves. "Keep her there until the hoopla dies down. You don't want to do anything that smacks of abuse or exploitation. Whatever you do, don't yell at her with the windows open."

Michael Rood III, saddlebag over his shoulder, stands tall on the porch and lights his pipe. The smoke boils straight up then flattens across the ceiling. He pats Biscuit on the head and walks like Abe Lincoln toward the road. He makes sure the charming old farm house is squarely behind him, so the television cameras

181

convey the proper Reaganesque message—farm family fighting for survival against the Big Brother liberal leviathan. As he walks he wishes the Cassowarys had an American flag flying.

He stops at the crime scene tape and waits until the microphones are in his face. Then he says:

"I am Michael Rood III. R-o-o-d. I'm the Cassowary's attorney. Rhea and her parents are quite distraught, as well you can imagine. But we are confident that this misunderstanding can—and will be—resolved quickly. There is simply no evidence that Rhea has been victimized in any way. She has feathers, yes. But she is normal in every other way."

A reporter shouts: "Is it true she doesn't go to school?"

Michael Rood III's head bobs up and down. "Rhea is home-schooled. Her father trained as a teacher before taking responsibility for the family farm. Her stepmother has an associate's degree in accounting. Her work is monitored regularly by the local school board. The Cassowarys are loving, responsible parents."

A reporter shouts: "They keep her in a cage!"

"They certainly do not. That chicken wire was there to protect Rhea from the occasional fairgoer who'd try to pluck one of her feathers. Concerned, loving father protecting his daughter. Any one of us would have done the same thing."

A reporter shouts: "I hear they only feed her bugs and worms."

"Absolutely ludicrous. I'd love to know your source on that one."

A reporter shouts: "What about the long hours they force her to work?"

"Rhea is a farm girl. Children on farms start helping their parents at an early age. I grew up on a farm myself, helped bale hay when I was nine."

A reporter shouts: "Being a side show freak is not the same as baling hay."

Michael Rood III feels the stem of his pipe begin to crack and he wiggles it out of his clenched teeth. "Rhea is not a freak. She is a beautiful, intelligent girl. And she was not in a side show. She was participating in a county fair, as thousands of farm children do every summer. There is nothing more American than a county fair, my friends."

Norman Marek shows his business card to the deputy, and, getting a thoughtful nod of approval, stoops under the crime tape and jogs up the driveway. He climbs to the porch, ignoring Biscuit's appeal for a pat on the head, and rattles the screen door with his knuckles. When Donna lets him in, he goes straight to the Mr. Coffee. His eyes are blinking like railroad crossing lights. "Who's the horse's ass talking to the press out there?"

Calvin, still at the table, pushes out a chair with his foot. "That's the second-best lawyer in town you told me to hire."

Norman sips his way across the kitchen and sits. "You have confidence in him, do you?"

"Not especially. But he has quite a bit of confidence in himself."

"Good enough. I tried calling you all morning."

"We unplugged the phone."

"Wise move." Norman leans and peeks through the blinds. "At least the trucks got through. Eggs have to keep moving no matter what—rain, shine or media circus. Christ, Cal! What in the hell were you thinking?"

"I had to do something."

"You got Bob's attention, that's for sure."

"Mr. Gallinipper knows already?"

"It was in this morning's *New York Times.*"

"That was fast."

"Those liberal pukes at the *Times* have been out to get the chicken people for years. Every time a fish dies downstream from a processing plant—take a free swing at the chicken people."

"So the story mentioned that I supplied eggs to Gallinipper Foods?"

"First paragraph. Bob is really pissed at you, Cal. *El pisso grande.*"

"I'm pissed at me, too."

"In case you didn't see it, Cal, there's a Good Citizen clause in your contract. You're expected to behave like a decent human being. First you get sued by your neighbors, then this." Norman presses the coffee mug against his hurting head. "You've got to trust Bob, Cal. These depressed prices are a temporary thing. Our Egg-ceptional Breakfast campaign has already boosted consumption point-three-five percent. And we're about ready to release a study showing that cholesterol can prevent impotence in men over fifty-five."

"Does it prevent foreclosure?"

Norman slumps sympathetically. "Why didn't you come to me, Cal?"

"Cassowarys solve their own problems."

"And *make* their own problems, apparently."

"So where do we stand? Is Gallinipper going to rip up my contract?"

"Cal! Shame on you! The Gallinipper family is exactly that— a family. Bob loves you like a son."

"He's never met me."

Norman points at him and winks. "But he reads your spreadsheets, Cal."

Betsy Betz has to park three hundreds yards up the road. She may be 65, but she can still jump a country ditch. She lands as gracefully as a young doe. Wades into the shoulder-high weeds. Were this fifteen years ago, and Betsy Betz still Betsy Cassowary, this field would have been filled with neat rows of green corn, just starting to tassel. Now the field is choking with thistles and teasel, wild carrot and wild rose, even some damn blackberry briars.

Storming between two of the long layer houses, she spots Biscuit. The old dog spots her. They run stiff-legged toward each other. "Bisky! Bisky!" she baby-coos. "Do you remember me?"

Biscuit does remember her. He licks the makeup off her face and runs around her in circles all the way to the house. He accepts her invitation to come inside. He hasn't been invited inside since Donna arrived.

The slamming screen door doesn't turn Calvin's head, but the plink of Biscuit's toenails on the linoleum does. "Mother?"

Betsy Betz comes at him with her arm extended like a fly swatter. Calls him a stupid bastard and smacks him hard on the forehead.

"Where's Ben?" Calvin asks her.

"Still in Columbus begging me not to drive when I'm this worked up." She goes to the cupboard and gets down a cereal bowl. Fills it with water for Biscuit. "Where's Rhea?"

"Upstairs. Donna, too."

She starts for the stairs, then turns back and smacks him across the forehead again. "You've got a million chickens and you can't make a living?"

He tells her it's only 810,000 now. He tries to explain the depressed market and corresponding low wholesale prices. He holds up his thumb and forefinger. "I'm that close to losing the farm."

"Then lose it! Sell the damn place if you can't make a go."

"I can't sell the farm and you know it."

"But you can sell your daughter?"

The stairs squeak. A sneeze echoes down. Donna appears, blurry eyed from trying to nap. "You didn't drive up by yourself, did you?"

Betsy holds out her arms, inviting a hug. "You holding up okay, honey?"

Donna bends over and hugs, her nose immediately stuffing up from the makeup, perfume and polyester pantsuit. "Why don't you go up and surprise Rhea? She's reading that book you sent her, I think."

"What book is that?"

"The one about the birds. She absolutely loves it. She sneaks out at night and reads it to her chickens. I'll make us some soup."

And so Betsy Betz goes upstairs and finds her granddaughter curled on her bed, huge stereo earphones over the crown of her feathered head, a book with birds on the cover in front of her face.

"Knock knock," Betsy sings out.

"Gammy Betz!" Rhea tosses the book and the earphones and crawls across the bed into her grandmother's arms. There are tears. Assurances that everything is going to be fine.

"Now tell me all about this wonderful book I didn't send you," Betsy says.

Betsy Betz is not upstairs five minutes when the screen door bangs again. A woman with tight gray curls hobbles in on a three-legged aluminum cane. It is Kitty Marabout, Jeanie's mom, Rhea's Toledo grandmother. "I'm filing for custody," she announces.

Twenty-eight

SITAREH ARAM FINDS her husband sitting on his yoga rug, in the lotus position, his toes tucked behind his knees. His face is as pink as a baked salmon, and glistening, as if the salmon had just been basted with butter. "Why are you crying, Pirooz?"

"I am not crying."

"Then you are leaking badly."

"I am meditating, my dear Sitareh."

"And crying."

Dr. Pirooz Aram surrenders. "Yes, dammit, I am crying. You are happy now?"

His wife bends over him, lifts his black felt beret like the lid of a kettle and kisses the hairless circle on the top of his head. "About what?"

"About one of my patients."

"They usually make you laugh."

"This one makes me cry."

"Anything I can do?"

"Other than leave me to my yoga?"

She replaces his beret and goes about collecting the newspapers he has tossed on the floor. It is his way: read a few pages then toss them, as if discarding pistachio shells after the meats are chewed and swallowed. "I know their sanity is your business, Pirooz. But your sadness is mine."

"You are tippy-toeing a delicate line, Sitareh. Don't you have some exams to grade? Your students are anxious to know how ignorant they are."

Pirooz finishes his yoga. Takes a shower. Eats his granola on the bedroom balcony, wearing nothing but baby powder and his beret. He does not put on a business suit today, but dresses in a pair of white slacks and one of the Hawaiian shirts he bought on vacation, the blue one with the white palm trees. He exchanges his black beret for a red one.

187

"Not working today, Pirooz?" his wife asks when she sees his outfit.

"You are tippy-toeing again," he says.

He leaves his house and drives his red Toyota to the interstate. Instead of going north toward the huge medical building where he keeps his office, he goes south, toward Wyssock County.

In the days before Abraham, he thinks as he drives, before religion became so filled with guilt and misery, a girl with Rhea's gifts would have been made a goddess, worshipped with wonderful feasts, wonderful poems, wonderful songs and dances. He is surprised to find the Cassowary farm after only a few wrong turns.

There are dozens of cars parked along the road. There are vans from television stations. There are police cars, some blinking red, some blinking blue. There are dozens of people, bunched like grapes, staring at the white farmhouse, as if at any moment it will metamorphosize into a huge flying saucer and screw itself into the sky. Just as he gets out of his Toyota, a phalanx of boys on bicycles charge the wide yellow ribbon someone has tied between the telephone poles. "Be careful Pirooz," he warns himself, "you have just landed in one of Salvador Dali's paintings."

For a few minutes he listens to a man with a pipe and a seersucker coat talking to the television cameras. He wonders if the man knows that the name of his coat comes from an old Persian word, *shíoshakar,* meaning milk and sugar. The Hindus stole the word to describe the light, bumpy fabric they wore to keep from boiling in the liquid heat of India. They passed it on to the British and the British passed it on to the Americans. And now here is this bumpy-coated American in front of the cameras, thinking he knows everything, but knowing nothing. How is it, Pirooz wonders, that these Americans have conquered the world so easily when they know nothing about it? He knows the answer, of course. It is because they are blissfully ignorant. The tactic of all barbarians.

Now Dr. Pirooz Aram meanders through the crowd, wishing he hadn't driven here this morning, wishing he had worn something a little less flashy. More people are looking at him than at the house. Perhaps they think he is the captain of the flying saucer.

He wants to mind his own business, to see for himself what greed and stupidity have done to the beautiful swan named Rhea. But the words flying between the two men standing next to him wriggle into his ears.

"It's all a publicity stunt," one of the men says. "You've been had, Sam."

"I wish it was a stunt," says the man named Sam. "But the poor girl is covered with feathers all right."

Suddenly Pirooz finds himself in the conversation. "Why do you call her poor? She is very rich."

The man named Sam shakes his head impatiently. "I don't mean poor as in not having any money. I mean poor as in pitiful."

Pirooz bubbles with anger. "Sir! My English may have an accent, but I know that poor has two meanings. And I know which one you meant. And when I said *rich* I did not mean money either. She is rich in her beauty, inside and out. No one needs to pity her."

"You know her then?" asks Sam.

"Sort of."

"Sort of?"

Pirooz wishes he had kept his mouth shut. "Sort of is all you're going to get."

The man named Sam yawns and starts talking to his friend about Ohio State's chances of beating Michigan. Knowing and caring nothing about the crazy American game of football, Pirooz is about to resume his meandering when the man named Sam asks him, "How does something like this happen? Growing feathers? Exposure to toxic chemicals, maybe?"

"There are many things more toxic than chemicals," Pirooz says.

"Such as?"

"Such as living on a concentration camp for chickens."

"She's allergic to chickens?"

"To the way they are forced to live perhaps."

"A psychological allergy you mean?"

Pirooz nods and shrugs at the same time. "Perhaps a spiritual one." He says this knowing that he shouldn't. Not for Rhea's sake.

Or his own. She was his patient, his friend. A doctor cannot discuss a patient's problems. And a friend should never betray a friend. No tippy-toeing. But these two barbarians are so incredibly ignorant. He tells them of St. Francis's wounds, of the stigmata suffered by so many others. "They bleed from their hands as if the Romans had crucified *them*."

"Can my Toledo grandmother really make me live with her?" Rhea asks Gammy Betz as they shuffle through the dark. They have a flashlight but they're not using it. It's ten o'clock but the road in front of the farm is still crowded with police cars and television crews.

"Of course she can't."

"If I had to go live with anybody it would be you."

"And if I had to have somebody live with me it would be you."

They reach the chicken coop. A nervous cluck works it way up the perches when the latch rattles. Rhea pulls the door open just an inch. "It's only me and Gammy," she says. The chickens relax.

Rhea clicks on her flashlight now and moves the beam from face to face. Sideway eyes beam back like buttons of neon. "Your old Buff Orpingtons are all gone," Rhea tells her grandmother.

"Nobody lives forever," Gammy Betz says, "but there's more than a little Orpington in these new girls." The beam reaches the big head of a rooster. "And who is that ugly cuss?"

"Mr. Shakyshiver. He took over sperm duty when the coyotes killed Blackbutt."

Gammy Betz laughs, surprised and delighted by her granddaughter's maturity. "Sperm duty?"

Rhea laughs back, embarrassed but proud that she is old enough to say adult things to her grandmother. She washes the flashlight across the empty bottom perch to make sure it is free of manure. They sit, side by side. Rhea hands her grandmother the flashlight and takes her book from the big pocket on the bib of her overalls. She'd told her grandmother what it was about when they were in her room, just before her Toledo grandmother stormed in

190

and promised she'd get her out of *this hell hole* just as soon as she could. So Gammy Betz is up to speed on the story about the cowardly birds following the Hoopoe through the seven valleys. Rhea reads:

> *"Next comes the Valley of Bewilderment,*
> *A place of pain and gnawing discontent—*
> *Each second you will sigh, and every breath*
> *Will be a sword to make you long for death."*

Gammy Betz and the chickens listen without a single cluck as the poem rhymes on and on, to a story about a princess:

> *"A great king had a daughter whose fair face*
> *Was like the full moon in its radiant grace,*
> *She seemed a Joseph, and her dimpled chin*
> *The well that lovely youth was hidden in—"*

In this poem the king brings a young slave into the court. The slave is so incredibly handsome that when he goes to the market, crowds gather around him just to see his face. It is only a matter of time before the princess sees him:

> *"One day the princess, by some fateful chance,*
> *Caught sight of this surpassing elegance,*
> *And as she glimpsed his face she felt her heart,*
> *Her intellect, her self-control depart—"*

Rhea closes the book and wedges it between her knees. "Gammy, did I ever tell you about Joon?"

Calvin Cassowary opens the screen door just wide enough for Jimmy Faldstool to slide that morning's *Gazette* into his hand. Jimmy salutes and heads for the layer houses.

Calvin unfolds the paper. The headline across the top screams:

The smaller headline under that asks this:

DID DAUGHTER GROW FEATHERS OUT OF SYMPATHY FOR DAD'S
CHICKENS?

"This is all I need," he says calmly, before kicking the screen
door and screaming, "SON. OF. A. BITCH!"

The story quotes a knowledgeable unnamed source who
claims that the horrible treatment of the farm's chickens may be
responsible for Rhea's condition. The story also quotes a Cleveland dermatologist, a Dr. Kimberly Kolacky, who cautions that
while she has never met the Wyssock County girl, or studied her
particular case, it is a well-documented medical fact that "psychological distress can have physiological manifestations."

The story also quotes Brother Edward Nogasto, adjunct
professor of comparative religion at Lewis Lutwidge University:
"Obviously I can't say whether this girl's feathers are a stigmatic
reaction, but the cases of Christians bleeding from their palms and
feet—usually middle-aged women in England and teen-aged girls
in South America—are quite genuine."

Bob Gallinipper crumples his *New York Times* into a ball, the
entire paper. "Dinky!" he screams to his secretary: "Get Norman
Marek on the horn—pronto!"

Scott Snitzen, national president of Animals Are People Too,
the AAPT, is in his kitchen making a broccoli, cauliflower and
peanut stir fry when Brenda Berdache, his Midwest coordinator,
calls. "You see the CBS News?" she asks.

"Nada. Dan Rather gives me the heebie-jeebies."

And so Brenda tells him what she saw: "Well, they did this
story on this girl from Ohio, who—"

192

Fifteen minutes later an AAPT ACTION ALERT is being faxed all over the United States and Canada.

All night the low rumble-hum of the window fan helped Rhea sleep. Now it wakes her up. She squeaks across the floor and turns it off. Closes her eyes and listens to the quiet.

It is only seven but already the AAPT is demonstrating. They showed up three mornings ago. Twenty or thirty of them. Their signs say SAINT RHEA. When the television crews turn on their cameras they begin their chant:

Free Rhea! Free the hens! Free Rhea! Free the hens!

She puts on her sweatshirt and overalls and squeaks down to the kitchen. The man in the uniform leaning against the refrigerator smiles grimly at her. She smiles grimly back. She goes to the cupboard where the cereal boxes are kept. The man in the black and blue uniform is not just a deputy, but Sheriff Skip Affenpinscher himself. Rhea knows that because yesterday when he came to the door Donna said, "Come in, deputy."

And he tugged on the brim of his black cowboy hat and corrected her, "Sheriff Skip Affenpinscher, Mrs. Cassowary."

Rhea chooses the box of miniature shredded wheats.

"The point is this," the sheriff says to her father. "We've got to tie this old shoe and walk on."

"I didn't invite these TV people," her father says. "And I sure as hell didn't invite those animal rights nuts." He is sitting at the table in the breakfast nook. He practically lives there now. It has become his cage.

The sheriff moves from the refrigerator to the stove so that Rhea can get the milk. "You are somewhat responsible, Mr. Cassowary."

"Judge and jury, are we sheriff?"

Her father's hostility makes Rhea miss her bowl. Milk runs under the toaster, drips off the countertop.

The sheriff holds up his hands in surrender. "Whatever legal problems you have are between you and Children Services. My only concern is keeping the road clear. So anything you can do to help us out."

"I could set my chickens free," Calvin says. "How would that be? How would you like 810,000 hens running all over the county?"

Sheriff Skip Affenpinscher leaves, the old shoe still untied. Only now does her father acknowledge Rhea's presence at the table. "What's up, buttercup?"

The downstairs toilet flushes and Norman Marek appears in the kitchen, still making sure his zipper is zipped. "This AAPT thing completely changes the complexion of this thing," he says to Calvin. To underscore how completely he now spells the word out. "C-o-m-p-l-e-t-e-l-y."

"Is this where Bob evokes the Good Citizen Clause in my contract?"

Norman Marek blanches as white as a Grade A Leghorn egg. Then he laughs and makes his hands into imaginary six-shooters. He fires away. "You are a funny man, Cal. F-u-n-n-y. Of course we're not going to invoke the Good Citizen clause. Bob's ridin' to your rescue, Cal."

"Raising prices, is he?"

Norman Marek twirls his imaginary six-shooters and puts them in his imaginary holsters. "Better than that." He explains how the AAPT has been a burr in the poultry industry's saddle for years. Crying about treatment of laying hens and broilers. Scaring the holy hell out of people about diseases. Turning people into celery eaters. Costing Bob Gallinipper millions. "So Bob and the other poultry bigwigs—pork and beef bigwigs, too—are fighting fire with fire. They've created their own public interest group. The PAAT. People Are Animals, Too. Turn the words around. Turn the debate around. Those kooks out there want people to believe animals have feelings. So we say: No way, José. Not only aren't animals people—people *are* animals. And all animals eat other animals. That's the way the Almighty wants it. Vegetarians are nothing but malnourished malcontents who worship wind chimes."

Rhea watches the headache gathering on her father's brow as Norman Marek pulls out his six-shooters and starts firing away again.

"Bob's pouring big bucks into PAAT," says Norman. "Studies. Lawsuits. Campaign contributions. Proactive advertising. Counter-picketing."

Rhea watches the headache spread to her father's temples.

"No, Norman," Calvin says. "Not more picketers."

"They'll be here about nine," says Norman.

Rhea puts her bowl in the sink and goes to the living room to watch TV. Donna is in her rocking chair, head bent over the ledger book spread across her knees, Kleenex in one hand, pencil in the other. A live shot of their house fills the TV screen. A wild-eyed reporter is trying to shout over the chanting.

Free Rhea! Free the hens! Free Rhea! Free the hens!

Weird, Rhea thinks. I'm inside that house right now.

At nine the demonstrators from PAAT arrive, blowing the horns of their pickups, gathering with their American flags and their bullhorns and their cardboard signs. The signs are hand-made but they all say the same thing:

STAND PAAT WITH CAL

As soon as the cameras swing their way, the PAAT people begin to chant:

Eat eggs! Eat meat! Stand pat! Or taste defeat!

At noon Michael Rood III arrives to update Donna and Calvin on the homeowners' association lawsuit as well as the effort by Children Services to place her in a foster home. When Rhea comes into the kitchen to make a peanut butter and jelly sandwich all three of them smile grimly at her and she grimly smiles back.

At two o'clock, a strange man in a no-nonsense gray suit

195

strides confidently into the kitchen and introduces himself as Bartholomew Gumboro, president of Gumboro Brothers Development. "We're prepared to offer you well above market," he tells Calvin, who is still seated at the table. "And we'll eat the entire cost of disposing of your flock and the manure. You and your family can walk away clean and free and rich."

"I'm not selling," Calvin says.

Bartholomew Gumboro tempts him. "It would make a lot of your problems go away."

"Suppose you go away?"

At four o'clock Norman Marek calls. "Cal—you got cable TV, right?"

"Assuming Donna found the money to pay the bill, sure."

"Well, if it's still working be sure to watch *In The Crosshairs* at seven. You'll see exactly what those bunny huggers are up against."

Twenty-nine

ECHO-BOOMING DRUMS. Simmering bassoons. Boiling trumpets. A voice from heaven: *"Tonight on* In the Crosshairs: *Rhea the Feather Girl. Liberal flight of fancy? Or a fight for animal dignity? Now here's your moderator, Carlotta Aqouti Brown.*

Carlotta Aqouti Brown: "Good evening. On this side of the barbed wire we have Scott Snitzen, national president of Animals Are People, Too. And on this side, Robert P. Gallinipper, chairman and chief operating officer of Gallinipper Foods, one of the nation's largest egg and poultry wholesalers."

Scott Snitzen frowns at the host. Bob Gallinipper smiles at the camera.

Carlotta Aqouti Brown: "Let's start with you, Mr. Snitzen. By now the entire world has heard of Rhea Cassowary, the Ohio farm girl with feathers. Now, as the family faces allegations of child abuse, your group is demonstrating in front of their farm, claiming Rhea as some sort of messiah for the animal rights movement. Aren't you just taking advantage of a sad situation?"

Scott Snitzen: "The sad situation is how animals are being treated. Rhea Cassowary has grown up seeing first hand how chickens are treated. Squashed into cages like so many sardines. Forced to breath putrid air. Forced to lay an obscene number of eggs. Murdered when their uteruses wear out."

Bob Gallinipper: "Murdered? Animals are just that, Mr. Snitzen—animals. God put them here for us to use."

Scott Snitzen: "Use is not the same as abuse."

Carlotta Aqouti Brown: "He has a point there, doesn't he, Mr. Gallinipper? Today's factory farms show no respect to animals whatsoever."

Bob Gallinipper: "Carlotta! Please! Farms are farms, whether you have six chickens or a million chickens. That factory farm stuff is nothing but liberal mumbo jumbo."

Carlotta Aqouti Brown: "We'll be back after these important messages."

Thirty

THE LILAC BUSH calls out, "Joon."

That startles Joon Faldstool, until he realizes it's not the lilac calling out his name, but Rhea. For some reason she's sitting inside the tree's ring of spindly limbs. He jumps from the snow cone wagon, where he's been working all evening scraping the dried egg off the floor, and sneaks low across the lawn, keeping, he hopes, out of sight from the house.

"Come on in," Rhea says.

So Joon squeezes between the spindly limbs and sits next to Rhea. Their arms and hips are touching. She tells him how she used to hide inside the lilac when she was little, pretending she was wearing a magic cloak that made her invisible, watching Phil Bunyip's crew load the crates of Leghorns.

"It's a lot like a cage in here," says Joon. A limb is digging in his back.

From the lilac they can see the sheriff's cars and the demonstrators. See the gawkers and the television crews. They talk about their few short days on the county fair circuit. They agree it seems like a long time ago. Agree it wasn't all that bad. "I was prepared for all that," Rhea says. "It was like being in the movies, you know? And there was a reason to do it. But all this. I don't think I can take this."

Joon puts his arm around her. She rests her feathered head on his cheek. "Most people really liked me," she says. "I know Jelly Bean and Robert Charles did."

It is only a bit after seven and the sun is just now beginning to tilt toward the horizon. "I'm driving down to see my grandfather on Thursday," Joon says.

"The one you got the big ears from?"

"Yup. Grampa Hap."

"The one who lives in the trailer by the swamp?"

"It's a cool place."

Rhea bends back his thumb, playfully, until he winces. "Cooler than my lilac?"

"Way cooler."

It is now that they decide to kiss for the first time. Neither has been kissed before, not a girl-boy on-the-mouth kiss. But they have been watching people kiss on television all their lives and they have practiced it on the back of their hands. So now, when they kiss, it is a good kiss.

In the Crosshairs isn't over two minutes when Norman Marek calls. "Great job, wasn't it?"

"It's just going to add to the hoopla," Calvin Cassowary says.

"It's also going to endear you to Bob Gallinipper. When Bob goes to war he doesn't leave his wounded on the field. Your copaceticness runneth over."

Calvin has the phone cord stretched as far as it will go, so he can lean his forehead against the screen door and let whatever breeze there is outside work on his headache. "Lucky me."

"Now there's one thing I want you to do, Cal. First thing tomorrow call Bob and tell him what a great job he did. Tell him how proud you were."

"To tell you the truth, I'm not so sure that—"

"And invite him to the farm for dinner. He eats that kind of thing up. But don't—whatever you do—try to tie him down to a specific date. Just make it general. Just say, 'You know Mr. Gallinipper, Donna, Rhea and I would like you and Bunny over for dinner sometime.'"

Calvin watches Joon Faldstool jump from the snow cone wagon and sneak across the lawn, heading toward the lilac by the garage. "Just sometime?"

"That way he won't feel guilty when he can't come."

Joon's sneaking worries Calvin. "Talk to you soon, Norm," he says and hangs the phone cord over the brass hat hooks on the wall. He slides out the screen door, making sure it doesn't slam. He trots to the garage and slips around the back, sneaking low across the grass to the lilac, where inside Joon and his daughter are locked at the lips.

Calvin reaches through the limbs, clamps onto Joon's ear, and jerks, and screams, "I should fire your ass on the spot!"

Calvin Cassowary does not fire Joon on the spot. Doesn't fire him at all. So for the next two days Joon comes to work as scheduled and shovels as much chicken manure as he can. On Thursday, even though it's his day off, he comes to work anyway, at 5:30 in the morning, and shovels until noon. Then he washes up and changes into a clean pair of jeans and a denim shirt and takes off in his Gremlin for Acorn County. He is thirty miles down Route 83 when Rhea pops up in the back seat, throwing back her cowl and kissing him first on the left ear and then on the right.

Joon pulls into a driveway and starts to turn around. "Don't you dare," Rhea says.

Joon needs no more of a threat than that. He's glad Rhea is in his back seat. Glad that they can spend an afternoon together. Even if it means that later tonight his ass will be fired for real.

Acorn County is real country. No developments. No strip malls. They pass through the townlets of Pym Center and Amberjack, Kellicott and McKelvey. They cross the bridge over Chippewa Creek and take a left on Bear Swamp Road. NO OUTLET the sign says. The dust flies.

Bear Swamp Road is straight and flat for maybe a half mile. The thick scrub woods on both sides muffles the sound of the Gremlin's tires on the gravel. Suddenly the road gets curvy. The scrub woods gives way to weedy fields. The sun gets hot. There is a corrugated metal culvert to bump over and then a final steep descent to the swamp and Grampa Hap's small silver house trailer.

They find Joon's grandfather behind the trailer, sitting in an aluminum lawn chair. He is just a few feet from a rotting dog house and a circle of bare ground littered with sun-baked logs of beagle manure. The beagle is sleeping on top of the dog house. A rusted lawnmower is submerged in the knee-high grass, right where it ran out of gas, maybe a summer or two ago.

Hap Aspergres is clearly in his seventies or eighties. He is clearly a thinner man than he used to be. His extra skin hangs in folds. His ears, even bigger than Joon's, are flower pots for thickets of bristly white hair.

"Joonbug!" he growls when they appear around the end of the trailer. "I've been waiting forever." When his eyes adjust to the distance, and he sees Rhea, he unfolds from the chair. He stares and shakes his head slowly. "I didn't know she was coming, too."

Joon skirts the beagle manure and hugs his grandfather. "I didn't either."

"You look a lot more normal than I figured," Hap Aspergres tells Rhea. He is studying her without embarrassment or apology. "What a wonderful world we live in."

He brings them tall glasses of orange juice and a new bag of Oreo cookies, and they sit on broken lawn chairs in the high grass and listen while he tells them the history of Bear Swamp: There are no bears. It really isn't a swamp. More of a marsh that spends all summer trying to dry out, succeeding just a week or two before the first snow. It runs east as far as the Bailey farm and west as far as the Wunkerschmidt farm and north as far as the new county landfill. "I own all but a corner of it," he says. "But nobody really owns anything, do they? Everybody's a renter in God's eyes."

Joon and Rhea tell him about their days on the county fair circuit. About her father's current trouble with Children Services, the Maple Creek Homeowner's Association, the AAPT and the PAAT, and the television crews.

"I've only had one television set in my life," Hap tells them. "When it fizzled out I saw no reason to buy another. But I've got several radios." He tells them that both radio and television are broadcast on radio waves. He tells them what radio waves are. Explains the electromagnetic spectrum to them, and Planck's constant, the theory by nineteenth-century German physicist Max Planck, that established the mathematical relationship between the frequency of an electromagnetic wave and the amount of energy in that wave.

It is now that Rhea remembers Joon telling her about her grandfather's gift for retaining information that has no direct bearing on his own life.

"You got time for a witching lesson?" Hap asks his grandson.

Joon loves to go water witching with his grandfather. Loves gripping that Y of springy willow, barely able to breathe while he walks, waiting for the end to tug downward, waiting for that pat on the head and the praise, "You're a natural, Joonbug!"

"Sorry. We've got to get back," Joon says.

Hap understands. Walks them to the Gremlin. The beagle comes along, his upright tail skimming the top of the tall grass like the periscope of a submarine. By the time they reach the car, Hap has explained the history of Daylight Savings Time to them.

Joon will have to push the Gremlin hard to get Rhea home in time for supper. He grips the steering wheel with both hands and leans into it. "Too bad we couldn't stay longer," he says.

Rhea leans against his shoulder. "It was worth it. "

Joon knows exactly what she means. He feels that way, too. A few hours of freedom. A few hours of respect. "Hap's really something, isn't he?"

Answers Rhea, "He reminds me of the Hoopoe."

They hurry north, through McKelvey, Kellicott, Amberjack and Pym Center. They hurry through a dozen plans to get Rhea into the house without Donna or her father ever realizing she was gone. They realize it will be next to impossible. But necessary that they try. If they're caught, Joon will lose his job. There'll be screaming and swearing and the smashing of coffee mugs and the sheriff's deputies guarding the driveway will hear it all and report it to April Poulard of Children Services. Rhea will find herself in a foster home. Maybe living with her Toledo grandmother. They will never see each other again. "You can't let yourself get caught," Joon says.

"I won't," says Rhea, tightening her grip on his arm.

A half mile from the farm they pull over and Rhea crawls over the seat. She puts on her cloak and melts against the floor. Joon drives on. The sheriff's deputy recognizes the Gremlin and motions him in. They crackle up the drive. Park alongside the garage. Joon half opens the door for Rhea. She slides out. He leans back and closes his eyes, waiting for the screaming and swearing and the smashing of mugs.

Rhea slips along the back of the garage and then ducks under the willow, its drooping yellow-green branches concealing her all the way to the corner of the house. She crawls to the rusted iron coal chute behind the snowball bush. She lifts the heavy lid and slides into the coal bin. The Cassowarys haven't heated with coal since 1965, when Rhea's grandfather got sick of the dirt and the lugging and had an oil furnace installed. Now the bin's cement block walls are painted white and instead of coal, it's filled with junk not good enough for the attic. She climbs down the metal shelving. The door to the basement is latched. She knew it would be. But she knows where the emergency coat hanger is. Her great-grandmother Dorothy got a coat hanger and stretched it out like the neck of a goose and hung it on a nail just to the right of the door in 1944, after getting locked inside herself. She'd been inside setting mousetraps when her husband Alfred came by and saw that the door was open a crack. He shut it and latched it and went outside to milk his cows and Dorothy was trapped inside there for two hours and the Swiss steak in the oven baked as hard as boot heels.

Rhea gets the emergency coat hanger and lifts the latch and after leaning against the washing machine for ten minutes or so, trying to hear what's going on upstairs, she climbs confidently to the kitchen.

"There you are," her father says. There is a frown on his face but his eyes are happy.

"I was looking at the junk in the coal bin."

Donna is draining spaghetti noodles in the sink. "That must have made for a fun afternoon."

"I was looking for that drawing of my mother feeding the chickens."

Donna turns, the dripping colander still in her hands. She stares at Calvin and makes a decision. "It's in the fruit cellar. Behind the wine jugs."

Rhea starts for the basement steps. Not only has she fooled them, but she finally knows where that drawing is.

Her father erupts: "Wwwwait!"

She orbits on her heels, expecting to see anger and betrayal rippling across his face. But his eyes are still happy.

"Children Services called," he says. "They're dropping their investigation. We didn't do anything wrong."

"We're going to do more fairs then?" Rhea isn't thinking about the gawkers or the chicken wire, but about Joon and Jelly Bean and Robert Charles.

Her father's entire head is happy now. "No need. We're going to work for Galiinipper Foods."

"We already work for Gallinipper Foods."

"Not that kind of work—we're still going to do that—but working with them at the corporate level. Norman called just fifteen minutes ago. I can't believe you didn't hear us yell for you. You're going to be the company mascot. Commercials. Public appearances. And not only that, pumpkin seed—they're also giving us the first commercial flock of their new 7-52 Super Hens. Seven eggs a week, fifty-two weeks a year."

Rhea looks at Donna. "Can I get the drawing now?"

Donna, without checking her husband's eyes for approval, nods that she can.

Rhea descends the steps, each step deeper and wider and mushier. Her father's voice is descending the steps with her: "We're flying to Chicago next week. Your first photo shoot."

Thirty-one

THE FLIGHT FROM Cleveland to Chicago takes an hour. That hour takes a hundred hours. Rhea Cassowary has never flown before. Each thump, bump and wiggle of the egg yolk-yellow corporate jet glues her fingers to the armrests. But they land and an egg yolk-yellow limousine whisks them downtown.

It is not a good morning in Chicago. The sky is as gray as the pavement. The limousine zips through neighborhoods filled with people every color but white. Elevated trains rumble past the dirty windows of dirty buildings. The limo driver—a Haitian or a Jamaican—sings questions to them: "Have you been to Chicago before?"

"No," Rhea's father answers.

"Ahhhh. Then you have never been to Uno's for deep-dish pizza?"

"Can't say that we have."

"Ahhhh. Everyone want to go there."

The limousine makes a series of right turns, each street getting narrower. They pull into a parking lot littered with small expensive cars. The driver helps them out. "I will be waiting right here," he assures them.

Rhea follows her father up a set of concrete steps. He pushes a button by the steel door. The ring throws the door open. "Rhea! Calvin! Come in!"

The voice belongs to a willowy woman with very white skin and very black hair. She is wearing a pin-striped man's suit. Her glasses have thick red rims. "I'm Rikki Coquina," she says and hands Rhea's father a business card, as if it were an admission ticket to her special world. Rhea manages to read it before her father slips it into his shirt pocket. It says: Alpenhorn & Coquina Talent Representation.

A freight elevator jerks them up several stories. "Jaret has been working on the lighting all morning," Rikki says as they jerk along. "Sooooo, with a little luck we can get right to work."

They enter the studio. Styrofoam coffee cups sit on chairs. People in baggy jeans sit on the floor. There is an upside-down moose head on the wall. In the center of the studio a bald black woman wearing red hightops is sitting motionless on a bale of straw, holding a large stuffed white goose. A man with a crazy grin, ponytail to his belt loops, is twisting the black light booms and white umbrellas. Rikki apologizes for the stuffed goose. "It was the only thing Jaret could find for a stand-in. To get the lighting on Rhea's feathers right."

Jaret suddenly leaps away from his camera and shoos the goose woman off the set. He floats like a helium balloon to Rhea and studies her, his hands folded in front of his lips as if in prayer. He extends a forefinger and lightly touches her face, then pulls it back quickly, as if he's in a museum and the guard will see him touching some priceless antiquity. "Fabulous!" he repeats several times.

Rikki ushers Rhea in to a dressing room where the bald black woman, no longer holding the stuffed goose, helps her dress. There are several costumes on the rack. The one they choose first is a sleeveless egg yolk-yellow tee shirt and a snug-fitting pair of bib overalls, the legs of which are cut and cuffed just above the knee. Rhea watches in the mirror as Rikki gently lowers a wide-brimmed straw hat onto the back of her head.

After she's dressed, Jaret spends an hour making sure Rhea is sitting just right on the straw bale. Then he takes another twenty-five minutes resetting the lights he'd spent all morning setting. Then he fires off several rolls of film. "Excellent! Fabulous! Excellent! Fabulous!"

At noon the alley bell rings, the elevator jerks up, and a man with a turban brings a bag of foil-wrapped sandwiches. After lunch, Rhea is dressed in a sky-blue gingham dress, sleeveless and short. Rikki slips sparkling slippers on her bare feathery feet. They are just like the red ruby slippers Dorothy wore in the Wizard of Oz, except that they are egg yolk-yellow.

While Jaret fiddles with his lights and umbrellas, assistants tear open the straw bale and scatter it. Then a backdrop is unrolled.

It is a painting of the inside of a rustic barn. Better than anything Calvin Cassowary could paint. There are no rows of cages inside this barn, no automatic feeders or manure conveyors, no skin-and-bone hens with snipped-off beaks or combs. There are just a dozen or so fat hens with perfect feathers, pointy beaks and floppy red combs, standing wherever they please. There is even a big rooster in the painting, silently crowing his happy heart out. Rikki hands Rhea a red pail that says CHICKEN FEED. They stand her in front of the painting, straw scattered all around. Jaret takes a half hour to get her pose just right. Then he goes to his camera and buries his face, and moans, "For crying out loud. She's crying. Will somebody *please* dry her eyes?"

"It can't possibly work," Joon Faldstool says.

"I know," says Rhea, "but we're going to do it anyway."

Joon buries his face in his knees, wraps his hands around the back of his head. The perch bounces. The hens complain. "It's so goofy."

Rhea closes her book and drapes her arms around his nervous shoulders. She knows he is right. It is a goofy plan. Not a chance in the world it will work. Still, she knows she has to try. "I will not be the mascot for Gallinipper Foods, Joon." She playfully tugs on his ears until he lift his head. She kisses him.

"I'm not even seventeen yet," Joon says. "And you're only fourteen."

"The perfect ages to do dumb things," Rhea says.

So Joon agrees, knowing that Rhea's plan is goofy and dumb and probably illegal, even for someone not yet seventeen. A time and date is set. Eleven at night, on the fifth of September. Two weeks from now.

In the morning Rhea and her father fly to Chicago again. To do the radio spots. Rikki Coquina practices the lines with her. "Sound as happy as you can," she says. "Even try to put a little giggle in your voice here and there."

Rhea sits in front of the microphone. An engineer eases

earphones over her feathered head. Happy piano music trickles into her ears. The engineer points. Rhea reads:

"Hi, I'm Rhea Cassowary.
The Feather Girl.
I bet you've heard of me.
I love our little farm in Ohio.
And I love our chickens.
Just as much as our chickens love
laying big tasty fresh eggs for Gallinipper Foods.
And eggs are good food.
Where would breakfast be without them?
Where would a birthday cake be without them?
Next time you're at the supermarket
Pick up a dozen Grade A Gallinipper eggs.
That's my picture on the carton."

"Perfect," the engineer says. "Let's try it again."

By seven they are back at the farm, eating canned ravioli and canned green beans. At eight Rhea goes upstairs and chooses a pair of overalls and a tee shirt and puts them in a paper shopping bag. She creeps down the basement stairs while the television blares. She crawls out the coal chute. Runs to the back of the garage. Biscuit follows on his short fast legs. The number of demonstrators has dwindled. But there are a few. Some from AAPT. Some from PAAT. Signs but no chanting. No television cameras. Two yawning deputies.

Rhea takes the tee shirt from the bag and dangles it in front of Biscuit's face until he gets the idea and takes it in his mouth. Rhea tugs and he tugs back. It takes some doing, getting this gentle family dog to behave like a wild beast. But Biscuit little by little gives into his primitive nature. When the tee shirt is shredded and soaked with spittle, Rhea stuffs it in the bag and pulls out the overalls. "This is denim, Bisky," Rhea whispers. "You've really got to work hard now."

Biscuit barks and snarls and grabs on.

The next night Rhea goes out to read to her chickens. Joon is already in the coop with a sewing needle and the test tube he stole from the chemistry lab at school. While Rhea reads, Joon pricks her finger tips and squeezes drops of blood into the tube. When she can take the pain no more, Joon plugs it with a cork and rushes it to the refrigerator in the employee locker room. He hides it in the bag of baloney sandwiches that's been in there for months.

It takes three more nights behind the garage for Biscuit to shred the overalls properly. Five more nights of finger pricking to fill the test tube.

Rhea's period arrives on schedule. She uses pieces of the shredded tee shirt and overalls instead of napkins. It's a messy affair. But necessary. There has to be a lot of blood.

Rhea keeps up with her homeschooling and pretends to be impatient about the radio commercials. "When are they going to start running?" she asks her father at least once a day.

"They'll let us know," he tells her.

On Labor Day Gammy Betz and Ben drive up from Columbus for a picnic. Because of the demonstrators, the picnic has to be held in the kitchen. But the hamburgers and hotdogs are cooked on the charcoal grill on the porch and they taste like outdoors. "Rhea made the macaroni salad all by herself," Donna tells everyone.

Rhea is properly defensive. "How hard is it to make macaroni salad?"

On the night of September fifth Rhea goes to the coop to read. She has been reading to her chickens for so many months now. She is nearly at the end of the book, yet not close enough to finish it tonight, or ever.

Joon comes and gives her the cold test tube of blood. They kiss longer than they have ever kissed. She lets him touch her feathered breasts. Their first time for that. "You know I love you," Joon says. "Right?"

The chickens are blinking and cackling, begging for more about the thirty birds who have flown so far, through so many valleys, to see the Simorgh, their king. "And you know I love you," Rhea answers.

210

Rhea goes back to the house. Says goodnight to Donna and her father. Goes upstairs. It will be eleven in just two hours.

About ten Donna and her father turn off the television and come upstairs. They turn on the television in their room. Which means they will be making love tonight. It will be eleven in just an hour.

Rhea slips out of her nightgown and dresses. Puts on her tennis shoes. She digs out an old pair of sweat socks from the dresser. In one she stuffs her birthday and Christmas cash, eighty-two dollars. In the other she puts the test tube of her blood. Then she takes her Nestlé's Quik can from her bookshelf. She scoops out the feathers and puts them in a Ziploc bag. She wishes she could take the Quik can with her. For years that old can has protected, and respected, not only the feathers from her body, but the feathers of Blackbutt and Nancy, killed while they scratched for spring grubs. She puts the empty can back on the shelf.

Rhea also wishes she could take that drawing of her mother with her. Her father drew it before she was born. It hung in the breakfast nook for a long time. Then it disappeared. Donna told her where to find it in the fruit cellar. She leaves the picture on her dresser.

Another thing she'd like to take is the book Dr. Pirooz Aram sent her. But like the Quik can and the drawing, the book would be missed. She leaves it under her pillow.

She creeps downstairs while the television in her parents' bedroom blares. It will be eleven in just thirty minutes.

She feels her way down the basement steps. Feels her way to the coal bin, making sure she ducks below the clotheslines. She leaves the coal bin door open. The shopping bag with her shredded bloody clothes is hidden behind the Christmas decorations. She pulls it out, unrolls the top, feels inside, just to make sure. The stench of her menses fills the blackened room. She climbs the shelving. Pushes the coal chute open. Crawls out. Leaves it open.

Out front on the road the blue lights of a single sheriff's car are blinking.

Rhea finds Biscuit asleep on the top of the picnic table. "Bye-bye Bisky-boo," she coos. She kisses his flat head and lets him lick her feathered face.

When she turns to walk away, he pulls himself up on his haunches, ready to follow. "Not tonight, Bisky. Tonight you guard the picnic table."

But by the time Rhea reaches the edge of the lawn, Biscuit is at her side, wagging and whimpering, knowing something's up. "You win. But you keep your yap shut about this, you hear?"

There is a moon tonight. Stars. The air is warm. Rhea walks between layer houses B and C and descends the manure-soaked fields toward the creek. She stays just outside of the woods, heading north. Head down, tail slowly swaying, Biscuit stays exactly one foot behind her, never once stopping to sniff or pee.

Rhea walks until she's on the back pastures of Andy Abram's dairy farm. The grass is short but thick. Her father says the coyotes gather here at night, climbing from their holes along Three Fish Creek, to tease the farmer's dogs with their howls.

A coyote killed Blackbutt and Nancy. Years ago now.

She opens the shopping bag and pulls out the shredded and bloody tee shirt and overalls. She scatters them. She pulls the cork on the test tube of her own blood and sprinkles it here and there on the grass. She pulls off her tennis shoes and sprinkles a little blood inside them, then throws them as far as she can.

Now she opens the Ziploc bag and retrieves a handful of feathers. She tosses them. Lets them twist and drift and fall. She begins walking, in a circle, tossing her feathers, until the bag is empty.

She knows this is a goofy plan. Knows it can't possibly work. No one will believe for a minute that coyotes ate her. But she will get her father's attention, that's for sure.

Rhea walks until she reaches the bridge on Townline Road. She waits underneath, scratching Biscuit until she hears a car pull up. She crawls up the embankment. Joon opens the door for her. Biscuit stands in the gravel, head tipping one way then the other, watching the green Gremlin chug away.

PART IV

"The first man I saw was of a meager aspect, with sooty hands and face, his hair and beard long, ragged and singed in several places. He had been eight years upon a project for extracting sunbeams out of cucumbers, which were to be put into vials hermetically sealed, and let out to warm the air in raw, inclement summers."

Lemuel Gulliver
Jonathan Swift's *Gulliver's Travels*, 1726

Thirty-two

CALVIN CASSOWARY REACHES over his wife and feels for the phone amongst the pill bottles and wadded Kleenexes on her nightstand. "Hello?"

"Bob Gallinipper, Calvin. I've just reserved the presidential suite for you and Donna at the Hyatt. Wednesday and Thursday night. How about that?"

And so on the eighth of July, Calvin and Donna fly to Chicago and spend the night in a huge room, in a huge bed, nibbling on fruit and drinking champagne, wondering what in the hell this is all about.

Why shouldn't they wonder? Calvin has been shipping eggs to Gallinipper Foods for twenty years and not once has Bob Gallinipper spoken to him. Business between them has been conducted through Norman Marek. Norman even delivered those wild strawberry plants after Jeanie died.

In the morning an egg yolk-yellow limo drives them to a sprawling office building in the suburbs. In front stands a thirty-foot revolving egg with gold longitude and latitude lines and buffed aluminum continents. They are met at the door by an emaciated woman in a gray suit. All the way to the fifth floor she tries to look pleasant, but simply does not have enough muscle in her face to pull it off.

The elevator empties onto a egg yolk-yellow hallway. They follow the woman toward a pair of golden doors. On both sides of the hallway, every three feet, huge photographs of beautiful white Leghorn roosters are hanging. Each rooster has a sign around its neck, reporting the number of eggs sold in a particular year:

1983
772.4 MILLION DOZEN

Under that, in script, with an exclamation point, is written:

The emaciated woman pushes a button on the wall. There is a *buzzt*. The golden doors swing open. A friendly Midwestern voice rolls out: "Cassowarys! Get your beautiful Ohio bee-hinds in here!"

Bob Gallinipper seats Calvin and Donna on a puffy white sofa. He lowers himself into a puffy yellow chair. Fifty feet below them is a pond with a fountain of bronze baby chicks spitting water from their open beaks.

For an hour Bob talks nonstop about his hardscrabble boyhood, his long and wonderful marriage to Bunny, his five wonderful children. He talks about how it saddened him to the roots when Rhea went home to live with the Lord. "How many years has it been since she passed?" he asks Calvin.

"Almost six," Calvin answers.

At precisely ten the golden doors swing open and the emaciated woman enters with a tray of sugar cookies and a decanter of hot chocolate. Bob pours the hot chocolate himself, making sure everyone got a few bobbing marshmallows. While Calvin and Donna sip and munch, and wonder what's coming next, he says this:

"Folks, the day Rhea joined the Gallinipper Family as company mascot was one of the happiest of my life. She was a gift from God. The most beautiful little creature ever born, inside and out. I've never lost a child, but I've lost people I loved. I know the sting never goes away. Anyhoo, your Rhea was a gift from God and all of a sudden here she was, helping Bob Gallinipper feed the world. And feeding the world is a wonderful thing, Calvin. And God is a wonderful God. Gave us big wonderful hearts. Gave us big wonderful brains to discover new and better ways of feeding the world. Jesus could just point at those few measly loaves and fishes with his holy fingers, and presto! There's enough there to feed the multitudes. We mortals got a tougher row to hoe. No divine abracadabra for us. But God gave us something just as magical. He gave us biotechnology.

"Take those 7-52 Super Hens of yours. Years of work went into those babies. All the other egg men said to me, 'Bob, you'll never design a hen that can lay the same number of eggs on half the feed. But Bob Gallinipper did it. Then they said, 'Bob, you'll never design a hen with a uterus strong enough to lay two eggs every three days.' But Bob Gallinipper did it. And when they heard about my idea to design a hen that could lay seven eggs a week, fifty-two weeks a year, they laughed their behinds off. Look who's laughing now. Bob Gallinipper and the Cassowarys.

"And look what we've done with the eggs themselves! Developed eggs low in cholesterol—not that cholesterol's bad for you—but people said they wanted them, and now they got them. Developed eggs that help with brain cell growth and blood clotting and digestion. Not a peep about this to anyone, but the wizkids in EggGenics are less than a year away from an estrogen-enriched egg for women going through the change. In five years we'll have a birth control egg.

"God shares his secrets. First the Bible, now genetics. So tell me—how much do you folks know about cloning?"

On his way to the cemetery, Calvin stops at the Pile Inn. It's nearly midnight and the place is empty except for a pair of sheriff's deputies at the far end of the counter. They recognize him and wave with their pie forks. He waves back with his coffee cup. He sips his way through three refills, then drives out South Mill. It's the fourth week of October and it's been raining on and off all day and every thermometer in the county has been clogged at forty for a week now.

Calvin doesn't pull directly into the cemetery. Too dangerous. Instead he drives another block and crunches into the gravel parking lot of St. Peregrine's Catholic Church, pulling right up to the rectory, parking right alongside the priests' dark blue Chevrolets. He closes the car door gently and sticks the garden trowel in his back pocket.

It's a big cemetery, but Calvin knows where he's going. He heads straight for the granite Union soldier and then weaves through the gravestones to the oak-covered knoll above the lily pond where Jeanie and Rhea Cassowary are buried. It's spooky being here at night.

Rhea's stone is right next to Jeanie's. It isn't a real big stone, just big enough for her name and a single soaring dove. How big does a stone have to be for an urn of feathers, after all? Like Jeanie's stone, and the other Cassowary stones, it is nestled in a bed of wild strawberry plants. Little white picket fences prevent the berry plants from being mowed over by the cemetery care-takers.

Calvin kneels at his daughter's grave. Rhea would have been twenty by now. Had she lived. And Jeanie? Had she lived. Forty-three? No, this is October already. She would be forty-four.

"Why did you drink all that coffee?" he whispers at himself. It's tough enough doing what he has to do without having to hold his urine. A man gets in his mid-forties and that prostate starts to swell and he just doesn't have the same control he once had. In college, he could drink 3.2 beer until two in the morning and wouldn't have to piss until he got back to his apartment. Now liquids just whistle through his bladder like the wind through these bare-naked oaks.

Calvin starts to dig. He skims off the grass and sod in wide strips and stacks them neatly to one side. When he's finished, he'll stomp the strips back into place.

Beneath the grass and sod he finds hard, gritty clay. It makes him cry. Rhea's death is still so hard to understand and there are still so many unsettled questions. Who ever heard of coyotes eating a human being? It just doesn't happen.

Yet it happened.

No one wanted to believe it at first. Maybe Rhea had escaped. But this is Wyssock County, not the goddamned Yukon. Rhea never showed up at anybody's house. Searchers never found her cowering high in a tree. Never found her at all. Not dead. Not alive. Just some feathers and a little blood and strewn clothing.

Sheriff Skip Affenpinscher was skeptical from the start, figuring Rhea was kidnapped by someone trying to get their hands on the Cassowary egg fortune. That blood and those feathers and those chewed up overalls were just a ruse until the kidnappers got far away. But kidnappers never called or sent a ransom note, and when he learned there was no egg fortune, only a huge egg debt, the sheriff changed theories and tried to get Calvin and Donna to confess to staging Rhea's disappearance themselves, as part of some sick money-making scheme.

"How could you think we'd do that?" Calvin asked, throwing his coffee cup against the kitchen wall.

"Number one, you're broke," answered the sheriff. "Number two, you've already demonstrated how desperate for money you are—carting her from county fair to county fair like she was a prize bull."

Sheriff Skip Affenpinscher wasn't the only one with theories. One evening after work, Joon Faldstool shuffled nervously across the porch and through the screen door and suggested that maybe Rhea had faked her own death and run away. "I don't think she was very happy about making those commercials," he said.

But Calvin assured him that Rhea was very happy making those commercials. "I know you were friends, Joon. But there's blood and feathers and Rhea's not coming back."

The trowel clunks the top of the urn. Calvin digs around it carefully, as if the urn was Rhea herself, a gentle treasure waiting to be resurrected.

The digging not only fills him with memories of Rhea—newborn baby Rhea, toddler Rhea, gangly Rhea, graceful Rhea, Rhea with feathers, Rhea without feathers, angry obstinate Rhea, sad brooding Rhea, sweet laughing Rhea—but also Biscuit. The old sheltie died just five weeks after Rhea's memorial service. Calvin found him in his house by the garage, faded dog nose poking out the rounded door. He figured he was just sleeping. But when he called his name—"Bisky! Bisky!"—Biscuit's ears didn't fly up, his brown eyes didn't explode with love. He buried Biscuit by the ceramic birdbath, inside the circle of marigolds. Donna watched from the kitchen window, allergic as she was to dog hair and marigolds. But Calvin could see that she, too, was crying.

Calvin lifts the urn from the hole. He takes the empty Ziploc bag from his pocket and opens it. He opens the urn and, one by one, transfers Rhea's feathers.

Calvin Cassowary is not a religious man. He hates church. Hates the hard benches. Hates having to sing all five verses of those impossible hymns. Hates the icky-picky Rube Goldberg rules for achieving salvation. But he believes in God. Believes that the souls of sweet children like his Rhea are rewarded with eternal happiness.

So Rhea is with God, and with Jeanie, and while that's all to the good, all Calvin has are his memories and this plastic bag of feathers. He cries all the way back to his car and all the way back to the farm. When he pulls in shortly before two, the gravel under his tires explodes like cherry bombs. Digging up Rhea's feathers after all these years is a bad and dangerous thing. But it still doesn't mean he's going along with the cloning thing.

The egg business started turning around about a year after Rhea's death. Weekly per capita consumption of eggs went up one entire egg. Retail prices rebounded and the bean counters at Gallinipper's found another penny per dozen to pay producers. And those 7-52 Super Hens!

The farm's finances got so much better, so fast, that Calvin, despite his resistance to divine interference, could not help feel that maybe Rhea's death was a family sacrifice of sorts. Dying for the farm the way Jesus died for our sins. A ridiculous notion, of course. But you can't stop notions like that from popping into your head when you're so full of guilt.

Adding to the spookiness was the way the lawsuit brought by the Maple Creek Homeowners' Association ended. The jury found in Calvin's favor, just as attorney Michael Rood III said it would. The jury foreman, Doug Chervil of D&D Tractor Sales, later told Sam Guss of the *Gazette* that "havin' a smelly farm ain't no crime."

The homeowners' association responded to the verdict by installing a ten-foot-high brick privacy fence. From the Cassowary farm it looked like the Great Wall of China. When Norman Marek first saw the fence he doubled over and laughed into his knees. "The stink'll pour over that fence like water over Niagara Falls," he said.

The lawsuit did get the attention of the Ohio Environmental Protection Administration and a van-load of biologists drove up from Columbus and took water samples from Three Fish Creek. They checked nearby wells and ponds and took soil samples, too.

"Let them test," Norman Marek said. "By the time they prove you've killed any little fishies, we'll be processing every squirt of poop your hens produce into livestock feed. I've heard through the grapevine that our Manure Management gnomes are just that far away from announcing a breakthrough." His thumb and forefinger were just a quarter-inch away when he said that.

Calvin Cassowary not only rebuilt his flock to a million hens, but with new loans, expanded it to a million-three.

The flight to Chicago seems to last forever, even though it only takes an hour. Calvin and Donna are a million miles away from each other, even though their shoulders are touching. The Ziploc bag of feathers is safely stored in the breast pocket of Calvin's sports jacket, making him look like he's got one breast.

The egg-yolk yellow limo again takes them to Gallinipper Foods and the emaciated woman again takes them up to Bob Gallinipper's office. Bob hugs them and leads them over the skyway to EggGenics. When they reach the windowless stainless steel door, Bob pulls an electronic card from his shirt pocket. "Even I need one of these to get inside," he says. He inserts the card in a slot that for all the world looks like the menacing mouth of a snake.

EggGenics is cleaner than a hospital. White floors. White wall tile. People in white scrubs and white tennis shoes, identification cards clipped to their collars.

In a small office with a stainless steel desk, Bob Gallinipper introduces them to Special Projects Director Sophia Theophaneia. Her curly Greek hair, despite the many barrettes, goes just everywhere. Under her lab coat she wears a EuroDisney tee shirt.

"Are those the *you-know-whats* in your coat there?" Sophia Theophancia asks, pointing at the bulge over Calvin's heart.

Calvin hands her the bag of feathers.

Sophia puts the bag in a plastic picnic cooler. Then she says this:

"Any day now the Roslin Institute in Edinburgh is going to announce to the world that they've successfully cloned a sheep. Half the world is going to pat them on the back and the other half is going to whine about them playing God. Truth is, we've been successfully cloning hens right here in this building for twenty-two months. So we can do this thing."

She lets those last five words of hers soak in. Then after an appreciative wink from Bob Gallinipper, she continues: "There is nothing illegal about human cloning. Nothing inherently unethical about it either. I consider myself a religious person. I see it as just another reproductive option, like adoption or artificial insemination. Children no different than other children except they have the exact superimposed physical image of the donor. *Imago dei* as we embryologists like to say. It's your decision to proceed, of course. But I want you to know that as a Christian and a woman and a scientist, I'm comfortable with it."

Calvin's eyes are glued on the picnic cooler. "We're comfortable with it, too, philosophically, but whether it's something we're actually going to do—"

Sophia is nodding. "It's a huge decision. One you won't have to make for some time yet. We'll have to successfully remove Rhea's DNA from the feathers first. Then see if we can activate it, so all the genetic codes are functioning, just as they would be in an egg cell. Then, Donna, we'll take some of your unfertilized eggs and remove the nuclei, where your genetic codes are kept. Then we'll implant Rhea's DNA in your eggs. If and when we get a healthy embryo, we'll attach it to the wall of your uterus. And pray for a successful pregnancy."

Bob Gallinipper claps his hands, startling everybody. "And bingo! Our new little Rhea!"

Sophia tugs nervously on her curly, everywhere hair, wishing the man who signs her paycheck hadn't said that. "Not really Rhea, of course, we all understand that. But, yes, an exact genetic copy of her. Your new baby would be a separate and unique individual. This isn't a resurrection."

Bob Gallinipper doesn't appreciate the religious reference. "They understand that," he growls.

Sophia Theophaneia didn't get to be Special Projects director by not understanding the corporate ladder as much as she understands those spiral staircases of life called the double helix. "We embryologists like to babble on," she says softly.

Donna sympathetically waves off her apology. "Cal and I haven't been able to have a baby. So this could be a godsend for us. Rhea was special and saw the world in a special way. Maybe we can have another special child."

"It could take many tries," Sophia cautions.

"We understand that," Donna says.

"So the first thing," says Sophia, studying Calvin's uncertain eyes, "is to get to work on these feathers. See if we can extract some good DNA. It could take months. Then we can proceed. If that's what you both finally decide."

Bob Gallinipper claps his hands again "I can almost feel that new little ball of feathers bouncing on my knee."

Thirty-three

BOB GALLINIPPER WALKS the Cassowarys back across the skyway, his arms tucked in their arms. "I'll call you the minute Sophia has something to report," he tells them when they reach the elevator. "It'll be good news, too. I can feel that in my ol' Indiana bones."

After the elevator door closes he pulls out his hanky and blows his nose, the *honk* echoing down the empty corridor. He does not want to go back to his office, not now, not after this. He wants to jump in his car and drive like a bat out of hell to that cemetery where his granddad is buried, just below that line of wonderful old hickory trees. He wants to sit by his granddad's granite gravestone, and run his hands through the wild strawberry leaves, the way he used to run his hands through the old man's bushy white beard when he was a kid. He wants to say, "Gramps, I'm doing something good for somebody again."

That's what he wants to do. But he has to go back to his office. He has three more meetings before lunch. Two meetings during lunch. Who knows how many meetings after lunch.

It's tough being The Rooster. Sure you get the perks of office—perching where you want, shitting where you want, riding the backs of all the hens you want—but you've also got The Responsibility. You've got to be the first one up every morning and crow like there's no tomorrow, even if your throat's sore. You've got to puff up and strut even though you're as frightened as everybody else. And it's always your carcass on the dining room table. Take, eat: this is Bob Gallinipper's body.

Bob Gallinipper was born in Pennibone, Indiana, at the height of the Great Depression. He was too young to truly understand how bad things were. But his father and mother were old enough to know how bad things were and they made sure he suffered right along with them. He grew up understanding that life was about working hard and going without, even if you didn't have to.

They had a farm right where the Wabash River swung south to begin its long fall to the Ohio. It was a good spot for a farm. Indianapolis to the east, Chicago to the north, two big cities where people had to eat food grown by somebody else. After World War II, his father saw the factories in these big cities sucking up even more people. The 1950s were coming. The suburbs were swelling. "Eggs," his father said one night at supper when young Bob was gnawing on a porkchop. "We're going to specialize in eggs."

And so the Gallinippers gave up cows and corn and built a long layer house and filled it with four thousand chickens. Bob learned all about gathering and candling eggs. Learned how to keep shoveling chicken manure when the ammonia was so thick he could barely breathe. By the time he was ready for college, they had three layer houses, each one bigger than the next, twenty thousand hens in all.

Bob Gallinipper wanted to go away to college. Wanted to major in architecture and be the next Frank Lloyd Wright. But Purdue University was just twenty-four miles up the road and it had a damn good agriculture department. So it was Purdue during the day, eggs at night. Even now he wonders how he ever found time to romance Bunny Yeddo. But where there's a will there's a way, and he sure had the will to romance pretty Bunny.

He hated the classes on animal husbandry and farm management. But those marketing classes—now that was fascinating stuff. Especially that one lecture by adjunct professor Edna Mills, about *middle men*, those logistical magicians who wore white shirts and neckties every day of the week, who knew how to make money in agriculture without ever going near the ass-end of a chicken.

He graduated the same year Dwight D. Eisenhower became president, 1953. Got married that year, too. "Daddy," he said the very afternoon he and Bunny returned from their honeymoon on Mackinac Island, "we'll never get anywhere selling our own eggs. We've got to start selling other people's eggs."

"Is that why I sent you to college?" his father asked.

"Daddy, that's exactly why you sent me to college."

By the time John F. Kennedy was taking the oath of office in January 1961, the Gallinippers had eleven farmers in their pockets and the eggs from 322,000 hens in their white and yellow cartons. Printed across the top of those cartons was this:

GALLINIPPER FARMS COUNTRY FRESH EGGS
We gather—You'll like them!

Bob thought up that final line himself. It helped them wrangle 38 percent of the egg market in Indianapolis, 53 percent of the egg market in Terre Haute, and 7.6 percent in metropolitan Chicago, the toughest damn egg market to crack in the Middle West.

So Bob Gallinipper today has forty years experience with little roosters like Calvin Cassowary. And he genuinely does admire Calvin's grit. Calvin was willing to risk the family farm, just as he'd risked his family's farm. He was willing to think big. Willing to submit to The Rooster.

Unfortunately, Calvin Cassowary also had a tendency to backslide into independent thinking from time to time, no better example than his carting poor little Rhea around to those county fairs. But God was looking down, and those bunny huggers from Animals Are People, Too, who'd been a burr in the poultry industry's saddle for years, finally bit off more than they could chew, and tumbled headfirst, with a little push from Bob Gallinipper, into the old poop pit of public opinion.

Deciding what to do with Calvin Cassowary was another bowl of peas. He prayed about it: "Lord, I ought to give that idiot the boot considering all the hoo-hah he's stirred up. I should just wash my hands of him, invoke that Good Citizens Clause in his contract. But, Lord, I know he was just trying to take care of his family. Same way I take care of mine and you take care of yours."

The Almighty responded, as He always did when the going got tough, filling his head with uncomplicated Indiana wisdom: when you're handed lemons you find some way to make a silk purse out of a sow's ear. So Bob Gallinipper made Rhea the company mascot. He put together the biggest advertising blitz in the company's history. Print ads. TV and radio spots. Public appearances. Then Rhea wandered into the woods and was eaten by coyotes. The Devil's doing, no doubt.

Despite the feathers and the blood, Calvin had refused to accept his daughter's death. Three weeks after the search teams disbanded, he was still walking the woods and fields screaming her name. According to Norman Marek, he screamed Rhea's name all through the memorial service.

Calvin finally accepted Rhea's death. Yes, he still spent several hours a day wandering the woods and fields, but instead of screaming her name, he reached deep into the holes of animals, hoping to find her bones, or a few scraps of her flesh, something he could bury. He got nothing for the effort but a skunk bite that required a tetanus shot. On the first anniversary of Rhea's death, Calvin and Donna buried an urn containing the feathers found by Sheriff Affenpinscher's deputies. Norman said that Calvin hugged Jeanie's gravestone and bawled like a baby.

Bob had wanted to go to Rhea's funeral, just as he had wanted to go to Jeanie's funeral, and the funerals of so many people he was either related to or responsible for. He even put the corporate jet on standby. But he just couldn't make himself go. Just as he couldn't make himself go to his granddad's funeral all those years ago. How do others do it? Stand over that box and look down at someone who just hours before was as alive as a butterfly?

So he did what he could do. He filled another clay pot with wild strawberries from his granddad's grave and had Norman deliver it. Over the years he must have done that two hundred times, feeling guilty as hell, hating himself for being so weak.

He was seven when his granddad drowned himself. The happy old man rowed his little fishing boat to the middle of the pond behind the cow barn, tied three cement blocks around his cancer-infested belly and jumped in. Two days before Easter.

Every June Bob and his granddad used to wander across the fields looking for wild strawberries. That June he had to go picking by himself. He cried the whole time but felt better afterwards. The next spring he dug up some of those strawberry plants and walked to the cemetery by himself, mile and a half, and planted them around his granddad's grave. Sending Calvin Cassowary a second pot of strawberries was just about the toughest thing he ever had to do in his life.

But it helped matters. And that's all that mattered.

Little by little, Calvin Cassowary recovered and went to work building one of the best egg operations in the Gallinipper family. According to Norman, Calvin and Donna also were trying to rebuild their family, trying like the devil to have a child of their own.

Then just a year ago when he and Bunny were in San Francisco to attend the high school graduation of their daughter Robin's oldest boy, Robbie, they wandered into a Border's bookstore, and there on the front table was C.W. Weed's best-selling book, *Of Course We Should: Making the Case For Human Cloning*. He stayed up all night reading and rereading. First thing the next morning he was on the horn to Sophia Theophaneia in Chicago.

Thirty-four

CALVIN CASSOWARY HAS already swatted about twenty flies this morning and he's yet to do the upstairs. He's got the swatter in one hand and a dustpan in the other. The flies are docile these first days of spring and you can walk right up to them and flatten them dead and let their black-jam carcasses bounce into the dustpan.

It's easy ridding the inside of flies. Outside it's impossible. The layer houses breed flies by the zillions. You can spray and hang fly strips every two feet but the flies keep coming. They swirl in swarms and escape through the roof vents like tracer bullets. They infest the garage and the tractor shed and use the flat top of the picnic table like an aircraft carrier. They venture far and wide across the manure-sodden fields, lingering on the muddy banks of Three Fish Creek and then buzz up the long slope toward Maple Creek Estates. They rest on the ten-foot privacy fence, then invade.

Calvin empties the dustpan and goes upstairs. Donna is still sleeping so he goes to Rhea's room first. The room isn't much different than it was the night Rhea disappeared. Her clothes are gone from the closet and the New Kids on the Block Posters aren't thumbtacked to the walls anymore, but her books and dolls and games are still on the shelves and the same tulips-and-daffodils comforter is on the bed. He goes for the flies on the window. There have to be a dozen of them.

Two years ago, the Maple Creek Homeowner's Association filed a new lawsuit over the flies. The jury was bused out to Maple Creek to see just how bad the infestation was. And it was bad. But Michael Rood III did a couple of clever things. First he called all the officers of the homeowners' association as witnesses and one by one asked them if they ever ate eggs. Every one of them admitted they did. Then he offered them a deal: Would they enter into a binding contract with Mr. Cassowary, promising never to eat eggs again? In exchange Mr. Cassowary would personally come to their homes every day, twice a day, and swat their flies.

It was silly idea, of course. A sarcastic idea. And of course not one officer of the Maple Creek Homeowners' Association bit. Then Michael Rood III said, "Then perhaps you can swat the flies yourself, and leave Mr. Cassowary to his enterprise, producing the eggs you can't live without."

The jury once again found in Calvin's favor. Then Michael Rood III did an astonishing thing. He called a press conference on the courthouse steps and announced that his client, although just exonerated, was a good and caring neighbor and a man of science always looking for ways to improve his operation. "Here's what Mr. Cassowary is going to do," he announced, taking his huge briar pipe from his seersucker sportscoat and rubbing it like a magic lamp. "At his own expense he's going to introduce *tenebrionids* to his manure pits." He lit his pipe and shook the match while reporters tried to spell the word in their heads. He chuckled. "In everyday language they're called darkling beetles. Cute little beetles that like dark stinky places. The beetles will eat the fly larvae and everybody will be happy. You see folks, people can get along just fine if they just trust one another and cooperate."

The darkling beetles arrived by UPS, and Calvin and Jimmy Faldstool sprinkled them into the manure pits. A month later the people living in the big houses in Maple Creek Estates not only had flies everywhere, but darkling beetles everywhere, crawling in their dresser drawers and kitchen cupboards, burrowing into their mattresses and sofa cushions, marching right across their breakfast plates, their twitchy little legs getting stuck in the egg yolk. The Maple Creek Homeowners' Association filed a $30 million lawsuit, now pending.

Junior Jr. dives from the perch and spears the darkling beetle ascending through the crack in the floor. He crunches and swallows. He puffs his breast and *brucks* victoriously.

Unfortunately, there are almost no other chickens left in the coop to admire—or envy—his performance. Over the years, disease and old age have taken a heavy toll on the flock. Today, there are just his brother George Herbert Walker Bush, at this moment cowering behind the water crock, and his bony sister Leili. Their mother was a mixed breed named Mary Mary Bo Berry. Their father was the terrifying Mr. Shakyshiver. They hatched just five months before the Feather Girl disappeared, in chicken terms a lifetime ago.

Yet as long ago as that was, Junior Jr. still remembers the Feather Girl coming into the coop at night to read to them from the little book she spread across her lap. He didn't understand a word she was reading. But he still remembers the soft and patient sounds that tumbled from her beakless face. He remembers this one collection of sounds in particular:

> *"By pain and grief the pilgrim is perplexed*
> *But struggles on through this world and the next—*
> *And if the goal seems endlessly concealed,*
> *Do not give up your quest; refuse to yield."*

The man named Calvin still comes and feeds them, and pours them a crock of clean water. But he won't let poor old Leili set. So it finally looks like the end of the line—the line that goes way back to that lusty Cuban with the black tail feathers, Maximo Gomez.

But Junior Jr. isn't complaining. He is The Rooster. He has a hen to ride and a brother to torment. He has a wire fence that keeps coyotes out and rotting floor boards that let plenty of those delicious darkling beetles in.

Calvin finishes with his morning fly-swatting and starts with his morning beetle-bagging. It's a gruesome process. He understands why Donna wants no part of it. You've got to snatch the little buggers between your thumb and forefinger—which is anything but easy—and then flick them in a plastic bag. Every morning you can catch about thirty or forty of them. Then you lay the bag on the porch and go at the beetles with a rubber mallet.

Calvin has nine beetles in his bag and a tenth wiggling under his thumb when the kitchen phone rings. "Hello?"

"Good news," Sophia Theophaneia says. "We've successfully removed DNA from Rhea's feathers."

"So soon?"

Sophia laughs a little. "It's been six months, Mr. Cassowary."

"I guess it has—so it's all gone well?"

"We were thrown for a loop once or twice," she admits. "Some of the feathers you brought us were real chicken feathers."

"What do you mean real chicken feathers?"

Sophia apologizes. "I didn't mean to say Rhea's feathers were fake chicken feathers. They're human feathers, aren't they? But there were chicken feathers in the bag you gave us. Somehow they got mixed in with Rhea's. When that chicken DNA showed up on our computer screens—*Whoa!*"

The apology does nothing to assuage Calvin's anxiety. "I took the feathers right from Rhea's cemetery urn. They're the same feathers the sheriff's deputies found."

"It's a mystery, to be sure," Sophia says. "But one we don't have to solve. The important thing is that we've successfully isolated and activated Rhea's DNA. All we need now are Donna's fresh eggs—and a decision to proceed, of course."

After the call, Calvin goes straight upstairs to the shower. He is quivering. His breaths are a half-inch long. He hops out of his jeans and underwear. He twists the knobs until the spray is the exact same temperature of a mother's womb. He sits on the shower floor and pulls his knees up to his chin.

Donna, surprisingly, has been for the cloning from the start. "It's a way for us to have a child," she whispered as they flew home from their first meeting in Chicago with Bob Gallinipper, "to put an end to all this frustration, this rift between us."

"There's no rift," Calvin whispered back.

Donna tore a wad of Kleenexes from the box in her lap. "You know damn well there's a rift. The Jeanie rift. The rift that kept me from being a good mother to Rhea because I wasn't her real mother. The rift that keeps me from being a real wife because I

232

can't give you the heir this farm demands. Now I can be a real mother and a real wife."

"But aren't there some bigger questions here?" Calvin asked.

That's when Donna's sinuses dried up the way they did during sex. "We can't afford to think about the bigger questions, Calvin. This farm is a financial house of cards. The second the economy goes bad or some new cholesterol study comes out, *pbbbbbt!*"

Calvin had always admired Donna's cool, accountant's view of life—focusing instantly and unambiguously on the bottom line—but at that moment he wanted to stuff Donna's *pbbbbbting* tongue right down her throat. "I am not going to recreate Rhea just to save the farm."

That's when Donna really let go with the psychological ice cubes. "Isn't that why you and Jeanie created her the first time?"

Calvin's whisper took on the intensity of a scream. "I can't believe you said that."

Donna answered calmly, and firmly, proving once again she was the adult in the marriage. "I'm not saying you and Jeanie didn't love her. Of course you loved her. She was a living expression of your great and wonderful love for each other. I understand that. I accept that. But don't tell me you weren't relieved to meet your ancestral obligation."

Calvin's brain was frozen on her *great and wonderful love* comment. "I love you as much as I—"

"I know—I know. You love me and I love you and Bob Gallinipper loves us to pieces."

"He's a good man."

"He's a businessman who lost his golden egg."

"So Bob and I are just a couple of cold capitalist bastards?"

"Get off your high horse," Donna said, peeling back her fingers one by one. "No. 1, we need a child for personal, psychological reasons. No. 2, the farm needs an heir. No. 3, Bob Gallinipper wants his mascot back so he can sell more of our eggs. In sum, this cloning thing isn't some filthy crime against God and nature. It's a good thing that makes everybody rich in every way."

The spray from the shower head pours over Calvin like rain over a toad, clogging his eyes, forming little puddles in the hollow of his ears. He has to decide—one way or the other. He wants another child. But this cloning thing is such a sick and dangerous thing. And it wouldn't be Rhea. It would just look like Rhea, a completely new child in Rhea's image. *Imago dei.* If only Donna could conceive on her own. The pressure would be off, Bob Gallinipper's offer not so damn tempting. What if they go ahead with this and God doesn't approve? Will he make the Cassowarys pay for a hundred generations? Still, when God wanted a son of his own He intervened with nature, didn't he? So maybe God does approve. Maybe there are some bigger issues here. Galactic issues that humans simply can't fathom. Maybe God wanted Rhea to have feathers. Maybe He wanted all humans to have feathers, to survive some strange and dangerous future not yet revealed. Then those coyotes spoiled it for everybody.

And so when Donna crawls out of bed, sniffing the salty phlegm from her throat, asking him what he's doing sitting on the shower floor, wasting all the hot water, Calvin looks up and says: "If you want to do it, it's all right with me."

After the eight slowest days in human history drag by, they are on the corporate jet to Chicago, and the stainless steel, lab-coated world of Special Projects Director Sophia Theophaneia.

There are contracts to sign. Secret contracts that can never see the light of day. One contract absolves Bob Gallinipper of any and all personal responsibility. Another absolves Gallinipper Foods of any and all corporate responsibility. Another prohibits any officer or employee of Gallinipper Foods from divulging the truth about Donna's pregnancy and the subsequent birth—should there be a pregnancy and subsequent birth.

Three days later Sophia Theophaneia gathers Donna's eggs and places them in laboratory dishes. The center of the cells, the nuclei, where Donna's own genetic codes are kept, are removed, and replaced with the genetic material rescued from Rhea's feathers.

Calvin and Donna take the egg yolk-yellow limo into Chicago and have pizza at Uno's, slow dance to jazz at the Moosehead Bar & Grille, try to forget they are waiting for important news. Back at the hotel they start to make love. But they can hear the TVs in the adjoining rooms. And if they can hear the TVs, then the people in those rooms surely can hear them huffing and puffing. So they watch TV, too.

During the night Calvin has a dream. He is in one of his layer houses trying to glue a broken egg back together. It is the last egg he has, and he needs it to complete a dozen. Norman Marek is standing next to him with the open carton, growling at him to hurry. The walls of the layer house suddenly dissolve and he sees Jeanie in the field below. She is twirling like Julie Andrews in *The Sound of Music*. Calvin hands the gooey, glue-dripping egg to Norman and rushes to her. But when she sees him coming, she begins to giggle and run toward the creek. He pursues her through the broken cornstalks. The hard ground turns to mud, the mud into manure. Calvin has had this dream so many times before that even in his sleep he knows what it means.

The next dream is a new dream. Even in his sleep, where anything can happen, it catches him by surprise. Donna is atop the picnic table, on her back, screaming, writhing, sneezing, trying to give birth. Norman Marek is telling him to remain calm, that Bob Gallinipper will be there any minute to deliver the baby. Sophia Theophaneia is there, but she is completely disinterested in Donna's plight, playing Frisbee with Biscuit instead. Then there is a great gush of water between Donna's legs. A monstrous egg slowly slides from her vagina. Calvin catches it. The shell crumbles in his hands. Squirming in the yolky goo is a creature half human, half Leghorn. It has huge unblinking eyes on the sides of its narrow face. Instead of a nose it has a beak. It has tiny human hands and ugly rooster's feet. Both fingers and talons are wriggling. It is covered with feathers. Bob Gallinipper is suddenly there, taking the creature from his hands, lifting it skyward, the way Kunta Kinte lifted Kizzy. When Sophia Theophaneia looks up and sees the wriggling creature, she shrugs and giggles impishly and says, "Whoops!"

That *Whoops!* slaps Calvin awake. He spends the rest of the night in a chair by the window, watching the sparse traffic on the interstate.

"Folks," Sophia tells them in a 5 a.m. phone call, "we've got oodles of healthy embryos."

And so one of them is implanted in Donna's uterus and, to everyone's delight, it keeps right on growing. Success the very first try. A triumph for science. Proof, perhaps, that God does indeed approve, that nightmares are only that.

They keep their secret all summer. On Labor Day, they have a picnic. Ben and Betsy Betz drive up from Columbus. Donna's parents drive all the way from their retirement condo in North Carolina. Jimmy Faldstool and his wife are invited, Norman Marek, too. Everyone fills up on hamburgers and sweet corn, and when everyone is sitting in a circle of lawn chairs spitting watermelon seeds, Calvin announces that he and Donna are going to have a baby.

"And you're announcing it on Labor Day," Donna's mother coos. "How cute is that?"

Early the next morning Joon Faldstool shows up on the porch.

Calvin, still in his bathrobe, is surprised to see him. He forces the worried frown that's been on his face for several months now into a welcoming smile. "Joon! How are you?"

Joon had quit his job at the Cassowary farm three years ago, to move down to his grandfather Hap Aspergres's place in Acorn County. He's taken over the dowsing business, finding new wells all over southern Ohio. Northern Kentucky, too. "I was visiting dad—figured I'd stop at the house and see how you and Mrs. Cassowary are doing."

"We're doing great. Your dad tell you that Donna's pregnant?"

"Yeah. Terrific news, huh?"

"You bet," says Calvin.

When Joon's cheek muscles start to twitch, Calvin knows he has something on his mind. Like father like son. "So, what can I do for you, Joon?"

"Those three old chickens of Rhea's you've still got? I was wondering if I could I have them. For my Grampa Hap's place."

Calvin Cassowary doesn't answer right away. He just stares at the little red coop. His memory sees Rhea inside the yard in her baggy sweatshirts and overalls, sun reflecting off her feathery face, tossing handfuls of cracked corn.

Then he grins. In just a few months his eyes will see Rhea, too. "You know what, Joon," he says, "I think Rhea would want you to have them."

Calvin wants to tell Joon about the new Rhea growing in Donna's uterus. But he can't tell anybody. And he never will tell anybody. Even if he wasn't under contract he wouldn't tell. He and Donna are going to keep their lips buttoned and when they have that baby girl and when people tell them how she looks just like Rhea, they'll scrunch their faces and ask, "You really think so?" And if the cloned Rhea starts growing feathers the way the original Rhea did, then no one will be able to see the similarity anyway. "I know you were just a boy when Rhea died," Calvin says to Joon. "But I know you had feelings for her. And I suppose she had—"

"We were in love."

Calvin finds himself pulling Joon Faldstool into his arms, kissing him square on the forehead.

Junior Jr. doesn't remember Joon Faldstool. George Herbert Walker Bush and Leili don't either. And they have never liked Calvin Cassowary much. So they resist being caught and caged and even after they are in the back of Joon's pickup they are *bruck-brucking*, their neck feathers flayed defiantly.

"You got time to see the new MAK carts?" Calvin asks Joon. "They're really something."

"MAKs?" Joon asks.

Calvin walks him to layer house F. He explains: "Modified

atmosphere killing. New way to dispose of our spent hens. Very economical."

Inside the layer house there's a guy about Joon's age, filthy jeans, backward baseball cap, high-school-dropout face. He's pushing a huge aluminum box along on its dolly wheels. "That's one of the MAKs," Calvin says.

Joon watches as the guy with the dropout face pulls a pleading hen from its cage and stuffs it in the top of the aluminum box. He pulls and stuffs until the cage is empty. Goes on to the next cage.

"As you know," Calvin says, "we used to ship our spent hens to soup and pet food plants. But that market's disappearing. Too many chickens being bred just for meat today. So now *rendering!*"

Joon watches how quickly the pleading hens disappear into the metal box, into that MAK. "Rendering into what?"

"Poultry rations."

"Food for other chickens?"

"Feathers and all. Extruded into high protein SHM. Spent hen meal. But the rendering plants don't want to mess with live hens. So—see that cylinder on the side of the box there? CO_2."

"So it's a little gas chamber?"

"They expire pretty quick," Calvin says.

They leave the layer house. Joon's eyes are burning. He'd forgotten how bad the air was in these buildings. They walk to Joon's pickup and shake hands. The three chickens in the back are confused but calm, good clean air circulating through the bars of their wooden cage.

Joon backs around and crackles down the driveway. He used to think shoveling manure was the worst job in the world. But that poor bastard pushing that MAK, he thinks, now that guy's got the worst job in the world.

Thirty-five

Joon Faldstool crosses the Chippewa Creek bridge and slides onto Bear Swamp Road. An endless cloud of dust follows the pickup. Ahead of him Grampa Hap's silver trailer glimmers like a UFO. Those three chickens in the back are really going to surprise Rhea.

He bounces past the house he's building for her. The outside is nearly completed—shingles on the roof and vinyl siding on the walls, windows and doors. The inside is another matter. No drywall, no plumbing, no nothing.

Joon reaches Hap's trailer and beeps. Rhea doesn't run out. So he takes the cage from the back of his truck and slips it under the trailer, to give the three chickens a bit of shade. "Rhea! Grampa Hap!"

Inside the trailer there's nobody but a note, stuck to the refrigerator with a Tweety Bird magnet. Says the note in Rhea's quick, scribbly hand:

> *Joooooooon—*
> *Couldn't talk Gramp out of witching Tink's new well.*
> *Soooooooo I went along.*

Joon gets a cold can of Dr. Pepper and heads back to his pickup. The dust on Bear Swamp Road has not even settled yet. He hops onto Route 83 and races south. Turns onto County Road 17 without making a complete stop. Pulls down the sun visor and squints all the way to Tink Shurebyrne's farm. Sees his grandfather's truck in Tink's drive.

Tink is outside his tractor barn, under his old John Deere, grease dribbled across his forehead. Fuzzy country music blares from a portable radio. Without saying hello, or anything else, Tink points Joon toward the hilly pastures east of the cow barn.

Joon nods his thanks and climbs the wooden gate. The pasture is a dangerous place. Bumblebees. Woodchuck holes to twist your

239

ankles. Thick-crusted cow pies that explode up your pantlegs if you step on them.

He knows why Tink wants a new well out here. Tink's daughter has finally found someone to marry—a long-distance trucker who raises Jack Russell terriers—and Tink has given them five acres of land. Just where those five acres will be depends on where the well will be.

Joon doesn't want Grampa Hap to dowse anymore. The old man has been hospitalized with congestive heart failure twice in the last year and he refuses to get the bypass surgery he needs. "I can handle the witching now, Gramps," Joon has told him a thousand times.

"I taught you how to witch so you could replace me after I was dead," his grandfather always growls back. "Which ain't yet."

So Grampa Hap goes on scheduling dowsing dates. And he always finds a good flow.

The first rule of dowsing is to find water where your client wants it found. So Joon figures he'll find Grampa Hap and Rhea fairly close to the road. He climbs the hill and battles his way through a hedgerow of thorny crabapple trees. There, not a hundred yards from him, is Rhea, sitting on a blanket, the brim of her straw hat shadowing her from shoulder to shoulder. Another hundred yards down the slope his grandfather is shuffling along with his Y of willow.

Joon squeezes his fists. He knows just how that willow rod in his grandfather's hands feels. Knows just what the tug of water feels like when you're over a good flow. It feels like you're bottom fishing for catfish and one of those big lunkers swallows your nightcrawler. A jolt that comes up your arms and shakes your spine from the tip of your tailbone to the top of your head.

Grampa Hap took his good time teaching Joon how to divine for water. Lectured him endlessly for three years as they walked the hot fields.

"Everybody thinks it's a bunch of hocus-pocus horse pucky,"

240

Grampa Hap would say. "They say there's water everywhere and all a dowser does is take money from fools. But there ain't water everywhere. Not sweet strong flows there ain't. So let them laugh at you, Joonbug. And when they come running to you, desperate for water, you just smile and take their money."

"Worse than those who say dowsing doesn't work are those who say they know how it works," his grandfather would say. Then he'd go into all the theories: "There's the *psycho-physiological* theory of the great German dowser Carl von Klinckowstroem. There's the magnetic and electrical current theories that got popular about the time Ben Franklin was playing with his kites. There's the mind-reaching theories of the sixteenth century Spanish *Zahoris*, who claimed they could see things hidden in the bowels of the earth—reaching out with their superior minds. It could be all those things, Joonbug. All those things or none of those things. All I know is that it works."

His grandfather would show him how to grasp the forked willow rod, palms up, fingers curled, so that the end of the rod was pointed skyward. "It don't much matter what a divining rod's made of. Some like to cut it from hazel or apple, some from wild cherry or peach. But me, I like a Y of willow, eighteen inches long, half-inch thick, branches angled out about seventy degrees. Gives you a good bob. But it don't matter. Your rod is just your instrument. It's you that finds the water."

They'd dowse for an hour or two, then find some shade. His grandfather would keep talking: "Bible says Moses struck a rock twice with his rod and water just poured out. Oh, Joonbug, it goes way back. The Scythians, the Persians, the Medes, and the Chinese, they all witched for water."

"For thousands of years no one doubted that it worked," he'd tell him. "Then the Christians came along and called it the work of witches and sorcerers. Even though Moses himself could raise his rod and divide the Red Sea! Then if the Christians weren't bad enough, along came the *scientists*, pooh-poohing a proven fact, calling practitioners of the old art charlatans and crooks. But it keeps on working."

Then they'd dowse some more. Rest some more. "Just because something can't be explained, don't mean it ain't true," Hap would say. "Nobody knows why Rhea's got those feathers. But she's got them. There's lots of things that can't be explained. Lost dogs and cats that find their way home, hundreds of miles away. Birds that migrate half way around the world, always ending up in the same tree in the same backyard. And women's intuition—every man alive knows that's true. So why can't a dowser know where there's a good flow of water?"

"Just believe you'll do it," he'd say as they walked the fields, Joon holding the willow rod in front of him. "Just relax and rely on your seventh sense. Divination means knowing something through your hidden senses. It's from the old Latin word *divinus*, don't you know, meaning one who's inspired by the gods."

And the tip of the rod would bow like a bamboo pole with a big catfish on the end. And Grampa Hap would grin and say, "There you go, Joonbug!"

So how can Joon be mad at his grandfather? Yet he worries about him. Doesn't want to lose him. Wants him to live on forever in that old silver trailer.

Joon sneaks across the field and kneels behind Rhea, kissing the back of her neck. "How long has he been at it?"

When Rhea turns, the wide brim of her hat slices across Joon's eyes. "Just half an hour."

"Water yet?"

"Right off the bat. But you know Hap. He wants to give Tink his money's worth."

Joon flops his head in Rhea's lap. Grins up at her. It's been two years since she lost her feathers. Her face is smooth as can be. For a long while after her feathers fell out, her skin was rough and red, like a bad case of pimples. You'd never know she'd had a single feather now.

"I've got a surprise for you," Joon teases as he plays with the soft skin under Rhea's chin.

"Drywall for the house, I hope."

"Better than drywall," he says.

She begs him to tell her but Joon just smiles. He's not about to tell her about the three chickens now. He wants her to see the cage and go running to them and call them by name, Junior Jr. and George Herbert Walker Bush and Leili. It's been six years since she's seen them. They were only chicks. But he knows she'll recognize them. Recognize their walks and the way they peck. Recognize their little souls.

After all these years Rhea and Joon are still amazed that they got away with their crazy plan. They wanted to get people's attention. Instead Rhea got a new life.

After Rhea's blood and feathers were scattered, they drove all night, arriving at Grampa Hap's early in the morning. They decided to sleep outside in the Gremlin until he stirred. It was Grampa Hap who woke them, rapping on the car window. They confessed immediately.

Grampa Hap made them breakfast. Soggy pancakes. Burned bacon. "And you just figured Rhea could live here happily ever after, did you?"

Joon knew his grandfather well enough to be honest with him. "Yeah."

"You know we'll get caught," Grampa Hap said.

Joon still remembers the relief he felt when his grandfather used that word, *we'll*. It meant he was going to let her stay. "I told Rhea about how the old Aspergres farm used to be a stop on the Underground Railroad. How your great-great granddad John once killed a southern slave tracker and buried him under the smoke house."

That made Grampa Hap smile. "I was just thinking about that story, too."

"So it's okay?" Joon asked.

"Under one condition. If we get caught, we get caught. We don't make up a lot of stuff about me not knowing she's only four-teen, or that I'm senile or something. If you're going to take a stand against injustice, then you take it. You don't piss and moan and say you're sorry when the law comes down. When word got around there was a slave tracker buried under the smokehouse, John Aspergres 'fessed up and said he was ready to spend the rest of his life in prison if that's what the law required."

"Did he?" Rhea asked. She'd never heard that part of the story before.

"Not a day. Acorn County was deeply abolitionist. The sheriff just said let sleeping dogs lie. But people in the know did stop buying John's smoked hams."

And so Grampa Hap took Rhea in and no one ever came looking for her. Sheriff's deputies had found her feathers and bloody clothes. She was dead. Joon kept working at the Cassowary farm shoveling chicken manure. He graduated from high school and announced that he was moving downstate to learn the dowsing business. His mother had a fit, but his father said, "Let the crazy boy go."

Joon began his tutelage learning how to dowse for water and how to grow vegetables in a weedy garden. He kept his hands off Rhea until she was eighteen, asking her to marry him the first night they made love, on a blanket on the knob above Grampa Hap's trailer, one evening when the spring frogs were croaking.

Rhea drove a harder bargain. "You want me to marry you, you build me a house first." And so right on the spot where they gave themselves to each other, Joon staked out a foundation and started digging a basement

It was after they started making love that Rhea's feathers began to fall off. Together they wondered if it was the sex, working some biological or psychological or even spiritual magic. "If it is," Rhea said, "then let's screw these feathers off as fast as we can."

Joon readily agreed.

As Joon began to learn the art and science of house building, Rhea took charge of the gardens and the yard, cleaning up Grampa

Hap's junk the best she could. She talked Joon into buying her a dozen Buff Orpingtons and she let them roam free. Occasionally one would get eaten by a fox or a coyote, but the flock survived and grew. Today there are twenty-four hens and three roosters. There are three goats and several cats, some tame and some feral. And because they live on the edge of the swamp, there are raccoons rattling things at night and rabbits so tame they don't bounce an inch when somebody walks by. There are Canada geese and mallard ducks and ghostly blue heron. When Rhea mows the lawn she watches out for the toads and garter snakes.

When Hap finishes, they walk back to Tink's. Tink pays for the witching in cash. They drive back to the swamp. Rhea recognizes the three chickens immediately, just as Joon expected. She calls them by name and sets them free. They immediately join the Buff Orpingtons. The Buff rooster—Joon named him Rooster von Klinckowstroem after the great German dowser—immediately goes after Junior Jr., sensing that he was once The Rooster and needs a readjustment in attitude. Junior Jr. quickly accepts his new station. Then Rooster von Klinckowstroem hops on the back of Leili. It is what roosters do. "I've got another surprise," Joon says as they watch.

Rhea studies his twitching cheeks. "Not a good one, I gather."

"Donna's pregnant," he says.

That night they cuddle on an air mattress on the plywood floor of their unfinished house. "Maybe now's the time to go see your dad," Joon says.

Rhea is not upset with him. He's tried to talk her into seeing her father a thousand times. "The baby means he's finally accepted my death," she says. "Why upset the applecart?"

Thirty-six

RHEA CASSOWARY'S BROWN egg business is up to thirty dozen a week—thirty-one when Louise Hoyle's arthritis takes a vacation and she can bake her famous poppyseed kuchens.

Joon and Grampa Hap still marvel at how many dozens Rhea sells. After all, Bear Swamp Road dead-ends into a swamp and anybody who wants eggs from Rhea's free-roaming flock has to go way out of their way. "It's the swamp bugs and the worms," Rhea tells her customers when they rave about the big brown eggs. "The windblown seeds. The freedom."

There are about a hundred chickens in the flock now. From April to November the chickens roost wherever they like—in trees, on top of the trucks, on the arms of Hap's many broken lawn chairs. In the winter they huddle inside the low-roofed coop Joon bought from Bud Miller. Joon had to take it apart, board by board, and then reassemble it.

Yes, the brown eggs are good. And getting better. Bigger and richer. Grampa Hap thinks it's the new genes being introduced into the flock by George Herbert Walker Bush. He's The Rooster now. Rooster von Klinckowstroem died trying to swallow a wasp and Junior Jr. died trying to mount one of the feral cats. That freed the way for George Herbert Walker Bush, whose ancestry goes all the way back to Maximo Gomez, the Black Spanish cockerel rescued from a Cuban brothel by Chuck Cowrie, during the Spanish-American War.

This warm May morning Rhea is trying to get the lawnmower started. Joon bought it last summer at a yard sale. It starts hard. Sometimes not at all. Midway through her seventh unsuccessful pull she sees a car coming down the hill. She hopes it's Gammy Betz and not another egg customer.

It's been two weeks since she called her grandmother. It was while Joon and Hap were dowsing a well down in Union County. "Hello?" the woman on the other end said.

"Hello," Rhea said. "Is this Betsy Betz?"

"Yes it is," the woman said.

"Gammy, we have to talk," Rhea said.

And they did talk, on the phone that morning two weeks ago—running up an enormous long-distance bill—and again the next day in the almost-finished living room of the new house on the knob above Hap's trailer. And now, just twenty-one hours before the wedding, Rhea's grandmother is driving up again, to walk her down the aisle and give her to James Faldstool, Jr.

Her grandmother had begged her to call her father—to tell him she is alive, beautiful and featherless, and about to be married—but she'd stopped begging as soon as she saw it wasn't going to do any good. Gammy Betz always knew when enough was enough. "Okay," she said, "it's your wedding. But as soon as that wedding music starts you're going to regret it."

"Probably," said Rhea. "But there's just so much ugly stuff between Daddy and me. Who knows what Daddy would do at the wedding. You know how he gets when there's too much pressure. I don't want him throwing dishes or jumping up and down on the cake. So we'll save the reunion for another time, Gammy. Though I'm dying to see the new baby."

That's when her grandmother said, "So am I."

"You haven't seen Donna's baby yet?"

"They're really protective," her grandmother said, adding in a whisper, "They're not saying anything, but I think the baby has Donna's allergies."

The car pulls up. The cloud of dust that followed it down the hill settles. It is Gammy Betz. Her husband has come, too. He pops the trunk and takes out a beautifully wrapped package that could only be a toaster oven.

Dr. Pirooz Aram, more rumpled than usual in his baggy Saturday shorts, goes to the mailbox. There is the usual collection of catalogs addressed to his wife and the offers of credit cards. There is one hand-written letter that forces him to sit on his front step and read it immediately. The return address simply says GRANDMA!

247

When the letter is read he stares at his azalea bushes for a while, then goes inside. "Sitareh," he yells, hoping his wife will hear him over the Yobisch Podka CD filling the house with monotonous New Age harmonies. "Do you remember that patient of mine who was eaten by wolves?"

Sitareh is in the kitchen chopping endive for a salad. "The one with the feathers?" she yells back. "I though it was coyotes!"

"Coyotes? Are you sure, Sitareh? I thought it was wolves."

"It was coyotes, Pirooz."

He is in the kitchen now, nibbling first on the endive, then on his wife's neck. "Anyway, this girl who was eaten by animals has just invited us to her wedding."

"Are we going?"

"We should, don't you think?"

And so three Saturdays later, Dr. Pirooz Aram and wife Sitareh drive deep into the state of Ohio, to Acorn County. The letter from GRANDMA! included a map. So they stumble across Bear Swamp Road rather easily.

They first spot the silver trailer and then the almost-completed house on the hill above it. They approach slowly, careful not to hit one of the many loose chickens. "What is it with this family and chickens?" Dr. Aram says to his wife. There is a collection of cars and pickup trucks already parked in a field of tall grass. They park next to a red truck with a blue camper on its back. Dr. Pirooz Aram gets a box from the trunk of his red Toyota. It is wrapped with silver paper. There is a toaster oven inside, something Sitareh says every young American couple needs. Sitareh carries the basket of painted eggs her husband insisted on bringing. They are the ancient Persian symbol of fertility.

A happy young woman runs toward them. She is wearing a short white dress. There is a circlet of yellow roses on her head. "Rhea, is that you?" Dr. Pirooz Aram asks.

She hugs him. "It's me."

"Where are your beautiful feathers?"

"Gone."

"And you weren't eaten by wolves?"

Rhea walks them, arm-in-arm, past the card tables covered with food and the coolers filled with pop and beer, to the short rows of folding chairs by a great drooping willow. "That fellow in the white tuxedo there, he is your husband?"

"Pretty soon he is," says Rhea. She sits them next to Jelly Bean and Robert Charles. "A beautiful day for a wedding, isn't it?" Pirooz says to them, his eyes marveling at their tiny turnip heads.

"Bingo!" answers Robert Charles.

A man starts playing an accordion. People scramble for chairs. Some have to stand.

Joon hugs his mother and then shakes his father's hand, without words thanking him for keeping their secret all these years. He trots to the willow and stands under a trellis woven thick with water lillies gathered from the swamp.

Now Rhea starts down the aisle, her arm locked in Gammy Betz's arm.

The service is conducted by a huge woman wearing a bright green pantsuit. Pirooz whispers to Sitareh that she looks like an avocado. Later he will learn that she is Rita Afflatus Ball, pastor of the Unitarian Universalist Church in Yellow Springs. To his delight, there is no talk of sacrifice or duty. No talk of better-or-worse. No talk of death. Or parting. There is only talk of love.

Says Rita Afflatus Ball: "We have not gathered here today to marry Rhea and Joon—as if we had the power or the right to do that. Rather, we have gathered as friends and family to acknowledge that they have already married themselves, many years ago, when they were children, and their eyes first met, and burned a secret passageway through space and time, through self and self-ishness, through apprehension and vulnerability, so that their souls could freely pass and entwine as one.

"Only Rhea and Joon can say they are married and only Rhea and Joon can decide how long their marriage will last. But Rhea and Joon have loved each other for a long time already, and it is my guess they will love each other for a long time to come. I would not be surprised if it proves to be the better part of eternity. So, Rhea

Jeanette Cassowary, it comes to this moment: Are you married to James Harold Faldstool Jr.?"

"I am," answers Rhea.

"And James Harold Faldstool Jr., are you married to Rhea Jeanette Cassowary?"

"I am," answers Joon.

"Then why am I talking when we should be eating and dancing?" asks Rita Afflatus Ball.

There is laughter and applause and the man with the accordion starts playing a polka. Rhea and Joon kiss.

Dr. Aram scoops Jelly Bean into his arms. Dances her around the trellis.

"You go, Mrs. Roosevelt!" Robert Charles bellows as he claps to the music.

A meaty red pick-up crackles to the edge of the hill and stops. Below, on the edge of the marsh, glistens a silver house trailer. There are a couple of dozen cars and trucks parked in front of it. One of those trucks has a blue camper on the back. Just up the slope from the silver trailer sits a small house. Behind that house a party is going on. People are dancing. When the driver of the pick-up rolls down his window, he hears polka music.

The driver takes his sweaty hands off the steering wheel and presses them against his cold cheeks. He looks to the woman next to him for guidance. She is holding a Kleenex to her nose. Between them, strapped into a plastic safety seat, is a baby. The baby's yellow sleeper is zipped to the chin. The baby's yellow knit cap hides everything but a pair of brown eyes and a nubby pink nose.

The woman smiles grimly. The man takes his foot off the brake. As they descend, the FRESH EGGS sign in the back of the truck, wrapped in beautiful blue paper and tied with beautiful white ribbons, rattles and rattles.

Thirty-seven

RHEA FALDSTOOL SITS by her mother's grave, Indian style. Inside the hollow diamond created by her folded legs she places the tiny girl named Joy. Joy is three years old now, squirmy and irritable. Rhea holds her in place with one hand and with the other opens the little book Dr. Pirooz Aram gave her when she was a child.

The wild strawberries already have been eaten and Joon and her father have wandered across the cemetery, searching for the graves of Civil War veterans. Donna is waiting in the truck, with the windows up, afraid of the thick June grass and the pollen-soaked air. So there is just Rhea and Joy and the half of Jeanie Cassowary not in heaven.

The book Dr. Aram gave Rhea, *The Conference of the Birds*, was written centuries ago by the Persian poet Farid ud-Din Attar. Rhea used to read it to her chickens at night with a flashlight. It was how she met Joon. It was how she made sense of the many senseless things that were happening to her. She remembers what Dr. Aram wrote to her: "The book is about a journey. And I hope that you will find the time to read it during your journey."

Rhea hopes the book will help tiny Joy on her journey. It is going to be a difficult journey. She finds the dog-earred page where she left off all those years ago. She reads:

> *"A world of birds set out, and there remained*
> *But thirty when the promised goal was gained . . ."*

Yes. That's right. Thousands of birds set out to find their king, the mysterious Simorgh. They were led by the Hoopoe. They flew through seven valleys, each one difficult and dangerous, until only thirty birds were left.

> *"Thirty exhausted, wretched, broken things,*
> *With hopeless hearts and tattered, trailing wings . . ."*

Joy stops squirming and nestles against Rhea's puffy belly. There is a baby inside that belly, a baby that won't be born for another five months. Genetic meddling has seen to it that Joy will be both its aunt and its sister—just as she is already both a sister and a daughter to Rhea. Such are the difficult and dangerous valleys created by this much-too-modern world.

Rhea reads on: The thirty remaining birds finally reach the Simorgh's palace. A herald warns them to turn back, but they refuse. So the herald unlocks the gate and takes them inside. A hundred veils are drawn back. He leads them through blinding light to a throne and gives each bird a written page, on which their life stories are recorded. Only after they have finished reading do they see their king.

But the king they have endured so much to find is only a mirror. A mirror! And they see only themselves!

The ending does not surprise Rhea one little bit. "Would you like to hear it from the beginning?" she asks. "I can't read it all today—it's a long book—but I could read you a little bit?"

"Read," says Joy. Her voice is as soft and sweet and vulnerable as the *peep* of a newly hatched chick.

So Rhea flips back to the first page:

"Dear Hoopoe, welcome! You will be our guide . . ."

Acknowledgments

Sometime in the 1950s my father cut a 26-inch section off a sheet of three-quarter-inch plywood. He first painted it white, then painted a half-inch black border around it. Then in bright red he painted this:

FRESH EGGS

He screwed hooks into the top of the sign and hung it on a post by the road. For years it swung there, inviting passersby to pull in for a dozen or two.

When the time came for me to begin a new novel in the summer of 1999, that FRESH EGGS sign started swinging in my mind. I searched the barn and found it. I scrubbed off the dust and mouse droppings, hung it on the wall above my computer and started writing. So thanks, Dad, for making that sign. And thanks, Mom, for not tossing it on the burn-up pile.

There are others to thank as well:

Like Karen Davis, Ph.D., whose book *Prisoned Chickens Poisoned Eggs*, proved to be an important resource, both technically and spiritually.

Like my dear friend and teacher, Dr. Manoucher Parvin, who introduced me to the rich history and culture of his homeland—in particular, the twelfth-century Persian masterpiece, *The Conference of the Birds*, by Sufi poet Faridud ud-Din Attar.

Like Dick Davis and Afkham Darbandi, whose beautiful translation of *The Conference of the Birds* I used.

Like Martin and Judith Shepard at The Permanent Press for making my dream—and the dreams of so many other writers—come true.

Like Anna Ghosh, my agent in faraway New York, who has waited patiently for me to find my way.

Like the Ohio Arts Council for its generous grant.

Like the helpful people at the Medina County District Library, which during the writing of this book, was named Library of the Year by the *American Library Journal.*

Like the Biliczky sisters, Carol and Joyce, and that ever-optimistic sheltie of theirs, Biscuit.

Like the little rag-tag flock of Buff Orpingtons and Bantams that run around our little farm here in Hinckley, Ohio.